Joltierre

Copyright © 2024 Joltierre Gonzalez

All rights reserved. Except as permitted under the U.S. Copyright Act of 1976, no part of this publication may be reproduced, distributed, or transmitted in any form or by any means, or stored in a database or retrieval system, without the prior written permission of the publisher.

The characters and events portrayed in this book are fictitious. Any similarity to real persons, living or dead, is coincidental and not intended by the author.

Table of Contents

Chapter 0.1	4
Chapter 1.1	5
Chapter 2.1	42
Chapter 3.1	73
Chapter 4.1	109
Chapter 5.1	144
Chapter 6.1	183
Chapter 7.1	207
Chapter 8.1	251
Chapter 9.1	291
Chapter 10.1	347

Enjoy each subchapter with a musical experience by scanning the QR code to listen to the corresponding song. Left side: Apple Music / Right side: Spotify.

Chapter 0.1

The Law of the Land Declaration of Unification — Lex Est Absoluta (The Law Is Absoluta) MMXXV

Enim Amicitia, (For Friendship)

Let it be known that all beings, living or dead, will be governed by this declaration: that in order to establish World Peace, as instructed by the man known as the Overseer, all kingdoms, empires, and dynasties alike must swear fealty to this document, the Amicitia Licentiam, and serve each other as one people under the Grand Organization.

Pacem. (Peace.)

Chapter 1.1

Dust clung to Juliet's skin as she rested her hand on the windowsill, her gaze out towards a weathered tree. Her face contorted with discomfort while other aged fingers combed through her hair. Angst welled up within her with each passing second.

The young woman's focus shifted to the last leaf clinging to a branch, as if it represented the last fragment of will holding her together. A gentle breeze threatened to break the leaf's grip, and in that moment filled with distress, the teeth of a wooden comb snapped her back to reality.

Juliet's eyes widened in surprise as her mother's deft fingers brushed against her scalp, coaxing out a tangled lock of hair. A nervous flutter danced in her chest, her breath hitching as her mother's touch grazed her skin. The constriction of her corset squeezed her ribs without mercy, a silent vice gripping her torso. Gasping for air, she fought against the suffocating pressure, fingers fumbling to loosen the laces.

With a sharp exhale, the corset relented, granting her lungs the freedom they craved, and a wave of relief washed over her as oxygen flooded her chest once more.

Silence enveloped the room, allowing Juliet's mind to wander to places she preferred not to dwell on. She fought back tears as memories of her upbringing surged forward. The prominent mark on her left wrist itched, causing her hand to clench into a fist as she contemplated its significance. The scar's discomfort echoed in her mind, reminding her of being labeled 'Marked One' in her youth, cast out into the wilderness with her mother. A rising storm of emotions flooded her gut, overwhelming her with each breath as she struggled to contain the turmoil.

"Please, remind me of the plan," Juliet blurted out, her voice laced with desperation. She sought solace in her mother's soothing presence, hoping it would anchor her in the present.

The older woman paused from brushing her daughter's auburn locks and sighed. She knew what troubled her and obliged, "My girl, we need an audience with the High Guardians. To achieve that, we must sneak past the main gates of the so-called 'Grand Organization' and befriend one of the nobles. You need to make it appear as though you belong there and establish connections. If we do that, then we all will be able to leave this wretched swinery and have somewhere to call home."

"I understand." Juliet's lips parted, her voice a mere whisper filled with both resignation and determination. With a subtle flicker in her eyes, she glanced down at her wrist, the memory of its branded mark lingering like a shadow from her childhood. The instinct to conceal it, ingrained through years of conditioning, surged within her. Yet, as she pondered the task ahead, doubt crept in like tendrils of ivy winding around her resolve. Could she maintain the facade, knowing the consequences if she faltered? The feeling of uncertainty pressed down upon her, casting a pall over her resolve.

Pressed for time, her mother resumed brushing her hair with quick and purposeful movements, striving to make it as presentable as that of a highborn noble. "You may need to seduce some of the men to get your foot in the door, but do not whore about! Stay presentable."

Juliet's features twisted in a visceral display of revulsion and defiance, her brows knitting together in a tight furrow. A wave of disgust washed over her, visible in the subtle curl of her lip and the flash of defiance in her eyes. "Gross," she spat out, the word punctuated by a sharp exhale, her disdain in every syllable. There was no masking the genuine repulsion that rippled through her at the mere suggestion, her reaction laying bare her innermost feelings.

She winced as her mother untangled the final knot in her hair, the physical discomfort mirroring the trials she faced both in the present and in the past. The pain served as a stark reminder of the challenges she had endured. "These are troubled times, and we haven't enjoyed a proper meal since our exile years ago," her mother remarked, emphasizing the harsh reality of their circumstances. "Remember who the true enemy is, love."

Taking a moment to regain her composure, Juliet replied, "I'll do my best."

Her mother's scanning held a mix of concern and determination. "Make sure your best is enough. We need you."

A comforting hand rested on Juliet's shoulder, grounding her in the present. She lifted her opposite hand to cover her mother's and returned the squeeze. With a nod, Juliet turned towards the cracked mirror, her hand dropping to her side. She took a moment to admire her appearance, but the style seemed antiquated, reminiscent of aristocratic portraits from times long past. Her wine red dress clashed and complemented the purple corset she wore over her eggshell colored blouse. Sighing, she doubted herself, but squared her shoulders and nodded, bolstering her self esteem. Juliet turned to her mother, and they exchanged a soft smile, reassured that she could accomplish this daunting mission.

The old woman's squint softened as she beheld her daughter with weathered eyes reflecting a deep reservoir of memories. A wistful smile tugged at the corners of her lips, hinting at a lifetime filled with tales untold. "You look beautiful," she murmured, her voice a gentle whisper laced with nostalgia, as if transported back to a bygone era of splendor and grace.

"Thank you, Mother. I got it from you," Juliet replied, noticing her mother's wistful look.

As they stood in the room, a sense of anticipation hung heavy in the air, threading its way between them like an unspoken vow. For a fleeting moment, their connection seemed to transcend time itself. But their solitude was short lived as the room filled with others, their presence casting shadows across the worn floorboards. In that instant, it felt as though all eyes were fixed upon Juliet, each pair a silent testament to the hopes and dreams of those who had weathered hardship alongside her.

She awaited the gathering crowd of migrants, their faces etched with the lines of resilience, bearing witness to the trials of displacement from their ancestral homes in the Calcite Empire. Juliet's mother, a pillar of strength in their shared struggle, stood beside them, her weathered hands clasped in silent prayer for her daughter's success.

A small child, his eyes alight with innocence, approached the auburn haired Marked One, offering a single larkspur as a token of good fortune. With a tender smile, she knelt down, accepting the delicate flower from his marked hand. Placing it with care on her vest, she embraced each member of the gathering with a warm hug, their silent blessings lingering in the air like whispers of hope.

With a nervous sigh, Juliet gathered her resolve, her footsteps tentative as she crossed the threshold of the shabby building. Taking one final deep breath, she squared her shoulders, determination burning bright in her eyes, as she embarked on the gravel road that led to the capital of the Grand Organization.

Chapter 1.2

Amidst an almost deafening silence, the Overseer's smooth voice resonated in the air, filling the room with a deep, reassuring tone. "Mercury..."

"Yes, Overseer." Mercury, his skin shimmering like gold, responded with his customary martial respect.

"Summon the rest of the High Guardians and return to me as soon as possible," the Overseer said, his voice indicating the confidential nature of the matter.

With a shaved head gleaming like brushed gold under the flickering torchlight, Mercury nodded in acceptance before departing the Great Hall. He traversed a labyrinth of winding hallways and shadowed corridors, the echoes of his footsteps reverberating against the ancient stone walls. His slender fingers danced across the pages of his leather bound handbook, recording the proceedings of the meeting as he navigated the labyrinthine passages.

Emerging into the grand foyer, bathed in the soft glow of the morning sun filtering through stained glass windows, Mercury's eyes were drawn towards a young handmaiden tending to a nearby tapestry. Pausing in his stride, he closed his notebook with a soft thud, his keen eyes observing her with a mixture of curiosity and intrigue. With measured steps, he approached her, the hem of his cloak trailing behind him while preparing for the conversation.

"Amelia, our guests have arrived. Please alert the kitchen staff," Mercury instructed.

"At once, M'lord," the young woman replied.

Grateful to serve her High Guardian, she made her way out of the foyer and towards the kitchen. Mercury watched her skip away, humming a high pitched melody that echoed through the hallways. Chuckling to himself, he resumed his journey towards the castle stables.

Mercury's hurried footsteps echoed down the final corridors, where working servants darted to and fro, their voices mingling with the clatter of dishes and the rustle of fabric. As he approached the reception area overlooking the bustling stalls, the soft rays of the morning sun filtered through the gauzy curtains, painting the room in a warm, golden hue. The gentle play of light and shadow danced upon the walls, imbuing the dim enclosure with a sense of whimsy and vitality. With a faint smile, Mercury paused to bask in the tranquil beauty of the scene before continuing on his way.

There, he met with the first of the High Guardians to arrive: Darakon of the Diamond Mortem Dynasty and Hari from the Emerald Empire. As he approached the two High Guardians, Mercury met Darakon's cold, dark glare, and scanned them for any hint of emotion, but to no avail. His features, etched with an air of unyielding determination, hinted at a relentless pursuit of duty. Dawned in armor that appeared to reflect the hardness of the diamonds from his lineage, Darakon exuded an aura of strength and discipline. Mercury then shifted his attention to Hari, a High Guardian notorious for his thick skin, both metaphorical and literal. Hari's physical appearance showcased the toughness that matched his reputation. His muscular build and rugged countenance spoke of battles weathered and challenges overcome. Clad in emerald-hued armor, Hari's presence exuded an earthy resilience, complementing Darakon's more austere demeanor.

With a final heavy and confident step, the golden figure stood before the two leaders. "I trust your journey was uneventful?"

Hari and Darakon both gave a short nod. Hari's tone dripped with sarcasm as he replied, "Yes, as uneventful as we can hope these days. Migrants often harass my company as soon as we leave the Emerald Empire."

Pressed for time, Mercury suppressed the urge to engage in a lengthy discussion about the migrants. It wasn't the time for it. Holding his tongue with practiced expertise, he focused on the urgent matters at hand. "Have you seen the others? The Overseer is waiting. . ."

Darakon's professional and calm tone, befitting a model soldier from the esteemed Diamond Mortem Dynasty, responded, "I saw the rest of the High Guardians not too far off. They were a little delayed upon entering the city, but I expect them to arrive within the hour."

As Darakon's words dwindled, a new figure emerged, his arrival marked by a descent from the skies. Haklo of the Hawke Empire touched down upon the balcony with the poise of a practiced acrobat. Clad in garments adorned with feathers mirroring the hues of his wings, his attire hinted at a profound connection with the avian realm. Perching for a moment upon the intricate balcony railing, Haklo exuded an air of relaxed assurance, suggesting a perpetual ease even amidst the chaos of unfolding events.

With a playful salutation on his lips, he greeted those below, his voice carrying the lightness of wind yet holding a hint of the shrewdness that marked a skilled diplomat and strategist. "Greetings, Mercury. I overheard you inquiring about the rest of the High Guardians. They are arriving as we spe—" Right before Haklo was able to finish his statement, the air was pierced by the metallic squeals and groans of the main portcullis gates swinging open, disrupting the tranquility of the moment. He paused, waiting for the noise to subside before continuing, "—speak."

Squinting for a bit, Mercury confirmed that the rest of the High Guardians were indeed arriving. He turned and saluted the three leaders. "Thank you, gentlemen. We will expect all of you in the Grand Hall. Enim Amicitia."

In a habitual response, Darakon, Hari, and Haklo saluted back, "Pacem."

Taking a final glance over the balcony's edge, Mercury observed the rest of the High Guardians' servants driving carriages through the open gates. Seeing no reason to linger in the entrance any longer, he executed a flawless about-face and began a brisk, composed walk towards the Grand Hall. With the message delivered to the rest of the High Guardians, he needed to return to his duties by the Overseer's side with haste.

Following Mercury's departure, Wingmen from both the Hawke and Emerald Empires joined the entourage of High Guardians outside the castle walls. They landed near the gates, assisting their fellow countrymen by unloading the burdens carried by their traveling beasts.

Inside the main antechamber, Darakon, Hari, and Haklo awaited the remaining High Guardians, deciding to walk together as a group towards the Grand Hall. Each donned a prestigious black uniform with a shimmering insignia adorning the left side of their chests. The Grand Organization of the Amicitia Licentiam's trademark, crafted from the finest steel, was both intimidating and beautiful. The insignia took the form of an arrowhead with two talons on either side, its arched crest gleaming whenever it caught the light—a representation of natural power.

The High Guardians filed into the Grand Hall, their footsteps echoing against the stone walls as they made their way to the heavy, weathered stone table positioned in the heart of the room. Each chair was adorned with elegant glassware and a bottle of wine, inviting them to partake during the discussion. At the center of the table rested a true to scale replica of the five sanctions, crafted decades ago during the inception of the Grand Organization. Despite the passage of time, the replica retained its amazing detail, a testament to the organization's enduring history.

Standing before them all, the Overseer extended his hands, his words resonating off the towering stone walls. "Welcome back! I am glad to see you all here today, united once again. Enim Amicitia!"

In unison, the High Guardian leaders replied, "Pacem," and took their seats, while their teams stood at attention behind them.

Mercury, the loyal friend and aide to the Overseer, occupied the seat to his immediate right, as duty demanded. Their evident friendship was recognized throughout the region, and the gold-skinned man had remained diligent by the Overseer's side for countless hours, fulfilling his role as an aide. He also kept detailed records of the Grand Organization's tasks and accomplishments. While not his preferred role, Mercury acknowledged the significance of serving in any capacity requested of him, crediting the world's newfound peace to the efforts of the Amicitia Licentiam.

The Overseer sat in silence, his expression neutral, his glances shifting from one High Guardian to another. He took his time, contemplating his next words with care.

In the ensuing silence, Mercury's mind began to wander. His attention roamed over the Overseer's remarkable skin, pale and translucent, untouched by light. Intricate patterns of black, twisting vines adorned his visage, their darkness vivid enough to devour the transparency around them. The man's appearance stood out, a rare sight at most seen by a privileged few. His hair stood tall, slicked back into a natural mohawk. Deep purple eyes matched the ambiance of his marks, burning with fiery intensity and youthful vigor.

The air grew thick with anticipation, the responsibility pressing upon every soul in the room. It was in moments like these that Mercury felt his martial training come to the fore. He was prepared to defend the peace they had fought so hard to achieve, and he knew the others were just as committed.

As the Overseer's voice resonated through the Grand Hall, its commanding tone captured the attention of all present. "I have important matters to attend to," he declared. "Later today, I will be meeting with the three largest nations, and our rendezvous shall take place at Zeller's castle, the closest location for such a gathering. In my absence, Mercury will assume the role of interim Overseer. You are to report to him as you would to me. Now, without delay, provide your reports."

Mercury suppressed a sigh, his golden-skinned hand moved with precision, transcribing the Overseer's commands in his notebook. He found himself juggling an even bigger load, his schedule already stretched to its limits. While grateful for the trust placed in him to protect the realm, the heaviness of the extra duties bore down upon him. Nonetheless, he approached his role with unwavering dedication and seriousness.

As the High Guardians exchanged glances, their silent communication indicating the unspoken protocol, Mercury's mind drifted back to his previous experience as interim Overseer. Memories flooded in: the dizzying whirlwind of challenges blending with the numbing monotony of administrative tasks. Reflecting on the past, he yearned for a more manageable journey ahead, a subtle wish for a smoother road this time around.

As one of the High Guardians commenced their report, Mercury's attention snapped into sharp focus. His pen danced across the paper, capturing every uttered word. There was a myriad of information to keep track of, and he couldn't afford to miss a single nuance. Each High Guardian led a company within their sanction, chosen for their experience and prestige. They took turns sharing updates on the economic, diplomatic, and political events within their respective domains, ensuring the nobles' satisfaction with the functioning of the Grand Organization.

Chapter 1.3

Mercury closed his notebook with a decisive snap, bracing himself for the trials to come, determined to demonstrate their value as guardians of peace. A subtle curve graced his lips, softening his stern countenance, as he met Mite's unwavering glare. Her piercing black eyes locked onto his, framed by the flow of her raven hair. The Wintersun, an intimidating race known for their fearless prowess in battle and unmatched ability in neutralizing all magic that approached them, stood as the formidable martial force of the Grand Organization.

Warriors from Mite's homeland, the Wintersun Dynasty, adorned themselves with minimal armor, displaying pale skin adorned with tribal patterns. Every inch of their flesh was marked, accentuating the multitude of jet black spikes protruding from their backs, instilling fear in their enemies.

Mite, the first female initiated into the High Guardians and the commander of its armed forces, eased out her chair and rose with confidence, thus poised to deliver a brief post meeting declaration. She glanced at the Overseer, ensuring his attention was on her, and evoked a subtle shift in the room's ambiance.

Mercury adjusted himself in his seat, waiting for Mite to speak her mind. She paused, struggling to find the right words to convey her thoughts.

He knew how difficult it was to overcome the intimidating shadow the Overseer casted. Mercury kept his gaze on the raven haired woman while biting the inside of his lip. In the extended quiet, the other High Guardians interpreted Mite's rise as a signal to gather their belongings, their patience waning as they awaited her next move. The subtle wave of a hand distracted her from her anxious trance.

"Enim Amicitia." A gentle goad from his golden grin granted just enough encouragement for Mite to regain her ground.

Mite's lips twitched into a strained smile as she responded, her discomfort evident in her voice as she uttered, "Pacem."

The Overseer regained control of the room, offering a genial farewell as he ushered them out. "I believe all is well. As always, I entrust the security of the sanctions to your capable hands. I have other matters to attend to. Unless there is something noteworthy, I wish peace and friendship upon all of you and your countrymen."

He approached Mite with grace, extending his arms for a hug, which she welcomed with a nod. As they embraced, a faint blush tinted her cheeks, and she turned away, concealing a smile. Sensing the need for propriety, she disengaged from the hug with a gentle motion just as he initiated, allowing their connection to remain respectful yet warm.

As he turned away, his movements portrayed a sense of weightlessness, gliding without effort towards the giant wooden door of the chamber. With a graceful gesture, he swept his hand, and the door swung open, granting him passage. The other High Guardians followed suit, filing in near silence into the antechamber behind him.

Mercury, seizing the moment, motioned for Mite to join him, gesturing with a tilt of his head. As she finished speaking to the rest of the group, he pretended to jot down notes in his book, creating the illusion of lingering business. "You go on ahead," Mite addressed the others, "I will catch up with you at the stables."

The others saluted and left the Grand Hall. Once alone, Mite turned to Mercury with a hint of trepidation. "What is it?"

Concerned, Mercury asked, "I noticed you were staring again. Are you two on another break?"

With closed eyes and an exasperated sigh, Mite replied under her breath as if others may be eavesdropping, "Yes, again. . ."

Mercury shook his head, chiding her. "You know, there is no shortage of women vying for The Overseer's attention. Why do you two not make it official?"

Mite snapped back, "And you think I haven't tried!?" Mercury bit his lip as she turned away, her fists clenched at her sides. After a moment, Mite looked back at his golden face, exhaling and relaxing her hands. "I am sorry. I didn't mean to snap at you. It is just very difficult to be with him. When he is not in a meeting he is planning with the High Guardians. When he is not with the others, he is with you. It is like he has no time for himself, or me, for that matter."

Mercury tutted before asking, "Well, the two of you have been courting each other for years. I have seen you around the headquarters quite a bit and a good portion of that time spent at his side. In fact, I would argue that when you are not on a mission, you are here more than your own home!"

Mite retorted, frustration evident as she threw her hands up in the air. "Because that is the single way for me to see him! He schedules no occasions for matters of the heart. He says that it is not the right time, but my heart belongs to him. I have no choice but to wait by his side until the time is right. For now, a few moments here and there will have to suffice."

Mercury hesitated before posing the question, his tone cautious. "Well, when was the last time you went out on a date?"

Mite's twisted face revealed her bemusement. "Does visiting the blacksmith count?"

"Not unless the product is a ring," he replied with a chuckle.

She rolled her eyes, "Perhaps in the future, but he is impossible to hold down right now, of course due to the upcoming expansion of the organization."

Mercury sighed. "Indeed, sometimes we lose sight of what matters most. Maybe it's time for an opportunity set aside just for the two of you. Maybe by the river? Maybe with a picnic?"

He winked as her eyebrows raised. A smile passed between them before Mercury opened his book again, pretending to study the page. "It seems he might have some time after he returns from the Zeller stronghold."

Mite shook her head. "No, it feels forced. I've tried scheduling things with him before, but his mind is always elsewhere. He's often preparing for whatever comes after our dates, which he never fails to attend, but something is missing. Even when we're together, I feel like he's worlds away. Don't get me wrong, he enjoys my company, but I want to be pursued. He hasn't arranged a single outing between us that didn't serve some diplomatic purpose. I just wish we could escape from all of this, but I think his one true love is his work. Perhaps, when the Grand Organization stretches from ocean to ocean, he'll need a new pursuit. When that day comes, I'll be waiting by his side."

Mercury let out a long breath, "My apologies Mite. I should not have meddled. I am sorry if I upset you. I just want the two of you to be happy."

She smiled and walked toward the exit. As she reached the door, she glanced back at Mercury, a single tear welling up in her eye. "Me too, Mercury. Me too. . . But I've already tried." Mite left Mercury in the room, enveloped in silence.

Chapter 1.4

    Mite walked down the familiar lone corridors, her steps slowing until she came to a complete stop. A quiet sigh escaped her as she found herself lost in a whirlwind of emotions. Her surveying drifted up towards an ornate chandelier hanging high above, triggering a wave of nostalgic memories.

    "Overseer, may I have a word with you?" she asked, her voice calm and composed. Despite her outward demeanor, nerves fluttered inside her, and she tried to ignore their growing intensity.

    "Of course, Mite. You know you never need to ask." The Overseer's smile expressed the humbleness in his heart.

Mite pondered the honesty in his words. "I wish to ask you about our plans for this week's end. I know the organization is still coming together. Of course, I will continue to be there for you every step of the way. However, I'm afraid that as we progress, you will soon have less time to build with me."

"Mite, this is the first time I've heard you getting sentimental. Are you ill?" He mused a playful and gentle laugh that bubbled up from his chest as he ran his fingers through her hair.

She smiled in response to the jest, but deep down, she yearned for a serious conversation. While their playful banter was enjoyable, this was a topic that deserved their full attention. "Well, I've given it a lot of thought. My country seldom involves itself in external affairs, and since we've been together for some time, I wonder about the future. . . our future."

The Overseer fell silent, allowing the weight of her words to settle in the air. Then, he sat up, turning his head to meet her stare, his voice gentle as he spoke. "Do you believe we could be more than just lovers? You know my heart lies with the pursuit of world peace. I must put this above all else."

At first, she remained in her position with her head resting on the plush pillow. But as he finished speaking, she sat up, meeting his level. "I understand that. I'll pursue this cause with you regardless. I just hope that after this goal of ours has been achieved you would consider taking my hand and solidifying our bond."

"I love you. . ." A sweet and tender utterance from his lips.

"I love you as well." she responded, her voice infused with a sudden surge of hope and excitement. She fought to contain her joy, managing to compose herself despite the slight twitch of her lips.

With such a keen eye, the Overseer did catch her reaction to his words, allowing her a moment for it, but no more than a moment. He spoke with deliberate slowness, capturing her full attention. "I love you but, as I said before, I need to focus on my mission. Our moments together I will always cherish but, I won't have time to settle down and commit to the relationship you seek."

Her burst of hope simmered down, replaced by a heavy weight in her stomach—a mix of anxiety and embarrassment. Her shoulders sagged, and she began to turn her head away. But before she could withdraw, he reached out, his hands grasping her chin, redirecting her attention towards him.

"To assure you, if there's ever the possibility, it is with you. It's unfortunate for both of us, that time will never come."

Releasing a heavy sigh, the raven-haired woman averted her attention from the chamber, her eyes fixed on the realization that still lay ahead of her.

Chapter 1.5

Juliet stood before the imposing castle gates, her hands clenched in nervousness. She tried to distract herself by repeating the plan in her head, but her anxiety was overwhelming. A thin sheen of sweat glistened on her freckled face as she surveyed the energetic scene before her. High Guardians mingled with the active crowd, their presence felt as they browsed the stalls, stocking up on supplies for their journeys homeward. The air was thick with the aroma of baked bread and sweet pastries, enticing passersby with their golden crusts and tantalizing fillings. Bakers stood proud as they displayed their creations, arranging them in neat rows on wooden carts adorned with colorful banners fluttering in the breeze. Nearby, the sound of looms filled the air as skilled tailors showcased their crafted garments, each stitch a testament to their expertise. Customers marveled at the complex designs and vibrant colors, eager while selecting their next prized possession. Amidst the hustle and bustle, children laughed and played, their voices echoing off the cobblestone streets as they chased each other with wooden swords and leather balls. Their joy was infectious, spreading smiles to all who passed by, adding to the atmosphere of the market.

"Harmony?" Juliet chuckled in disbelief at the opulence displayed even by the common folk near the Grand Organization headquarters.

Returning her admiration to the magnificent castle, she knew she had to proceed with careful precision. However, the churning in her stomach made it difficult to take the next step. She tried to push aside her nerves and focused on the doors of the castle as they opened, revealing a remarkable sight. Awe and fear battled within her as she mustered the courage to act.

An imposing figure stepped into the market plaza, bathed in the orange light of the setting sun. His iridescent complexion reflected the warm colors of his realm, and he smiled as he looked upon the peaceful and thriving community.

"The Overseer." Juliet seethed through clenched teeth, discerning his identity from the way others turned to bow.

She felt conflicted. Having been raised to dislike the man, Juliet blamed him for her people's exile and the hardships they endured in poverty. Yet, in that moment, she saw him as the people of the market square did—larger than life, exuding confidence and commanding respect.

His appearance stunned her; the marvel of such a man was beyond comprehension. Even though she had seen the giants from the Zircon Empire and the antlered druids from the Spinelle Kingdom, she had never fathomed a creature so bizarre it could make her heart shake with fear.

She was certain that if anyone could resolve the turmoil her mother faced, it was the most powerful man in the world. Despite holding him responsible for their situation, she hoped he could offer a solution.

As the Overseer and his group of High Guardians approached the entrance of the city, Juliet merged into the stream of travelers passing through the gate. She hurried by with purpose, those steps measured and deliberate, blending with the crowd of aristocratic figures. With each stride, she maintained a composed demeanor, her posture upright and confident, concealing any sign of anxiety or uncertainty. Despite the wild activity around her, Juliet remained focused, her senses attuned to her surroundings as she ensured that her branded wrist remained hidden from view.

Once inside, she separated from the travelers and made her way to the stables. She needed a moment to collect her thoughts and figure out the next steps of her plan. As she arrived at the stables, she overheard two High Guardians coming from the castle, engaged in a conversation about state matters.

"Bemus, you're misinformed and lacking common sense. The Diamond Mortem and the Zellers have a rivalry. Why else would they be having this meeting?" a deep voice echoed through the stalls.

Juliet couldn't resist eavesdropping, even though it wasn't her original intention. She found a hiding spot behind a small stack of hay and peeked out to observe the two men talking. Once she confirmed that they were not looking in her direction, she focused her attention on their conversation.

Bemus, a man with an athletic physique, shrugged and scrunched his face in disagreement. From their discussion, Juliet deduced that the other man, Vladsan, was the leader of their group. Bemus scoffed at Vladsan's insult and shook his head, offering his own retort.

"Listen Vladsan, just because you're the leader of this company it does not make you more informed than I am. Your guess is just as good as mine. This is just like you. Last time you said the Wintersun were immortal."

Vladsan sighed and placed his hand over his face. Tall with spiked, blond hair, his clothes accentuated his well chiseled physique. He spoke with a hint of exasperation, "You know we've all had our experiences, but you persist with this theory."

A soft spoken woman, accompanied by a stern man in a similar uniform, interrupted the two men. Juliet watched as they approached from the castle together. "Well, to be fair, they could be kind and yet suspicious of each other. Perhaps there's a communication barrier, and the Overseer is trying to eliminate any potential conflicts. Maybe he should come here and do the same with you," she said, trying to lighten the mood with a laugh. Her short, tousled hair framed her face in a rebellious dance, the strands mirroring the spirited nature of the world around her. Dressed in the sleek black High Guardian attire, she moved with an air of quiet confidence, her clothing a canvas for shadows to play upon.

The two disputing men shrugged and smiled in response. After pausing to absorb the vibrant surroundings, the group resumed their discussion, adopting a lighter tone while staying focused on the matter at hand.

Vladsan's attention shifted towards the castle's exit, following the sound of approaching footsteps. With a sharp adjustment to his posture, he remarked, "Omnibenevolence must have heard you, Golnesa. Here he comes now."

"Di meliora," Bemus exhaled, his voice filled with hesitation.

The High Guardians turned to acknowledge the Overseer's arrival, offering a slight bow. The assistant who accompanied Golnesa, Ovidius, a representative from the Romanite Empire, raised his olive-colored hand in respect. "Pardon me, Overseer, but we were discussing your travels and hoping for some answers."

Furrowing his brow, the Overseer responded, "You know I am not one for gossip, Ovidius."

Golnesa, representing the Azure Kingdom, interjected with confidence. Her uniform was adorned with excessive jewelry, and her face shimmered with various piercings like stars when they caught the light. "We don't mean to be disrespectful or rude, Overseer. I myself am curious and must ask the truth. I've heard the Zellers built their castles with marble, and their spires reach above the clouds!"

Bemus, an Alexandrite who was obsessed with his own country's culture, chimed in with a credence, "I heard they are xenophobic pompous snobs."

Vladsan gulped the air with a nervous inhale as the Overseer listened. He felt responsible for allowing the political conversation to reach the Overseer's ears and observed the man's annoyed expression.

Clenching his teeth, the Overseer raised a hand, cutting through the air to signal an end to the conversation. "These are rumors, and you shouldn't be spreading them. I can confirm that the Zellers indeed construct their architectural marvels with their own hands. They are beings of immense intelligence and deserve your utmost reverence."

Embarrassed murmurs of acknowledgment filled the air as the group understood their misstep. Juliet, standing nearby, was left dumbfounded by how the Overseer commanded respect and attention from the High Guardians without any effort.

Juliet watched the Overseer's departure and realized she needed to follow him. Her eyes swept the distance, scanning for a suitable mount. A solitary blue roan horse caught her attention, standing apart from the others, its presence calling out to her. She darted behind the barrels and bales of hay, her movements swift and purposeful as she approached the horse. With practiced ease, she saddled it up and swung herself onto its back. With a swift nudge of her heels, she urged the horse forward, intending to follow the Overseer's trail.

Juliet's eyes widened in disbelief as she surveyed the distance the Overseer had covered on foot. She had just saddled her horse when he disappeared beyond the gate. A mix of frustration and confusion washed over her features as she tried to comprehend how he could move so fast. She then spurred the horse forward, urging it into a gallop as she burst through the front gates. The horse's hooves thundered against the cobblestone road as she leaned forward, her determination driving her forward. In her haste, she failed to notice a servant crossing her path, and with a loud thud, the unfortunate individual was knocked to the ground. Ignoring the commotion she left behind, Juliet focused on catching up to the Overseer, who had already gained a considerable lead on foot. Disgruntled voices rose from behind her, signaling that her attempt to remain inconspicuous had failed.

Chapter 2.1

"Juliet!" The weathered voice, feminine and familiar, filled the air.

"Coming, Mother!" A high pitched cackle followed her exclamation, emerging from a patch of tall sage grass. Juliet burst forth, fragments of greenery clinging to her clothes before surrendering to gravity. Dandelion seeds swirled in the air as her skipping feet brushed against the plains. The scent of a nearby stream mingled with the exhilaration that curved her lips upwards. Her lavender dress billowed in the breeze, mirroring the surrounding flowers, and the sweet aroma clung not just to the fabric but also to her skin. As she reached her mother, her steps slowed, marking the impending conclusion of their time in the prairie.

"Mom, do we have to leave now? I was hoping to see the sunset," she implored, gazing up at her mother with pleading eyes.

A muted sigh offered a glimmer of hope, and anticipation swelled as Juliet waited for a nod of acceptance. A few seconds lingered before her plea yielded results. Her mother's weathered hands rubbed away the dark circles under her eyes. They settled in the field, with Juliet finding a place on her mother's lap.

The sky transformed into warm hues of orange and yellow as it descended toward the horizon. Light streamed through the grass, casting delicate shadows upon the swaying blades. Clouds painted the expanse above, some molding the sky in grace, while others carved bold shapes against their canvas.

A whispering wind swirled below, dictating the whimsical dance of foliage, leaves, and petals. Butterflies flitted by, their delicate wings tracing paths near a fluttering Calcite banner. As the sun sank lower, hues of blue and purple followed its descent. Colors streaked the sky in vibrant curves and lines, blending and bleeding into one another as darkness claimed the day. Juliet could feel her mother's heartbeat through their shared embrace, synchronized with the sharpening and deepening of the clouds' mark upon the sky.

Warmer tones surrendered to violets and deep blues, conceding to the growing chill as the sun submerged itself beneath the land, leaving the sky to unveil a beautiful night. Glistening stars adorned the distance, their light serving as mere candles in the embrace of darkness. Calmness reigned as the whispers exchanged between Juliet and her mother echoed: "I love you."

Chapter 2.2

The sky transformed into a soft shade of purple as the sun began its descent, casting its hues upon the Overseer's liquid-like outer layer of skin as he approached the meeting grounds. The castle, also serving as the Zeller's home, exuded an air of pride in its decorated decor.

His face held a surface of composure, yet beneath it lurked a faint flicker of concern, not for the potential derailment of his schemes, but for the chance of dampening the moods of those awaiting him. He feared any friction could prolong the process, hindering the progress he aimed to achieve. The idea of nurturing resentments within the ranks of those he sought to side with unsettled him, aware that lingering animosities could prove detrimental to peace, in particular when dealing with dignitaries. He demanded steadfast allegiance from them, viewing each interaction as a chance to solidify it.

The sound of crunching leaves beneath thick leather boots ceased as the Overseer approached the city's imposing front gates. He marveled at the architectural genius of the Zeller castle, unparalleled anywhere else. The brief moment between his pause at the gates and their magical opening reminded him to dispel any doubts. He understood that presenting himself with unwavering confidence was paramount for successful diplomacy. Any crack in his resolve could be exploited by opportunistic individuals.

The castle loomed tall, its sturdy marble walls stretching skyward, catching the last rays of the setting sun in a dazzling display. Perched atop the highest point in the Zeller capital, it commanded a commanding view over the city below, its presence akin to a vigilant guardian, silent yet steadfast.

Even at the gates, the Overseer's acute hearing caught snippets of conversation from within, familiar voices reaching his ears. As he allowed himself entry into the castle, the grand gates swung open, revealing Victor Zeller, Sothis, and Azrael—men he had traveled almost a hundred miles to meet. In the courtyard, they clustered near the entrance, their faces a canvas of intuition, their questioning looks hinting at lingering uncertainty about the Overseer's motives. These proud men guarded their ancestral land with jealousy, perceiving every interaction with the Grand Organization as a potential threat to their sovereignty.

On the other side, the Overseer emanated an aura of imposing presence, intimidating the three men. He ensured that his appearance projected an elegant symbol of unity and peace within the Grand Organization. His confidence served as his initial tool of diplomacy, aimed at disarming the distrust that lay before him.

Victor Zeller, the Grand Emperor of the Zeller Dynasty, exuded a charm that had endeared him to the people. His height was rivaled by Azrael, the Grand Emperor of the Diamond Mortem Dynasty. Azrael stood motionless, his hood drawn, allowing his black robe to sway in the autumn breeze. He remained silent as Victor and Sothis engaged in conversation about the matter at hand.

Sothis, with pale and weathered skin from years spent in the North's harsh climate, possessed a youthful spirit. His eyes reflected a man who often celebrated the thrill of battle. War paint accentuated the scars earned through countless conflicts, while his armor bore ornaments made of small bones, rumored to belong to those who had dared to claim the throne.

Once the gates had opened, the Overseer stepped within to greet the leaders.

"Enim Amicitia, Overseer, right on time as always. I trust your journey was uneventful?" Victor greeted the Overseer with an enthusiastic handshake.

"Pacem. It was a pleasant stroll." The Overseer's senses pricked up as a distant galloping reached his ears, a sound he couldn't ignore, having detected it the moment he departed from his own castle.

Suspicious of possible eavesdropping, he turned to the men and continued. "No time for further pleasantries my friend. We should head somewhere more private and comforting."

"Indeed, Overseer," Victor said, showing his excitement with a humble smile. "We shall head straight to Zeller Hall!"

"How original," scoffed Sothis with his eyes rolled.

Azrael spoke for the first time. "Now, now you two. Of course, the Overseer has important matters on his mind. Let us go inside."

The Overseer smiled and motioned towards the next set of gates. "I'd expect nothing less."

"Indeed! Let us go forth!" Victor said, brimming with enthusiasm at the Overseer's arrival. He then turned to pull a whistle from around his neck, playing a melodic tune that signaled for the guards to close the gate, and the four of them proceeded through the castle towards the Zeller Hall.

The Overseer took in all the details that few absorbed while within the castle. In the Zeller's realm, external prejudice prevented much influence from beyond their borders, resulting in a distinctive craftsmanship untouched by foreign hands. Every item, from armor to tapestries, bore the mark of meticulous handiwork and a unique style that reflected their cultural heritage. Within the castle's hallways, statues stood as silent sentinels, while vibrant paintings and woven tapestries adorned the walls, adding a sense of grandeur and beauty to the surroundings.

The four found their way into the Zeller Hall, a room as spacious as a cathedral's sanctuary, where they then sat around a round table set with food and drink.

"Help yourselves," Victor said with a smile, and after a few continued minutes of chatter, the feast began.

While amicable, the ambiance had the distinctive smell of tension and distrust coming from the three men who were waiting to settle this talk of treaties. They, like the Overseer, tried to hide their negative emotions and fears under the facade of proud royalty but the colorful man was quite well versed in the act of deception himself and could see very well behind their masks. He kept his smile to himself knowing that he would use this to his advantage.

Chapter 2.3

After some time, the atmosphere shifted from one filled with food and drink to a setting more conducive to debate and politics. The Overseer had waited for the right moment, knowing that what he was about to propose would provoke an unwanted rebuttal.

"Sothis, next time you must bring Ara as company. Unless, of course, you plan to keep that work of art all to yourself." Azrael's low tone almost concealed his desire to see the purebred Hawke's white eyes until his change in tone resulted in an awkward silence among the men.

"I will, but one question remains. How would your wife respond to your burning curiosity?" The group shared some hearty laughter at Azrael's expense before Sothis continued. "Our banners have grown close over the past few years, and Ara does, in fact, send his best wishes towards the Grand Organization.

Azrael slumped in his chair from embarrassment, "Well, I'm sure we appreciate the sentiment, but I am not getting any younger. Let's convene and be on our way."

At last, the moment had arrived. "Indeed," the Overseer said. "I have a very important proposition to make to you three."

The three leaders exchanged glances, their eyebrows arching in unison as they leaned forward to hear his proposal. The moment they had dreaded was at hand. The Overseer cleared his throat, commanding respect and silence from the Grand Emperors surrounding him with this gesture.

"I have no doubt in my mind that you all know what it takes to run a dynasty, in fact, each of you have built yours from nothing but the soil your lands provided. I also know you would do anything to keep your dynasties alive and well for generations to come. You three are great leaders and I expect you to remain so for a very long time." He raised his cup as a gesture of solidarity to appease the suspicious monarchs.

The three emperors lifted their cups in response, but the tension in the room felt as though it could be shattered by a gust of wind.

Seeing no improvements, the Overseer continued. "However, my brothers, time is the enemy of every living being. As Azrael can attest from his own mouth, death knocks on every man's door. I can assure you that no man outside your designated heir will wear the crown of your lands. This guarantee of your unending legacy extends beyond time itself quid pro quo you swear absolute allegiance to the Grand Organization, and sign onto the Amicitia Licentiam."

The chamber's atmosphere was coated in silence. What they had feared had happened, and now it was up to those three men to debate whether or not they would be willing to gamble their future with the leader of this Grand Organization.

A loud bang on the table ended the silence. "But our nations have stood for centuries and you wish us to be naive and sign it all away for a false promise? Overseer, do you take us for fools?" The Wintersun Grand Emperor interjected with his upper lip raised in disgust.

"Sothis," the Overseer bellowed in the great room, "all will be clear in a moment, if I may?" The fire in the Overseer's eyes that had shut down Sothis's protest faded, yielding to a softer but still stern glow. "As I was saying, under one unity there will be worldwide peace and together we would stand as one against any evil that may come to threaten these united lands. Not a single one of you will have to give up ownership of your dynasties, nor will your citizens have a new lord. You see, while your subjects bend their knees to you, all I ask is that as lords, you pledge your fealty in cooperation for a universal peace with the rest of the countries apart of the Grand Organization. Does this not sound reasonable to you? Imagine a world filled with no more wars. Imagine the possibility of absolute peace."

After a few moments of silence, Victor gave a calm response, but it was laced with a hint of disturbance. "With all due respect, Overseer, on the matters of the Grand Organization, are we expected to fight for lands not of our own? Should we sacrifice our swords for another banner? Who must we protect that we can not claim as our own people?"

"No, Victor. I would never ask the Zeller to wage war on another's behalf. Your nation is impressive and your people are strong and skilled, but I am not asking you to fight another banner's battle; I am telling you to fight for your own, for your children, their children, and your nation's future— de amor patriae. Do you not owe that to your people?"

Victor's head bobbed in a deliberate nod, though his furrowed brow hinted at the lingering thoughts occupying his mind.

Azrael continued with his own concerns. "And who shall enforce that your promise is fulfilled?"

"That brings me to the second component," the Overseer continued. "I have been enforcing the Amicitia Licentiam from day one. I have raised revenues and created a peace that stretches as far as the East is from the West. Not a single collective has been made to assist in a matter they were not willing to do in the first place and minimal donations are required to keep things running. I must add that this unity works if you become willing to allow this to work. It requires your faith above all."

He motioned with his hand to the three. "You three will have the same arrangement. You and your heirs are protected, since we respect lineages, and you have the added protection of the Grand Organization's High Guardians should you ever be subject to siege or rebellion. All we ask is that your actions be presented to me before they are to be implemented. There will be no need for the blood of our subjects to be spilled in a meaningless war under my rule. I am more powerful and cunning than anyone, therefore I can assure you that no one but myself is capable of enforcing it in such a capacity."

Victor and Sothis answered together, "No one but you?"

"Yes, my friends. You see, I am a timeless being beyond this world. I possess the wisdom that Azrael has acquired in his long life, I have wealth equal to the treasures of the Zeller, and I have acquired over time stronger magic than even you could handle, Sothis." The Wintersun cocked his head in disbelief and feeling insulted began to shake his head, feeling insulted as he listened to the man continue. "I am admitting that I have worked my entire life to be the person I need to be to fill this position. I will provide a ductus exemplo as a perfect being, a god amongst men, and as such, I ask you to witness that leadership."

Azrael spoke from his heart, "You are not the great Omnipotence, Overseer, and I warn you to not see yourself as even close to perfection, for even you have the heel of Achilleus. We must remind ourselves how familiar are the cases of prior men who held themselves in such high regard. We know how such ambitions ended, and I wish for such catastrophes to not show face again in my life nor my heir's. Overseer, I admire your vision, but you're losing me."

Chapter 2.4

Juliet's auburn hair billowed behind her as she slowed her horse to a trot. With the moon casting its dull glow, she sighed, her shoulders slumping in defeat as she glanced around, unable to discern any trace of the trail she had been following. The sky darkened even more as thick gray clouds rolled in, casting a shadow over the landscape and dimming the light, and a cascade of what appeared like liquid sapphire fell from the sky. Her determination to locate the Overseer waned toward hopelessness until something brilliant on the horizon captured her attention.

Amid the lush vegetation, majestic marble spires stood tall, catching her eye like a beacon of hope. A path flanked by ivory hibiscus flowers led to a welcoming marble gate, matching the pristine color of the spires. The open gate, with its cylindrical bars adorned by two lions flanking the letter 'Z,' was connected to towering walls, each at least twenty meters in height, ending with graceful merlons. Upon closer inspection, she realized that the very spires she noticed were an integral part of the walls themselves.

Overwhelmed by the splendid sight before her, Juliet couldn't help but voice her thoughts, "Is this the Zeller Kingdom they were talking about?"

"Dynasty, even." A male voice chimed nearby, startling Juliet and sending a shiver down her spine.

A tall young man with a pixie cut hairstyle appeared at the gates. His initial smile faded as he noticed Juliet clutching her chest. He clenched his teeth and flexed his neck in an apologetic gesture and then positioned himself on the other side of the gate, facing her. Without hesitation, he welcomed Juliet and assisted her with her horse. Once they had secured the horse's reins, they walked together under a sheltered path towards the main castle.

The young man continued, his natural smile returning, "Kingdoms aren't as large as true dynasties, you know. A kingdom encompasses between one and ten million acres with a population of at least a million. An empire, on the other hand, goes beyond those numbers, with a population exceeding a hundred million. Now, a genuine empire, or dynasty, has stricter criteria. There are three nations worldwide that meet these requirements. Their lineage needs to span over a century, and the land they own must exceed a billion acres, with a population matching that."

As Juliet adjusted her attire to appear more presentable and concealed her distinctive marking, she turned her attention to the man and admitted, "I never had the pleasure of experiencing the hospitality of an empire nor dynasty firsthand."

"Is that so?" He asked with a spike of curiosity before continuing, "I've never heard of anyone, above all a woman such as yourself, living without some knowledge of governance. It's rather peculiar, in my opinion. In our realm, we study subjects like history and mathematics with the utmost importance. We excel in many areas, among other things. But, pardon my digression. What is your name?"

After providing her name, the young man introduced himself, saying, "It's a pleasure to meet you. I am Vincent Zeller, a young cousin of the Grand Emperor himself," and bowed, a faint grin playing at the corners of his lips.

Juliet glanced to the side and displayed a smirk that would make her mother proud. "It's a pleasure to meet you. Please, enlighten me about the distinctions between an Emperor and a Grand Emperor."

Vincent offered her a tour amid his enthusiastic explanations, which she accepted. They first walked through the luxurious Town Square was a vast, open expanse of cobblestone streets, flanked by a symphony of styled architecture. It was not just a central gathering place but a living tapestry that showcased the synthesis of history and innovation. Here, the past and future mixed with grace to create a unique and thriving civilization, where every corner told a story of unity, knowledge, and prosperity. The centerpiece of the square was a majestic, carved marble fountain, its cascading waters adorned with statues of legendary heroes and mythical creatures. This fountain was surrounded by a lush garden of vibrant flowers and pruned hedges, which added a colorful contrast to the gray stone surroundings. Dominating one side of the square was the magnificent Zeller Castle, the epicenter of their power. Its towering walls, constructed from sturdy gray stone, were adorned with banners bearing the Zeller emblem. The main entrance was a pair of colossal wooden doors, abundant with ornate ironwork, depicting scenes from the dynasty's storied history.

Nestled in one corner of the square, the Grand Library of Wisdom was a hub of knowledge and enlightenment. Its architecture blended ancient design with modern advancements. The library boasted a vast collection of books and scrolls preserved through the ages. Scholars and curious minds from far and wide flocked to its grand entrance adorned with towering columns and a bronze owl sculpture, a symbol of wisdom. On the opposite side of the square stood the Temple of Unity, a place of spiritual significance. The temple was a sanctuary, a massive structure constructed with marble and adorned with intricate stained glass windows depicting scenes from various faiths. Inside, visitors could find a serene courtyard with lush gardens and tranquil reflection pools.

The square also hosted the Guildhall of Artisans, a hub for the dynasty's craftsmen and artists. Its exterior showcased crafted sculptures and beautiful murals, highlighting the artistic prowess of the Zeller citizens. Inside, various workshops and studios bustled with activity as craftsmen and artisans perfected their trade. On the far side of the square, the Merchant Exchange was an elegant building where traders, artisans, and merchants gathered. Its facade featured a blend of gothic arches and modern ironworks, signifying the city's position as a trade hub. The interior was filled with commerce, offering a rich variety of wares from across the land. Surrounding the square, open market stalls presented a delightful assortment of goods, from exotic spices and textiles to complex metalwork. Street performers entertained the passing crowds with music, acrobatics, and juggling. The aromatic scents of street food vendors added to the sensory feast, offering a delectable array of cuisine.

Juliet realized that she was one step closer to securing her people's salvation, and perhaps, she pondered, she wouldn't need the Overseer's aid in the end – which might even be for the best, as he bore some responsibility for the hardships that had befallen her people.

Chapter 2.5

The plan to enhance the Overseer's vision for world peace through the Amicitia Licentiam included a multi-faceted strategy. This involved diplomatic outreach, a willingness to address leaders' concerns by amending the agreement, centralizing authority while ensuring transparency and accountability, and creating an impartial conflict resolution mechanism. The plan emphasized the establishment of a common defense force to a significant reduction in military spending, foster economic cooperation, and initiate humanitarian initiatives aimed at promoting goodwill and diminishing incentives for conflicts. To gain public support, the plan included extensive public awareness campaigns and encouraged civil society engagement. Furthermore, it incorporated measures to respect national sovereignty and offered strategic concessions to appease various stakeholders. It emphasized the importance of continuous dialogue, mediation, and conflict prevention, all while implementing mechanisms to measure the success of these initiatives. This holistic approach aimed to bring about lasting global peace. The Overseer presented this plan with a perfect amount of confidence, though it was met with a somewhat subdued response.

A scoff from Sothis ruptured the room's tranquility, infusing it with unmistakable tension, creating a visible discomfort. In response to this atmosphere, the Overseer, acknowledging the skepticism, inquired with a note of concern, "You doubt me, Sothis?" It was evident that Sothis wasn't convinced.

"I don't doubt your power or wealth; your dominion is set clear at the heart of every nation. I don't even question your High Guardians, for among them is one of my own," he said in a frigid tone. "However, what I do doubt is your understanding of reality. History has never recorded the existence of a single government. Kings of the past have attempted and failed. Their actions resulted in more bloodshed and tarnished their legacies. I appreciate a good challenge, but not a futile one."

Sothis's arched eyebrows challenged the Overseer's position, yet the leader of the Grand Organization countered him. "Of course, such a feat has eluded the past. While I may appear to be a mere visionary, I possess the power to realize my vision. It is natural that I am relentless in this pursuit. Among the regents, the three of you are the ones yet to embrace the Grand Organization's ideology. You have left my invitation unanswered, and in addition, you've enjoyed its benefits without committing to the treaty."

Azrael, hooded, locked eyes with the Overseer before interjecting, "History tells us that power corrupts. What barriers are in place to prevent your ideals from succumbing to the same corruption that ensnared previous visionaries, great one?"

The Overseer savored the inquiry before responding, "Azrael, my old friend, actions speak louder than words. I have demonstrated my success through decades of ethical practice building the Grand Organization, surpassing all who came before me. My intentions are devoid of malice, evident in how I treat other regents. If, at any point in your lives, you've encountered someone with greater patience, empathy, and integrity, please speak now. I am more than willing to step aside if someone can exhibit greater leadership qualities than I have displayed over this time. I regret, there was one other Lord of Peace who epitomized perfection, and despite being mistreated and misunderstood thousands of years ago, his legacy still endures. Trust me when I say no one else alive can establish a functional system with the effectiveness that I can. All I desire is for peace to endure on this earth for all eternity, and this is the path to achieving it."

Azrael witnessed the Overseer's sincerity through his multi-colored eyes and lowered his hood, deep in thought.

Victor observed the relaxed response and posed his own question, "What do you gain from governing this Grand Organization? What motivates you to undertake the demanding task of unity?"

The Overseer stood poised as he replied, "It is a duty entrusted to me, Victor, in the name of true peace. Can you not see that when people have nowhere else to turn, they seek my aid? Why shouldn't I be proactive and protect them from war, disasters, plagues, famine, and any threat to our way of life? I would protect everyone, including yourselves. I do this not for personal gain, but because I am the one capable of doing so. You might call it an obligation, I suppose."

Sothis, however, couldn't contain his outrage any longer. "Hypocrite! You think we are unaware of the Marked Ones within the Grand Organization. You speak in rhetoric of prosperity and insinuate that we all seek your aid in attaining this utopia, while many who have already suffered under your rule are disregarded. How can you expect us not to question you?"

The remark unsettled the Overseer, his clear arms displaying raised hairs. Such a matter was unexpected.

Sothis, ready to depart, held his position for a final remark. "Furthermore, the Wintersun need not depend on your faulty protection. We possess the most potent magic known. If we wished, your Grand Organization would be ashes in a day. Nothing could even approach me, nor. . ."

Before he could complete his statement, a radiant burst of light emanated from the Overseer, blinding the three men. Waves of energy filled the Zeller Hall, scattering debris from the broken table between them, obscuring the vision of everyone present.

Sothis raised a hand to his face, a look of fear in his eyes. Ogling at his palm, he discovered a few drops of his own blood. His expression twisted with anger as he questioned the Overseer, "W-why did you. . .?"

The radiant man interrupted him as he wiped dust from his attire. "The Wintersun may possess the most potent magic known to you, but I am more than you can ever comprehend. It would serve you well to remember this, Sothis. Nothing with malicious intent can survive or challenge me. Be grateful that I stand for divine peace, my friend."

The three leaders fell silent in a contemplative fluster, their attention fixated on the Overseer.

Moments passed, feeling like hours, until Azrael's chuckle broke the silence. "Sothis, I warned you against being so outspoken, lest someone silences you for good and you become a soldier in my army."

Sothis rolled his eyes, and the hooded man redirected the conversation. "Overseer, your power is undeniable. However, do you, in your most genuine opinion, believe you possess the wisdom necessary to lead us? Knowledge and wisdom are both invaluable. As for your dramatic response, Sothis provoked you, so I can overlook that. But how can we be sure that you won't suppress the next leader who dares to question you? Would you resort to veiled threats to maintain control?"

The Overseer drew in a breath. "Azrael, you know there is no better way to get through to someone as headstrong as Sothis. As for your question, I have no intention of seizing your thrones or replacing you. I pledge to protect the dynasties, not to dismantle them. I trust I've made it clear that I do not intend to coerce your compliance."

Azrael lifted his hood, locking eyes with the Overseer once again. "Overseer, the road to every evil is paved with good intentions. You must recognize this. The path before you is filled with challenges, and it could lead to tyranny, jeopardizing everyone involved in your dream. As Grand Emperors, we understand that our authority exists as long as our people permit it. The moment we deviate from the path and the masses grow disenchanted is the moment our courts may decide we must be replaced. Your plans appear to lack such checks and balances."

The Overseer's glassy-like lips curled in contrast to the concerned look in the hooded man's eyes. "I have a duty to fulfill. I will allow my record to speak for itself. I am a unique being, free from the imperfections of lesser individuals. I wield the greatest power, possess the appropriate wisdom, and maintain the correct vision. My realm demonstrates that my system is now the most suitable for our world. I am the ideal candidate for this role, and I intend to remain so. Every other nation has acknowledged my qualifications to lead us to greatness. The question is: How long will you resist the realization of true global peace?"

The Overseer allowed a moment to pass before regaining the leaders' attention. "Gentlemen, I will take a short recess and return after you've had a chance to discuss. I leave the decision making in your hands for now. However, be aware that soon, the Grand Organization will extend to every corner of this planet. Divine peace will flow throughout the universe. It's not a matter of 'if,' but a matter of 'when.'"

As he exited the chambers, the three men released heavy sighs. It was apparent that, in their opinions, this had been a setback, and they couldn't see an immediate way to counter the proposal without perhaps provoking the Overseer further.

Sothis looked to the other monarchs, anticipating a similar fiery response, as he questioned, "If his system works without flaw, why does he ignore the plight of the Marked Ones? For all his confidence, he is allowing a crisis to escalate under his rule while pretending it doesn't exist. If we were to enter his organization, we would have to address a problem that originated within his reign. Are we to stand by as a group of migrants try their luck in our cities?"

Azrael, filled with conflict, cast his scorn downward. "You Wintersuns would have us wage war against the most powerful entity in the known world? You witnessed what such a rash action could lead to. Open hostility would leave your lands little different from the wastelands between realms. Perhaps, instead, we should focus on reconstructing our borders and provide a new home for those people."

Victor gestured to the two in an attempt to regain their attention. "Please, my friends, let us not sow further discord in my chambers. The Overseer has already done enough in that regard. We must not appear weak for the sake of our states, even if it means signing the agreement. Let us maintain our dignity as the royalty of vast lands, and let us explore if the terms can be negotiated with more favor. As for the matter of the migrants, it does not concern me, but I will instruct my scholars to study on the Marked Ones on your behalf, Sothis."

"I concur. For now, let us stall for time with the Overseer. During this period, we can develop a more refined plan. While I do not dispute the appeal of the Amicitia Licentiam, we must ensure we have safeguards in place to prevent potential despotism," Azrael suggested, noting the reluctant agreement in Sothis's demeanor.

Chapter 3.1

The grandeur of Victor's influence left a distinctive imprint on the land, its architecture radiating an unmistakable air of self assured dominance. This, however, had given the Zeller a reputation for arrogance. Both residential and commercial structures, ranging from towering skyscrapers to modest homes, emerged from the ground with an appearance of sculpted, man made elegance. Every street was lined with these impressive structures, from their ornate rooftops to the cobblestones that lined the exterior walls. The neighborhood the Overseer passed through exuded an air of tranquility. Small, multicolored gardens nestled between neighboring homes formed a tight knit community of self sufficient property owners. Even as he breathed in the atmosphere, he caught the scent of fresh baked bread wafting from an open window. Lost in his thoughts, he noticed a passing woman who bore a striking resemblance to Mite.

The Overseer's thoughts took over, and he contemplated, "At her home, none could rival her prestige, and few could beat her in a duel. Her people stand as the most resistant to the law, yet she somehow remains aligned with my goals. She's quick tempered and ruthless, yet a loyal and fierce woman I'm proud to have by my side. There's an undeniable chemistry between us. Perhaps I should reconsider? If it were that simple. My work comes first. I must stay focused."

As the first stars began to twinkle in the evening sky, the Overseer made his way back to the main castle, in search of the three leaders to check on their progress. To his delight, he found the Zeller Hall filled with a diverse array of sun kissed complexions. As he moved through the crowd, he encountered curious watchers, a common occurrence for someone with his captivating presence and reflective skin. His crystal eyes landed on familiar faces: Sothis and Azrael were engrossed in conversation, and Victor was engaged with Vincent on the other side of the room. A smile graced the Overseer's plain countenance, and he decided to engage with some of the attendees, but soon, someone else captured his attention.

This woman, with her auburn hair ablaze like fire against wood, possessed skin as smooth as champagne. She exuded an ethereal quality, as though divinity itself had carved her features. Her grace was evident in the way she sat and moved, in her melodious voice, and in the chosen words she spoke. At the moment, she was locked in a battle of wits with one of the Zeller subjects, discussing riddles and puzzles with an enchanting flair. The Overseer couldn't help but be enchanted by her beauty, not even noticing Victor's playful approach with a wine glass in hand.

"You're staring, your highness," Victor remarked, drawing the Overseer's attention.

In a casual tone, the Overseer looked away and asked, "Which kingdom does she represent?"

"Her? Juliet? As far as I know, she has no kingdom," Victor responded with a smirk, casting a similar glance in her direction. It was clear that Juliet had become the center of attention, as everyone in the room appeared to be entranced by her.

"She comes from a land with no king?" The Overseer couldn't help but scoff at the notion.

Victor's expression held mixed emotions. "And no allegiances, Overseer. But isn't this meeting about more than just one woman?"

The Overseer ignored Victor, his attention fixed on Juliet. She was an enigma, free from any man's rule or any land's dominion. To him, this meant she held potential and value that needed to be explored. The idea formed in his mind: he must speak with her in private.

Yet, as the debate among the attendees continued to gain momentum, The Overseer scanned the room, his surveying darted from one corner to another, searching for a glimpse of Juliet's fiery locks. Her sudden disappearance left him unsettled, a nagging feeling gnawing at him. Was it possible she didn't recognize him, or worse, didn't care? The idea was unsettling, an affront to his authority that he wouldn't let slide. Yet, instead of irritation, he found himself intrigued in the most strange way by her disregard.

"Well, gentlemen, have we come to a decision?" An inattentive Overseer asked, his focus still on the place where Juliet had been.

Azrael, who had approached them, chuckled. "I'm quite sure you were just as captivated by her beauty and wit, weren't you?"

The Overseer sighed. "I suppose, but is one woman worth the risk, even if she is as beautiful and intriguing as her?"

Victor couldn't contain his laughter. "Ah, you admit it. We will reconvene at a later time and provide you with an answer within a week."

The Overseer's flushed face betrayed his embarrassment. "Alright, one week from today, gentlemen. I will await your responses." With that, the Overseer left, heading back to the capital, where he would be consumed by thoughts of Juliet, who was now imprinted in his mind as firm as the dirt beneath his feet.

Chapter 3.2

Impatient footsteps echoed in the corridors of the Grand Organization's main castle as the Overseer awaited a critical report. The silence was broken when Mercury entered, and they exchanged a significant look before the Overseer motioned for Mercury to proceed.

Mercury unstrapped a black leather satchel and placed it on the table. "Sir, unless you want to read them yourself, I can read them aloud to you."

"Go ahead. Read me your report," the Overseer said, maintaining a composed demeanor.

Mercury withdrew a notebook from the satchel and began to share his findings. "Very well then," he began, flipping through the pages of his journal, "We have two of the world's most skilled spies tracking her. We've kept our presence hidden from the other nations. Just you, the spies, and I have knowledge of this information. To begin, it didn't take us long to locate her home. She lives in a modest building, I presume with her mother, outside a rustic village situated between the Calcite and the Shadow Empire. Juliet herself often does not leave her home, but when she does, it's to a nearby pub, about a quarter mile from that road. She often travels alone."

The Overseer nodded, taking in this information. "Thank you, Mercury. I will consider this and take action in correspondence with what I learn on my own accord. You will act as interim Overseer while I'm away. That's all for now."

Recognizing that he should leave, Mercury bowed and exited the room, leaving the satchel behind. The Overseer, however, couldn't resist a brief look at the contents of the satchel. Among the documents, he found a sketch that caught his attention. It was unmistakable, Juliet. The drawing depicted her with an enchanting likeness, and her eyes seemed to pierce his soul. He couldn't help but smile as he admired the sketch.

"You are flawless," he whispered while his translucent thumb traced the edge of the illustration. With care, he placed the study back in the satchel for Mercury to find later and headed out to pursue his next mission – meeting Juliet.

Mite's curiosity got the best of her, prompting her to approach Mercury. As the door closed behind them, she seized his arm, eager to engage in conversation.

"What's going on between you two?" Her urgent whisper carried a hint of suspicion.

Startled, Mercury tried to deflect her, but their brief struggle ended with both of them tripping, landing on the floor, and Mite straddling him, a dagger aimed at his neck. "Mite what are you going on about? Stop this!" Mercury protested, a touch of urgency in his voice.

"What secrets are you hiding from me? What happened at that meeting?" Mite's snarl revealed her growing concern.

Mercury managed to roll her off him and stood up, responding, "You need to stop being so paranoid. It's as if you think the Overseer and I have some secret romance."

Mite blinked a few times, processing this unexpected possibility. "Well, do you?"

"No!" Mercury exclaimed, trying to keep his voice down. "But you know I can't reveal any of the Overseer's plans. If you're concerned, ask him yourself."

Mite's expression became more contemplative as she looked down. "What's happening between us, Merc? I feel like I'm losing him."

While Mercury's response was somewhat cold, he empathized with her. "He was never meant to be yours, Mite. Let's get out of the hallways before we're discovered."

Mite accepted his hand, but the unease of impending change lingered in her gut as they left the room. She wanted nothing more than for everything to remain as they were. Without warning, the servant Amelia cracked the door open, and both High Guardians ducked from fear of being caught and withdrew from the area in surprise.

Chapter 3.3

As the Overseer made his way along the dusty road that led to the Calcite Empire, he contemplated the secretive nature of the Shadow Empire. In a world where nations displayed their power in pride with towering castles, its determination to remain concealed was abnormal, shrouded in mystery and intrigue. This land, however, kept itself shrouded in myths, making it challenging to discern fact from fiction. One thing he did know was that its population was rumored to match that of the Diamond Mortem, yet they remained hidden, their presence unknown to most. All Mercury had brought with him was a sketch of a representative from the Shadow Empire and a document of allegiance to the Grand Organization, lending little insight into this enigmatic land.

The Overseer's walk shifted when he glimpsed Juliet strolling along the path near the hills, just as Mercury had depicted. The sight captivated him, igniting a blend of emotions. He attempted to rationalize it as mere fascination or interest, but the rapid thud of his heart revealed otherwise.

As Juliet vanished into a nearby pub, maneuvering like melted butter through the weathered wooden door, the Overseer hastened his steps to prevent losing sight of her. Despite the discord of voices resonating from inside, posing potential challenges, his determination to confront Juliet outweighed any doubts. This uncharacteristic feeling bewildered him, leaving a perplexed expression on his face, but he pushed it aside.

Stepping into the timeworn pub, both Juliet and Arvid, an exile from the Calcite Empire, halted their conversation to focus on the unexpected arrival.

"Please, continue. I didn't mean to intrude," the Overseer responded to their curious looks, shattering the silence.

As expected, the pub's occupants, including Juliet and Arvid, recognized the Overseer and sensed his visit held significance. It was unconventional for someone of his stature to venture into such a rustic establishment. Nevertheless, the peculiar circumstances demanded their conversation to come to an awkward halt.

Then, Juliet's voice, sultry yet unwavering, cut through the thick tension, revealing a boldness the Overseer had not encountered before. "Overseer, are you stalking me?"

The Overseer's toes curled as embarrassment crept over him, despite his efforts to project confidence. "Well. . ." he began, clearing his throat to regain his composure, "In all my existence, you are the first of your kind that I have encountered, and I cannot help but notice a certain. . . stench about you, m'lady." He managed a slight bow and a wry smile. "Curiosity got the better of me, I suppose," he added with a genuine smile.

Juliet shot a glance at Arvid. "I guess I can add that to the list then. . ."

A momentary surprise crossed the Overseer's face. "A list of. . . what?"

"It's Juliet, Overseer," she corrected him, a note of sarcasm in her tone, "and do you refer to the women you are intrigued by by their kind in most cases? Seems a bit odd."

The Overseer could feel the blood from his cheeks hit the floor, his embarrassment evident, but he regained his composure within seconds and replied, "I use names for individuals once I've come to know them more. Not everyone has that honor."

"Ah, 'honor' it is, then? My apologies, Your Lordship," Juliet quipped. She then rose, mocking a curtsy before resuming her seat. "This list has to do with a dream I had."

The Overseer's interest was piqued, and he leaned in. "A dream? Please, elaborate."

With a sardonic smile, Juliet began, "Just a dream I had of somebody who used their tongue to—"

"To explore what your outer layer tasted like." the Overseer finished her sentence, suggesting that he knew the nature of her dream. Their eyes locked, and the beauty in her eyes drew him in, like a gateway to a realm of captivating enchantment. Their smiles broadened, and they shared a soft laugh. Juliet's glances darted away as their conversation continued. "Well, you know how those dreams can be. You'll have to forgive them."

"I don't. . . won't," she replied, furrowing her brow. "Besides, if you are the Overseer, shouldn't you already know everyone in your lands by name?"

The Overseer paused, feeling both intrigued and challenged by her, before responding, "Not everyone, Juliet. As of yet, you seem to be an exception to every rule!" His tone light, he considered, "How dare she speak to me this way. She is not incorrect but she is out of place. . ."

Juliet interjected, her voice unwavering. "Overseer, I meant no disrespect, but please understand that in my short life, I've learned that fear is not more potent than an actual punch to the gut, and those who growl the loudest often have the softest underbellies. I will not be your victim."

"I am not seeking a victim, Juliet; I am nothing more than bound by interest. That is all. I mean no harm, nor do I require anything from you." The Overseer put on his most sincere expression, and after a few seconds of silence, he tried to pull himself away, but Juliet's lascivious look held him captive, drawing him in deeper with each passing moment. He wondered, "What is it about this woman? Why am I so invested?"

"Well, Overseer, I gave you my name. I think it's fair if you give me yours?" He hesitated for a moment, contemplating the risk of entrusting this crucial truth to her enigmatic hands, before regaining his composure and saying in a composed tone, "Just call me your Overseer," as he walked out into the moonlight.

The Overseer's perception of an innocent Juliet was shattered. Her purity was not the defining characteristic; it was her calculated bluntness that stood out. Strange, he was drawn to it, just as he was to the depths of her eyes. Desire stirred within him, though she seemed to just tolerate him.

"I can work with that," the Overseer pondered, considering Juliet's predictable routine. "So, she takes the same route to the same pub every day. Interesting," he muttered under his breath. Juliet's performance had not deterred his determination to study her. He continued his relentless pursuit of the warmth her presence brought him, even leading him to leave Mercury in charge of his duties as he concealed himself behind a tree, observing the woman who had captured his fancy.

"You can stop hiding; I know you're there, Mr. Overseer," Juliet stated as she exited the pub. Her narrowed eyes honed in on his location, compelling him to reveal himself. A mixture of annoyance and disbelief flashed across Juliet's face as she placed her hand on her hip.

"You got me this time, Juliet," he acknowledged with a wry smile. Although embarrassment danced in through his words, he regained his confidence with ease. This was the perfect opportunity to initiate a conversation, a small victory, perhaps.

"Have you been following women since you were little, or is this a new hobby of yours?" she mocked him, her brow raised in self defense.

The Overseer's stomach churned at the quick witted retort, as sharp as ever. "I'd rather discuss my past in front of a drink, but I can assure you it's not common for me to be deliberate in my pursuit of a woman."

Juliet let out a slow exhale, her words inaudible as she murmured to herself. "There was no way to escape this one, no matter how much she would rather argue." She gathered an air of hospitality, looked up at him, and said, "Come, let's have a drink, so I can get to know your past."

"At last," he pressed through his teeth with enthusiasm. He gathered his belongings, eager to join her as she led the way back into the pub.

Arvid cleaned a glass as they sat, casting cautious glances at the Overseer while preparing their drinks. The room wasn't crowded, but enough regulars were present, engaging in awkward coughs and shifts in their seats as they talked amongst themselves about the unwelcome newcomer, creating an atmosphere thick with tension, marked by the clamor of creaking and squeaking chairs and tables.

Juliet wasted no time before launching into her investigation. "So, how did the Overseer come to be?"

Numerous eyes remained locked on the Overseer, as he continued to admire the sheen of Juliet's red hair, captivated by her presence. He was too engrossed to consider not answering. "Well, from what I recall, over time, I acquired the abilities of every species. This gave me the best traits of any living being, just short of god-like."

"Are you claiming to be a god?" Juliet scrutinized, her brows furrowing at the thought.

The Overseer threw up his hands and backtracked. "By no means would I ever consider myself a deity. I am just someone who feels he has earned his place and is respected by Omnipotence himself."

"And how did you earn your powers, Overseer?" Juliet inquired with intense interest.

A smirk grew on his dark lips. He was aware of the impact his words held, knowing and confident. "Through just a little bit of contact. The tiniest of fluids is all I need: blood, sweat, saliva. . . quom," he stated with a lowered tone of seduction.

Arvid almost dropped his glass from what he overheard, but he caught himself in time to avoid interrupting the conversation. His shock was nothing compared to the sheer horror that seized Juliet, visible through the tension in her hands as she brought her drink to her lips and finished it. The Overseer failed to register her response, and the full implications of his words escaped him. However, for the very first time, the commoners present had gained a valuable clue to a sinister secret about him.

Chapter 3.4

"I'm still surprised you accepted my dinner invitation," the Overseer mused as they sat together. Despite the Marked Ones feeling uneasy in his presence, they had grown accustomed to the fact that Juliet was his focus. Over the week since their first encounter in the pub, he had mustered the courage to ask Juliet to dinner, even though she had been reluctant to meet him at sunset in his castle. However, she didn't reject his invitation.

She stifled a laugh as she looked out over the headquarters balcony towards the horizon. "Why would I dare turn down the opportunity for a free meal with the true king of the world?"

Absolute terror was etched on the face of the dark haired woman, Mite. She hid away, avoiding the staff working along the corridors while watching the scene unfold like a predator stalking its prey. Her confusion was evident, and the anger within this Wintersun bubbled to such a degree that her seething could pierce through flesh and bone if it were possible. Her ears perked up, tuning in to the conversation between this foreigner and the man she loved.

Servants waltzed in, setting down plates in front of them with grace, filling the table with a variety of dishes. Among them, Juliet recognized baked salmon drizzled with garlic, parsley, basil, and lemon, served on a bed of steamed rice. Her stomach grumbled with envy at the wondrous aroma. The servants gestured for the unforeseen couple to enjoy their meal as they poured them each an aged glass of red wine. At first, the Overseer and Juliet exchanged a few words, but with time, he grew more comfortable, speaking of things he knew, desired, and had achieved. However, nothing quite matched the grace of Juliet's presence—her mind, her voice, from that of otherworlds. Yet, she offered a sincere smile and thanked him for the compliments, with no banter or scorn to offer. Their dinner remained pleasant and civil all the way through, and soon their plates were empty, and their stomachs full.

"I didn't anticipate it, but I enjoyed this evening," Juliet said as she wiped her mouth with a handkerchief.

She was just about to excuse herself when the Overseer interrupted with a bold kiss. The servants watched in awe as Juliet blushed, taken aback by the unexpected yet not troubling turn of events. Mite gawked at the sight but turned away as tears welled up in her eyes. She almost ran, her heart shattering, trying to escape further embarrassment.

She would retire to a guest bedroom that night, and by morning, she was gone. It became a familiar sight for the servants, who grew accustomed to her presence, expecting her to grace the halls with her quiet elegance. Despite her regular visits, little changed in the grand scheme of things. Each evening concluded in much the same manner, leaving the Overseer undisturbed in his solitude, a recess from the demands of his duties.

Even the locals began to take note of Juliet's frequent appearances, recognizing her as a fixture in the Overseer's sanctuary. She had, in essence, become a part of the fabric of his life. Over time, the moments shared with Juliet became precious to him, something to be nurtured and cherished above all else. In her company, he found solace from the pressures of leadership and responsibility. Each encounter with her brought a sense of calm and contentment, as a shell upon the shore of a beach.

Until one day, one such moment was disrupted by a familiar voice.

"Uhm, excuse me, Overseer?" Mercury crept up behind him, stopping at a reasonable distance to ensure that the news he was about to deliver wouldn't result in his premature end.

"Yes, Mercury?" He suppressed his irritation, remembering that there were still duties that needed attention.

The golden figure responded in his humble cadence, "It's the High Guardians, Overseer. They need to meet with you at your earliest convenience."

"Fine. Get the itineraries ready." The Overseer waved his hand with annoyance, although the gesture was unnecessary, as the golden arches in the room shifted to match his attitude. Mercury eyed them under cautious pretenses, aware that this signaled trouble. He was uncertain but feared for the stability of the Grand Organization. He chose not to verify his theories, leaving as soon as he could without being disrespectful. Still, something felt off, and Mercury couldn't quite shake the feeling that there was something peculiar about Juliet.

"There is another meeting?" Juliet asked with a disappointed groan, as the answer was both clear and unpleasant. "Why can't they just leave us be?"

"Yes, dear, there is another meeting. Since I am the Overseer, they need my guidance, and we are expecting an update from the last meeting at the Zeller castle. It has been a while longer than I would allow, but I have been rather distracted in the past few days." The revealing statement carried no remorse for his choice of words.

"Well, what happens at these meetings?" she asked with a playful laugh.

He looked at her dumbfounded, "What do you mean? You have been to them before."

Juliet rose to exclaim, "Correction! I have been to one and that was because. . ." she paused, unsure what to say next before dismissing her intrusive thoughts with a shake of her head, "Well, that is no longer important. The situation was handled."

The Overseer added, "You know that the High Guardians and the emperors they represent are the ones who may attend, and you are not with any faction at all. The fact that you were there at all is unheard of."

"Yes, of course," she said with a growing grin. "I attend those types of meetings because I must! Don't you see that those who represent their kingdoms do not disseminate the minutes of those meetings? The people of those lands deserve to know what their leaders are plotting."

He chuckled. "Plotting? m'lady, you make me out to be a fiend!"

She gave a light smack on his shoulder, infusing a hint of strength into the gesture. "You are a fiend!" They laughed together. "If it were me, I would want to know what my king was deciding for me, wouldn't you agree?"

"You are an interesting one, Juliet," The Overseer replied with genuine humility.

"I like to think so," she smiled. "It's just that so many people grow tired of being lied to by their superiors."

"I just want to maintain a certain level of unity and peace, and sometimes. . ." he trailed off.

"Sometimes what?" she asked with a lighthearted tone, choosing her words with care to avoid arousing his suspicion.

"Well, sometimes sacrifices have to be made. Something small has to be done to prevent something larger from coming to fruition," he said, his voice filled with confidence. He looked away, hesitating to see her face, and thus, he didn't notice her eyes glazing over with boredom.

When he decided to look back at her, he found her fixated on him. He started to pull away, but she guided his face back to hers, determined to keep him engaged. "Sounds to me like even the big, bad Overseer needs some reassurance."

During the meeting, the Overseer celebrated the welcome news of both the Zeller and Diamond Mortem dynasties joining the Grand Organization in full. However, a month had passed, and the Wintersun had not yet accepted the invitation. The castle buzzed with festivities for world peace, with everyone appearing joyous, except for Juliet, who remained in deep concern about the well being of her mother and the other Marked Ones.

The subsequent month was a time of uninterrupted togetherness for the new couple. The Overseer bestowed upon Juliet a wardrobe filled with a variety of elegant dresses and took her on journeys to far off lands, revealing a world of diverse wonders. Over time, Juliet grew to accept his idiosyncrasies and quirks, relishing in the royal treatment he lavished upon her. As the next meeting approached, the Overseer made a surprising decision to skip it, passing the responsibility on to Mercury. This stirred resentment among some of the High Guardians towards Juliet. Mite, in particular, decided it was time to voice her frustration.

She seized the opportunity to confront Juliet while the Overseer was away, pinning the redhead against a wall with her lips just inches away from Juliet's ear. In a harsh whisper, she hissed, "Listen here, bitch."

Juliet's breath caught in her throat as she stepped back, but Mite closed the distance, her hands gripping Juliet's shoulders, preventing her escape. With a quick response, Juliet delivered a knee between the High Guardian's thighs, causing an agonizing shriek to escape the pale woman's lips. As the redhead retreated, she could hear Mite's weak but irritated voice hurling a barrage of threats and insults.

Since that moment, Juliet clung to her newfound love, embracing him and cherishing the safety and comfort he provided.

The Overseer had been delaying an acknowledgment to himself, but one day, he decided to voice an idea that had been ringing in his mind like a bell in a church. "Juliet?" He eased into the quiet, breaking its comfort with gentle words, "Would you accompany me to the next meeting?"

Her silver tongue twisted and shot out, "I thought you would never ask!" she said, her smile gaining an intriguing edge that was difficult to interpret.

After a few more minutes spent in intimacy, the Overseer pulled back and said, "In all of my two hundred years—"

"Two hundred? What in the blaze are you?" Juliet scrutinized him with a mix of alarm and curiosity.

"Oh Juliet, as I said before, I am above all things except the gods. I am the living being closest to perfection, second to none other than you." He flattered her with a dramatic dance with his hands before leaning down for a kiss. In that embrace, he felt her touch as an integral part of his most private self – his emotions, his soul. He was almost certain that her overwhelming warmth would have consumed a normal man, but he had not tasted her enough to expire just yet. "So this is what it must feel like to kiss a goddess," his thoughts resonated.

Juliet felt it all through the kiss as well, and couldn't discern her feelings apart from his. She received his openness with a warm heart, showing empathy rather than disdain. Juliet contemplated his yearning, and with a soft whisper embraced his love, "delicious." She did not intend to let the Overseer get addicted, but it was a soothing experience that they both shared.

She asked with tantalizing fingers tracing the pearlescent reflection of his chest, "What makes your skin so. . . unique?" The Overseer closed his eyes and soaked in her presence, engraving this moment inside his memory so the feeling would never leave him even when she's away.

The Overseer closed his eyes and savored her touch, exhaling with subtle pleasure. "It's what happens when my kind assimilates the qualities of all others."

"Your kind?" She posed a curious question, her lips trailing behind her fingers, skimming down his abdomen, eliciting subtle shivers.

"I belong to a breed assumed to be extinct, I'm the last of my kind, the Justitiarius Cryptonym." The Overseer sighed in relief as Juliet was left in a state of perplexity.

Chapter 3.5

In an abandoned church on the outskirts of the Calcite Empire, those who had been exiled from the realm gathered to convene. Men, women, and children alike sought refuge within the old building to escape the night air's cool breeze. They were joined by a flock of

Wingmen from the Hawke Empire, who perched on withered, ancient trees. The crowd continued to swell as visitors from foreign lands arrived, and in the center, one figure towered above the others nearby.

"Ara, we stand by your side, my lord!" A Wingman called out, encouraging others to voice their agreement.

Ara's mere presence possessed a charisma that quieted the dense congregation that had filled the church. Standing before the crowd, he squared his shoulders and began to address them. "Thank you all for gathering here today to bear witness to this proclamation. I must ask that you take my words at face value, for I speak the truth."

People who were already seated were compelled to rise to their feet to make space for the increasing number of attendees. Ara waited until the room fell silent before continuing, "Today, we have assembled members of the Hawke Empire, the Howlitte, the Blood Moon, the Kristos, and even a representative from the Carnelian Empire."

As he mentioned each nation, cheers and applause echoed through the room as the representatives from those lands stood and nodded in respect.

"My fellow countrymen, I have called you here today to focus on one particular group, the Marked Ones, who bear no banner. Many nations, including the Calcite Empire, have stripped them of their property and well being. We, the privileged, must understand that these former citizens have no sanctuary to turn to. No other nation will accept them. Why is that? Why must these families endure a life of destitution and hardship, homeless and poor?" Ara's voice echoed.

A hushed silence filled the room.

Ara's wings gave a brief and subtle flap before he continued with fervor, "My friends, the nation that abandons its people should be held accountable. However, we are deceived by a hidden monster pulling the strings. These refugees suffer because they cannot seek refuge under another banner. We have all been manipulated into a facade of a united nation, controlled by the Grand Organization of the Amicitia Licentiam."

A unanimous uproar erupted, shaking the church's windows and walls as passionate cries filled the room.

"Ladies and gentlemen, I speak of vengeance and vindication. Our current monarchs have wronged the people with impunity. Our leaders remain protected by the Overseer's authority and become reckless, insulting other nations as if we cannot hold our own against them."

Chants of Ara's name began, and he continued his speech, shouting with tears in his eyes.

"Empires and kingdoms assembled here with me today, I tell you we must fight for the common folk! We must strive to support one another, not just make hollow promises of unity! Our nations exist to serve all within our borders, not just those who swear allegiance! The people's welfare is our priority! We must seek justice for these injustices. We must fight for independence from the Grand Organization because through that independence, we must stand united!"

As the crowd celebrated and chanted, a hooded woman approached the speaker from behind. Ara crouched so she could whisper in his ear, revealing a cunning plan that would aid their mission. Every detail had to be perfect, as any slip up could be fatal to their cause. A revolution was brewing, and the Hawke Empire was on the brink of acquiring the most valuable weapon to assist in their victory; a gateway to infiltrate the heart of the Grand Organization. The woman moved her aged hands in the air as she explained Juliet's role and how it might create an opening for the Marked Ones to rise and claim a space they could call home.

Ara responded with hope, not just for a small piece of land but to expose the Overseer's fallacious concept of peace. He elaborated on how the world would never attain true peace by accepting a law created by one man. He cited historical treaties that had led to larger wars, kingdoms that had fallen to give rise to empires, and lineages that had been extinguished due to the diseases caused by interbreeding. The core of his message was that the Marked Ones were victims of the Overseer's cunning, and that due to this loophole, which the Calcite Empire had exploited, these exiles would be hated and hunted over years still to come. Ara concluded that the nations that continued to support this system had one final opportunity to change, or else be consumed by the flames of rebellion.

What they didn't realize was that there was one faction that had been overlooked amid all the talk of revolution. This banner, which had yet to accept or reject the Grand Organization's invitation, would become the deciding factor in the conflict if war broke out. This dynasty was not just one of the three most influential nations, but their soldiers possessed the unique ability to nullify the powers of others, ensuring their opponents would be defenseless in the upcoming war. A few critical decisions remained to determine which side the great Wintersun Dynasty would align with.

Chapter 4.1

"Enim Amicitia." The Overseer's voice resonated through the Grand Hall, carrying an unusual sense of cheerfulness.

In unison, the High Guardians responded in a soft spoken "Pacem."

As the meeting drew to a close, Mite's eyes flickered towards the red headed woman seated beside him. Juliet felt the weight of the other woman's sharp glare, but she didn't flinch. Instead, she met Mite's obsidian eyes head on, a mischievous grin playing on her lips, unfazed by the evident hostility. The porcelain-like woman averted her gaze, trying but failing to conceal the anguish that burned within her heart. The Overseer walked with Juliet towards the exit, and many of the High Guardians followed them out, but a select few remained, including the now irate Mite.

"She burns me up!" Her emotions bubbled to the surface, manifesting as visible tension in her posture and a sharp exhale that betrayed the simmering frustration within her.

"You don't seem to be on fire," Hari chuckled.

Pretending to ignore him, she continued, "I pity the Overseer for falling for some sleaze. We don't know her intentions; anyone who pledges allegiance to no one is suspicious." She took a deep breath to calm her nerves before adding, "It just does not sit well."

"With whom? You?" Hari teased, his half smile more playful than sincere.

"As well as many others!" Mite snapped at the insinuation that her anger might be nothing but petty jealousy. "Are you okay with her? Do you trust her? Is she justified to be a part of these meetings, or is she in effect jeopardizing our peace?"

"Well, maybe you should try looking at it from a different perspective," Mercury interjected, sensing that the tense atmosphere might escalate into a more significant problem.

"And what might that be?" Mite refocused her attention on the golden man.

"He is the Overseer. He also pledges to no one." Mercury pointed out, "Therefore, it is fitting that he ends up with yet another who does the same." He concluded with a nonchalant shrug.

Haklo's curiosity was piqued, prompting him to comment on the situation. "The Overseer has been seen around town with her. Plenty of folks support them and recite poems about blooming flowers. This isn't the issue. What about her presence within our walls? How long until she becomes the de facto Overseer instead of Mercury? It appears as though the Overseer is entrusting the entire organization to her silver tongue."

"Of Course!" the pale woman exclaimed. "Soon Juliet will be sitting in his seat and speaking on his behalf."

Darakon saw this as the right moment to chime in. "No one can deny her debating prowess—"

"She's overconfident." Mite retorted, cutting his compliment of Juliet short.

Mercury, not bothered by her ire, continued to defend the Overseer. "The agenda hasn't changed, and the Grand Organization remains intact. If Juliet is the one who has captured his heart, then who better to lead alongside him? Peace is still being maintained, and not much has changed. In the Overseer's view, this is paradise."

"It's a fool's paradise." Mite muttered under her breath, but Mercury heard and sighed in disbelief. He figured no amount of logic would change her mind.

He let his golden eyes shift to Haklo, Darakon, and then to the defeated woman, offering all the sympathy he could muster. "I understand where your hearts are, my friends, but it is still his choice."

Chapter 4.2

Juliet exhaled in sudden, unexpected relief at the sight of a familiar face defined by a mirror-like complexion. She could see her eyes in his, and his breath even echoed her own. Hair from the top of his head dangled and tickled her forehead. She couldn't help but smile at his calm demeanor. She admired his lips and how succulent they tasted. The Overseer's body highlighted hers as the colors danced in different tints. His chiseled abs hovered over her plain stomach, his chest almost touching her breasts.

He smiled as she welcomed him, biting down on her lower lip as he moved in closer. Her warm tone moved against him, and he reached his heavy hand for her neck, placing it around her throat with a delicate touch. He felt the blood flow in her veins as he lifted her jaw in the process, pinning her further down with enough strength to make her spine arch in submission. He could see one of her hands lift up, and as she did he gripped her wrist with his free hand and pinned it down. Her mouth opened with her cheeks flushed. She enjoyed being manhandled, and he enjoyed taking control. This new position was different from what he was used to, but he enjoyed that too. He reminisced for a moment.—

Mite's porcelain-like hands gripped onto the leather strap that was tied around his neck. The Overseer looked up as her muscles flexed, his knees cold from the floor he knelt on. She stood over him with her bare legs touching his shoulders. Her cold stare from this angle made the hairs on his arms and back rise. He smiled through his shallow breathing, hoping she would smile back. She instead pulled tighter, to where his nose tickled the top of her inner thigh. He was surprised that he enjoyed the fact that even though she looked as cold as snow, she felt warm.—

The Overseer scrunched his face as he came back to the present, and even though Juliet noticed, she paid it no mind. Her rose-like hair matched and blended with the red petals scattered around her head, somewhat disappearing into the creases of the pearl colored satin bed sheets she layed on. They moved along as her fingers curled into a clenched fist, pulling on the fabric as she tried to ground herself. He put on the sweetest of grins as he put more of his weight onto her still focused on and mesmerized by Juliet's awestruck gasps. His lips roamed over every mark. He searched every imperfect crevice. Touching every glistening patch. He even admired the way her curves casted shadows. They reminded him of the dark patterns he memorized from her skin.—

Her pitch black hair covered his face as she pressed her body onto him, the spikes that protruded from her back appeared menacing, and yet beautiful. Her tribal markings twisted all throughout her pale topless body, complementing her curves. The symmetrical design began on the outside of her calf muscle, then spiraled up her thick thighs. They stretched around from the back and curved over her abs to almost touch her navel but then pushed away to intertwine with the spikes on her back. The pattern was elegant and smooth, a near perfect work of art. At last, the tips of the design rounded over her shoulder and ended just before touching each of her snow white nipples.—

The Overseer opened his eyes once again to admire the set on Juliet's breasts that resembled honey roasted pecans. As they moved back and forth he began to crave the taste, and used his mouth to accompany that desire. He pressed his body into Juliet as his pulse quickened. The pure bliss reduced them both into a needy mess, letting out keen whines for each other to hear. Juliet began lifting her hips to contrast against his, matching his pace in a delicious dance. They both shared a joyous clamor that thundered in his ears, in sync with the sound of the headboard crashing against the wall which then echoed throughout the castle as if its foundations were being shaken by some kind of military assault.—

The Overseer adored how his general dominated the field and his bed. She pressed against the greyscale of his chest as she began to straddle him. While on top of him, and he in her, she in turn curled her snowlike fingers and dragged her nails down his chest, leaving red scars of pleasure. As he winced, she ran the palm of her hand across his cheek to silence him. She began again as he bit his lip in obedience. His heart raced as Mite started digging deeper. Deeper. Deeper.—

Juliet pulled him closer, spreading her thighs and letting his lower body fit into the exhilarating warmth that radiated between them. His crystal eyes looked into hers and he saw his own elation being matched by his lover, the thought of Mite came to him once again. Guilt caught up to him in an overwhelming presence, and in a desperate effort to get rid of any imagined resemblance with his previous partner, he switched up Juliet's position without slowing his pace, continuing to make both her pleasure and his grow into something sharper. Hotter. Higher**.** He admired every inch of her from this new point of view before latching onto her hair, going from light strokes to grabbing a fistful of soft red strands and pulling them into a fist, bringing her mindless pleasure to a stuttering stop before tipping her off the edge. All at once, this new rush reached a peak and made the Overseer explode with roaring enjoyment**.** She could feel him spill and fill inside her as they both reached their peaks. The room grew quiet as they took some time to share a moment of tenderness in the afterglow of it all, listening to each other's heartbeat slow down once more and soaking in the simple feeling of tranquility they exuded, before cleaning each other and their room up.

"Love, does this gown accentuate my figure?" Juliet's fingers toyed with her locks as she admired into the mirror, her curiosity piqued by the reflection staring back at her. Despite the wild tangle of strands, there was a certain allure to the mess, a subtle reminder of the events that had led to her current disarray.

"Yes, dear, it does." The Overseer marveled at the simple pleasure he found in assisting Juliet with her wardrobe choices. How had he, a man of power and authority, come to derive such contentment from such a mundane task? The answer eluded him, yet he knew that Juliet possessed a rare and extraordinary quality that captivated him. Something about her made him unable to even consider breathing too far away from her, as the world felt dull in comparison to the fascinating array of color she seemed to spread everywhere she went. Nothing else in the entire world could quite match her in the Overseer's eyes, even when she did things such as lingering in the closet because none of her outfits appealed to her. He took this hesitation as his cue to intervene and with but a wave of his hand, a sky blue dress was recolored to match the kind of dark crimson he knew she preferred.

His musings were interrupted by a sharp rap at the door. "Come in!" they both shouted out and shared a laugh, reveling in the simple joy of being in sync, a testament to their growing connection.

Mercury entered the bedroom in a hurry, addressing the Overseer. "Sir?"

The Overseer, noticing the unusual urgency in Mercury's voice, inquired, "Yes, Mercury, what is it now? Another meeting?"

The devoted messenger hesitated, struggling to suppress the tension in his words. "Well, sir, you're half right."

The Overseer leaned forward, intrigued. "And the other half?"

"Mite is requesting a private meeting with you. . . alone." Mercury glanced at Juliet with subtle intent, hoping to convey something to her, before continuing. "It appears she needs to discuss an urgent matter concerning another sanction."

The Overseer's brow furrowed in a muted sign of anger and impending trouble. Mercury could sense the shift in his demeanor, and it didn't bode well for whoever had triggered it.

"We have another meeting in a few days," the Overseer replied, "if it's of dire urgency, why didn't she come to report herself? I'll take care of it when I can."

"Indeed, sir. Thank you." Mercury responded, nodding in obedience. He left the room in a hurry, closing the door behind him to create some distance between himself and the already irritable Overseer. In the presence of both the Overseer and Mite, he often felt surrounded by formidable individuals who had the potential for destructive wrath. "If that woman would just let her fiery temper simmer," he thought to himself. However, he couldn't deny that he appreciated Mite's spirited behavior when she directed her antagonism towards Juliet rather than the Overseer. Mite's feistiness was refreshing and bold, traits Mercury couldn't afford to have himself.

The Overseer's blank stare met Juliet's pursed lips. She approached him with an air of elegance, adorn in flowing crimson fabric that danced behind her with each long stride. Coming to a halt mere inches from his face, she tilted her head, a silent question in her eyes.

"Go, check on your other lover," she said, her tone teasing and light, meant to provide comfort but failing.

He countered, "You know I have no other lover, but I am going to see her." There was a rigid glint in his eyes, betraying his unwavering commitment to his words, even in the face of potential conflict.

The Overseer gave Juliet a brief kiss before leaving. He couldn't deny the hints of truth in her comments, and they did irk him somewhat. However, he couldn't deny that Mite had always been a reliable and unwavering pillar of support for him and the Grand Organization. Since the day they met, her competence had been beyond reproach, she was consistent in offering wise and sound advice that he had no qualms listening to. She provided her presence and assistance as a loyal woman, and he felt indebted to her for any meeting she requested.

As he approached the entrance to the Grand Hall, he spotted the familiar figure. "Hello, Mite. You beckoned me?"

Mite scanned the area over the Overseer's shoulder, searching for any potential eavesdroppers. She decided it was safer to discuss the matter in the relative secrecy of the empty Grand Hall. Within seconds and without explanation, she ushered him inside, locked the door behind them, and then turned to face him.

"There is drama brewing in the barren lands," she began, her tone grave but not displaying the urgency of the situation. "The Calcite Empire has exiled even more of their citizens."

The Overseer's voice grew serious. "How many?"

"At least twenty thousand, including women and children," she replied without hesitation. She continued to glance at the hall's various entry points, vigilant for eavesdroppers.

"What madness is this? What reason could they have for such extensive exile? Everything seemed fine on my last visit."

"No, everything is not fine!" Mite exclaimed, slamming her fists against the table. Her sudden rage surprised him. "You're distracted with your new. . . acquaintance. Mercury has been suspicious of them for a while now, thinking you'd resolve the issue on your own. We've had proof for months!"

"What?" The Overseer exclaimed, his expression closer to shock than a question, his skin shifting through various shades in response to Mite's anxious pacing. "Why didn't anyone inform me before today?"

"Mercury has mentioned it to you several times. It gives the High Guardians the impression that you're not serious at being the Overseer because of this," Mite cried out, trying to ensure her voice reached the walls around them, even if it seemed to fall on deaf ears.

"That's absurd. How can I not be me? What was the reason for the exiles?" He retorted, displaying defiance in response to Mite's claim.

Mite sighed in subtle frustration. "Accusations of tyranny, targeting you."

Chapter 4.3

The walk through the countryside felt rather dreary to the Overseer as he contemplated the news Mite had given him. Juliet had not been in his chambers when he had returned, so he decided to see if she had gone to the pub she often visited. It was odd that she had vanished without notifying him, but he also accepted responsibility for leaving her side.

To his surprise, the bar was almost empty, and the place had been renovated, appearing cleaner, brighter, and almost brand new. The renovations included a fresh coat of maroon paint and an ornate figurehead of a siren over the pub's new door. A large wooden sign hung underneath, reading "The Muse."

Upon entering, he found a refurbished interior with oak tables and chairs, and various hunting trophies adorning the walls. It took a moment for him to grasp that this was the same bar he had walked into months ago.

Arvid, the bartender, was cleaning a glass as usual and called the Overseer over. "Old friend! Welcome back. You look like you need a drink. Come over here post-haste, good sir! What troubles the great Overseer?"

Despite the comfort Arvid provided, the Overseer hesitated to discuss the latest developments with a bartender, knowing it would become the talk of the town. However, this was no ordinary tapster. The Muse had become an oasis of neutrality in a political world, where all could speak without fear of reprisals. Moreover, the Overseer had developed a level of trust in Arvid. He thought, "Arvid is trustworthy, but to what extent?"

The Overseer had learned much about Arvid through Mercury's memoirs. Arvid had grown up in a world plagued by conflicts over territory and banners, and he had built this bar in the badlands as a refuge for peace. He had experienced the darkest horrors but refused to let anger consume him. Meeting the Overseer had been a relief, as he believed this new friend could help him maintain his composure.

Arvid had a profound realization that some individuals, fueled by nationalism or the honor of their species, could commit unthinkable acts. Still, he had learned to remain composed, avoiding succumbing to a raging, destructive inner self. This trust was something the Overseer felt he should return.

The two men drew together, sharing a smile as Arvid poured a glass for the Overseer. Arvid pushed his wild hair back and rolled up his sleeves, discussing the newest commodities at the bar. They exchanged pleasantries for a few minutes before the Overseer withdrew into his thoughts, sighing as he sat there nursing his ale. "It feels like everyone wants to commit treason these days."

Arvid kept his eyes on the mug he was cleaning but raised a questioning eyebrow. "Ah, you must be referring to the mass exile?" He replied, trying to keep the conversation casual given the gravity of the situation.

"So you have heard then?" the Overseer responded, curious about how the news had reached this isolated bar.

"Uhmm. . ." Arvid's ears perked up, and he looked away from the glass he was cleaning, his squint narrowing towards two young patrons seated at the back of the bar. The Overseer followed his stare, and left his stool in a flash, making his way toward the two young men.

Chapter 4.4

As the Overseer advanced, the murmurs of conversation surrounding them intensified, swirling into a discord of hushed tones. It was as if the air itself held its breath, bracing for the inevitable clash. By the time he arrived, the two young men were ready to brawl until they realized their situation, distracted by the imposing figure that stood before them, the Overseer himself.

It was apparent to the Overseer that the two young men were Calcite soldiers, and he wasted no time in demanding to know why they were there.

"Excuse us, Overseer, Kalroth and I—"

"I don't care," the Overseer interrupted, glaring down at the young men. "Where is Juliet?"

They looked at each other for a moment before responding, "Sir, as far as we know she resides outside of our borders. That is, at least, where we last saw her."

The Overseer felt a wave of relief wash over him at this news, but he needed more information. He turned to the second soldier.

"What else?" His question was met with silence, as the young man struggled to speak due to fear and panic. "Out with it," the Overseer pressed, his tone carrying an unspoken threat.

The second soldier shifted on his feet, his movements betraying his unease as he summoned the courage to speak. "Sir, it was also confirmed that there was a gathering of Calcite rebels near a run down church, and we have been told they will be exterminated soon."

"But was she seen with the rebels?" the Overseer asked, his patience waning.

"Well, no, but. . ."

"Then, there you have it," the Overseer snapped. "She could have been outside the church for any number of reasons."

The two young men exchanged confused glances. "Yes, Overseer, but. . ."

"For all you know, she could have been out for a walk or tending to the garden. The point is, we do not make quick judgments about what we see."

The two men answered in unison, "Yes, sir!"

"Do not bother with your drinks. Go. Begin your exile, away from my sight."

The two men bowed in a pathetic attempt at making up for whatever offense they were guilty of. "Overseer, our deepest apologies—"

"Have fallen on deaf ears," the Overseer interrupted with a sneer. "But before you two begin your exile for treason, please enlighten me with the reason you pissed on the Amicitia Licentiam."

At these words, a few ears perked up all around the bar but nobody dared turn their head. As interesting as the topic was, it brought danger some knew and all feared, and the Overseer's presence made that weariness feel all the more justified.

With tears welling in his eyes, Kalroth choked up, "We committed no treason, Overseer, all we did was tell the truth. We would have told you everything else, but we wish not to further upset you."

"Well, you will do as you are commanded, now speak!"

The young man knew there was no point in trying to tame his anger now, as the truth would just condemn them further in his eyes. The first soldier blew a heavy exhale from his nose, a silent agreement passing between them, before he launched into his words. "Overseer, word has it that your. . . Juliet was responsible for the mass exile—"

Before the words had even left the young man's lips, the Overseer's saber was out, firm in his wrathful grip. The bar's warm candlelight gave the blade a sharp gleam where it rested against the young man's throat.

"Be wise in your rhetoric, young man," The Overseer's voice was calm, his stance unwavering, as he spoke without any hint of movement. There was no escape possible as he had pinned Kalroth against a post, and would not hesitate to draw blood nor take a life.

The young man continued with a low breath after a loud gulp, as if he feared every word would bring his friend closer to his imminent death. "She was the one who advised the rebels in the first place. She has been coordinating attacks from that church. You may kill us, sir, but it is the truth I speak."

The Overseer reeled with the new information and released Kalroth.

"That is impossible! It cannot be!" he yelled, to himself more than the ones who revealed it to him.

All objectivity had been shunned out the bar's small windows, as irrational disbelief threw the Overseer into mindless shock. These were non-truths to him, even though there was no reason for the lies. His glare flitted back and forth between the two men as if he were questioning everything down to their existence, and the second one, who felt less shaken than his colleague, stepped forth.

"Sir, my sources do not lie—"

"Your sources?" he snapped, gathering enough of himself to let out his rage, "You mean your ailing mother with a brain as addled as an old mare? I think I can find at least ten more reliable sources in a day. No wonder you are the lowest of the Calcite men."

The soldier tensed at the insulting words, his muscle gave an involuntary flex as though he would consider attacking the Overseer then and there, but he kept himself in check, as the outcome of such a fight would not benefit him in any way.

"Sir, with all due respect, my sources have not been wrong before. When talk of rebellion started I received everything."

"That is enough." The Overseer couldn't handle the near blasphemous thought of his dear Julict raiding with bandits unworthy of her attention, coercing to unravel all the efforts he had invested in building. It tore his heart asunder, but there was no proof of such an unthinkable betrayal.

"Leave," he commanded through clenched teeth, his scorn fixed on the table before him. The two young men, sensing the gravity of the situation, bowed and scurried out of the bar, fearing the consequences of lingering even a moment longer.

The Overseer returned to the bar with heavy feet and a heavier heart. "Arvid, what do I do?"

Arvid sighed and pretended to check an already clean glass for the slightest smudge, trying to bring a sense of familiar calm to the distraught man. "Well, Overseer, there isn't much you can do. If I were you I would ask your lady friend why she was seen hanging out with rebel scum. Worst case scenario, she gets mad at you for a day or two and then you two lovebirds will patch things up right quick. Now man up and get to it! The fate of the Grand Organization rests upon it."

These were wise words he did not want to, but had to hear. The Overseer nodded in acceptance. He finished his drink in one swig under Arvid's sympathetic glance, and headed home hoping Juliet would be there.

When he arrived at the castle, he saw the lights in his chamber, and his heart leapt with joy at the thought of Juliet's company. However, his mind was still clouded with doubt. He decided to address the issue, and as he climbed the stairs, he thought of the various ways to bring up the topic.

Juliet was waiting for him, sitting by the door in her nightgown. As soon as the door swung open, she rushed to greet him with a kiss, but he met her with a suspicious inquiry.

"Where were you?" he probed, bypassing any pleasantries.

Juliet's eyes betrayed a sense of hurt and shock at the accusing tone. "I went home for the afternoon to check in, as I spend weeks at a time here with you. Then, I went for a walk to run some errands in town, Overseer." She answered, giving him a sarcastic curtsy and a defiant glare before asking a question of her own, "Where were you? I have waited half the night here in a cold bed."

Ignoring her question, he continued to press her. "So you were nowhere near the old, abandoned church where these 'Marked Ones' had been meeting?"

"No. Why would you even ask me that?" Juliet inhaled in shock, appearing hurt by the accusation. "Come dear, let me soothe your troubled mind." She let her hand rest on his cheek, and it was met with warmth rushing to his face, but it felt off. What used to feel like true love turned into a nauseating sweetness and almost repulsive, tainted by doubt as it was.

He moved Juliet's hand with deliberate slowness, each second between the transition careful and delicate. "Juliet, you were seen leaving the premises."

Juliet hesitated, and then replied, "Well, I may have taken a walk in that direction, but I don't recall anything significant."

There was no denying that Juliet was manipulating him, but even this knowledge was not enough to keep his will strong as he looked into her eyes, searching for a hint of reassurance in those depths. He thought, "After all, what did he have but the secondhand testimony from a Calcite boy? What was it compared to the word of his lover, untrue as it might be?"

The accusation shook their love as he decided to confront her. "Why are you being dishonest with me?"

Juliet's reaction was a mixture of hurt and defensiveness. "Come, dear, let me soothe your troubled mind."

He lowered her hand, stating to himself, "What does she stand to gain? She is unclaimed, and she pledges allegiance to no one. Why would she dabble in politics?"

Juliet allowed herself to be provocative, and let her robe fall to the floor, but the Overseer was too preoccupied with his doubts to notice her advance. He muttered to himself about her actions.

Juliet became more direct in her tone, "Mr. Overseer, are you second guessing me?"

His crystal eyes met hers, but it was tainted by doubt, no longer exuding the love he once felt.

After some time, he chose to undress, and Juliet attempted to reassure him. "I have nothing to do with this land or that church, and what could I stand to gain from any sort of rebellion when I have you?"

However, he couldn't suppress the doubt that had taken root in his mind. The Overseer felt conflicted, as he both desired Juliet's comfort and was tormented by his suspicion.

Juliet's hand touched his chest as she moved closer, but he hesitated for a moment before deciding to climb into bed. Despite his doubts, he found himself in her arms for the night.

Chapter 4.5

In the morning that followed, the Overseer woke up to an empty bed and a scrawled note laid on the pillow where Juliet should have been.

Don't fret, I just left downstairs to get some fruit to snack on. If you didn't look so damn adorable while you slept, I would have woken you up to come with me.

-Juliet

He sat up, yawned, and blinked away his sleepiness. Just as he started stretching, a loud knock resounded at the door. It seemed like people always had a knack for interrupting his moments of peace. It was as if everyone realized he was available the instant he opened his eyes, and it never failed to exasperate him.

"Come in!" he shouted. He was too annoyed to even open the door himself, and he hadn't had time to dress yet.

After a few seconds, the door opened to reveal Mite. She was hesitant in her tense and uncertain steps.

"Good morning, Overseer," she greeted but said no more, standing there as if she wanted to be anywhere else but near him.

"Good morning, Mite. I sense you haven't come to my chambers just to wish me well," he remarked.

She cast her stare toward the floor, jaw clenched. "No, sir."

"Well then speak your piece. It's just the two of us here. What's troubling you?"

"I would hate to ever disrupt your time and I would hate to ever get between you and someone else but. . ."

Mite's voice softened, her words measured and cautious. Each word seemed to be spoken as if it could cause some great offense. Her next words were about to disrupt his blossoming relationship, a relationship that she knew made him enamored for the first time in fifteen years. Even though it wasn't with her, she cherished his happiness. Still, she had to reveal the truth, even if it meant ruining that happiness.

"Juliet is not who you think she is. She is a manipulator and a parasite, and right now, the person she is draining is you. I do not trust her, and you shouldn't either."

That struck a nerve, and the Overseer turned away from Mite before looking at her from the corner of his eye, as though he could not bear the sight of her anymore. The deep scowl that was etched onto his face did nothing to change that impression.

His next words were cold, and the formality stung like frostbite. "Will that be all, High Guardian?"

Mite was taken aback by his words and the complete dismissal of her revelations. He hadn't even used her name. His words stung like frostbite. In response, she gave a polite bow and replied with a quiet and defeated, "Yes."

But were these words enough to convey the turmoil that she felt within her? The deep seated emotions were trapped inside, intertwined into the fabric of her being. Had she spoken enough to feel satisfied? No, not in the slightest. She was just a woman, restricted from expressing her opinion except when granted permission by man, viewed as the lesser sex according to society. One who had no right to demand more than she was given, which was very little, regardless of her position that was well earned; useful but not valued. In this moment, as she faced the Overseer's wicked glare, Mite knew she would never have the true opportunity to say her piece.

The Overseer, unmoved by her apparent distress, got up, unclothed, and approached her. He looked down at the porcelain woman, and her defeated demeanor did little to soften his scorn.

"Leave then," he said with a harsh, growling anger evident in each syllable.

Mite rushed away, horrified by the Overseer's coldness, almost stumbling over her own feet as she heard the door slam shut behind her. His reaction filled her with terror. It felt as if he saw her as worthless, a loathsome creature he had expelled from his home.

"Something wicked is going on," she struggled to admit, fighting back the overwhelming heartbreak that riddled her inner core.

Chapter 5.1

"Marked One!"

Beyond the horizon Bemus' voice rang out, and the snapping of twigs and branches drowned out the wheezing of an older male. As he vanished into the dense forest, the High Guardians gathered near the undergrowth where he was last seen.

"Spread out, but do not make too many sudden movements. Expect him to try to hide in this terrain instead of running," Vladsan spoke with experience. Although tracking would be difficult, he knew that the shoulder high thickets would present a problem for both chase and escape.

Golnesa nudged Ovidius and signaled for him to follow her lead. "We'll take the north end."

Ovidius complied, being cautious as they maneuvered through the tall weeds, making sure not to attract any unwanted pests. They ended up a few yards apart, their attention focused on the trees ahead. The sound of crunching leaves beneath their feet led to eerie sounds in the distance. While Golnesa pressed on, Ovidius grew curious and whispered, "What's so important about this spurius?"

Golnesa whispered back, "He's an enemy of the Grand Organization, a traitor."

Ovidius probed further, "Aren't Marked Ones more like migrants than traitors? I'm a bit confused."

Golnesa stopped to face him, "We don't know much other than that they don't belong here. They defected from their empire and we have to ensure they don't infect the rest of the Grand Organization."

Ovidius continued to follow her but questioned, "Well, where do we send them then? And why do you seem offended?"

"I don't know!" Golnesa exclaimed, her frustration evident. "I'm getting irritated because I'm standing in an overgrown forest with hundreds of bugs trying to feast on me, and you're bombarding me with questions."

Meanwhile, Vladsan led Bemus along the southern perimeter where the sun struggled to penetrate the thick canopy. The denser tree trunks provided better cover, so their search became meticulous. After some time, they decided to move downhill, where they saw a conspicuous boulder amidst the dense vegetation. Bemus grew cautious and called out while holding a steel falcata.

"Come on out now," he demanded, hoping his suspicions were correct.

A few seconds passed before a pair of raised hands appeared from behind the large rock. The old man revealed himself soon after. Vladsan signaled the others by letting out a sharp whistle, and Bemus approached the Marked One. The High Guardian moved closer until he was within striking range, almost tackling the old man onto the boulder behind him. Bemus then forced him onto the ground and began kicking at his back and sides. Vladsan waited until blood began to flow from the man's lips before intervening.

With his arm on Bemus' shoulder, he said, "that's enough."

"Filthy Marked One," the insular Alexandrite projected his disgust towards the man sprawled on the ground.

As Ovidius and Golnesa reached their partners, they witnessed the aftermath of the assault and came to a halt.

Golnesa let out a nervous exhale, "May Omnibenevolence have mercy on you, Bemus."

Bemus ignored her, lifting the man from his prone position and propping him up against the stone. The Marked One looked up at him in pain from the assault. Golnesa, the sole High Guardian showing a hint of sympathy, looked away just as the other three crowded around the Marked One to begin their interrogation. The man winced as Bemus' grip on his shoulder tightened.

"What's your name?" Bemus growled, his patience wearing thin.

In pain, the Marked One managed to gasp out, "Udiah, from the Calcite Empire."

Ovidius interjected, "Udiah, the Calcite Emperor has branded you as a deserter and enemy of the Grand Organization. Why do you still show your face as if you're wanted?"

"What choice do I have?" Udiah cried out.

His suffering caused Golnesa to turn away. She empathized with Udiah but refused to show it, positioning herself as if she was scanning the area for potential witnesses. She fought the urge to intervene but continued to listen.

"Marked Ones aren't welcomed within the Grand Organization." Vladsan's calm but firm nature influenced the others to reduce their aggression.

Udiah gasped for breath and pleaded, "I understand that, but where can we go?"

"You should've thought about that before committing treason." Bemus shot back.

Vladsan faced a barrage of questions from the Marked One. "Is it treason because I have my own opinions? Must I follow the Emperor's orders, even if they harm me? I don't mind being evicted from my home, but we're prevented from ever finding a new one because of the policies of this tyrant Overseer!"

Golnesa moved forward as he spoke the last words. She raised her fist and struck the fresh cut between Udiah's eye socket and temple. Ovidius and Bemus grabbed the unconscious migrant. Vladsan stood still, looking at Golnesa with a mix of awe and concern.

Chapter 5.2

The heavy canter of an albino Friesian horse alerted the guards at the main gates. As the steed approached, its ears perked forward through a long, thick mane, listening to the sounds of the metal barriers being moved aside from its path. As instructed, the horse slowed to a walk and turned towards the stable. Mite dismounted, praised the horse for the ride, and began removing the saddle. The horse stayed in the stable, its head drooping, while she headed towards the Grand Organization's main castle.

Mite maintained a solemn demeanor as she fulfilled her duties, her emotions bubbling beneath the surface. Mercury, noticing her distress, gave a playful bump into her and quipped, "Why the long face?"

"He is just so blind!" Mite exploded, her fists clenched at her sides.

Mercury gave her a nudge and whispered, "Hush now Mite, lest you be the next one charged with treason."

"Treason? What are you on about?" Mite asked, her surprise evident as her anger subsided for a moment.

"There's a Marked One on trial today. It was a long wait, but at least now the Overseer will be dealing with the migrant situation." Mercury explained, raising his shoulders with his palms up.

"That's a relief. Have you spoken with him?" Mite's demeanor shifted from anger to curiosity.

With raised eyebrows, Mercury replied, "Not just yet. However, I'll remind him that his decision affects way more than just this one man. It can be problematic if we come to wage war against the homeless."

"You should do that now, before anyone else gets a chance to add their opinion." Mite added.

Mercury smiled, then placed his hands on her shoulders.. "Great idea, Mite. I'll be on my way."

Mite's chest tightened with a mix of anger and anguish as Mercury turned away. Her face remained locked in thought as she contemplated taking advantage of the situation. A plan began to form in her mind as she sought to resolve the deep heartache she felt. She wanted to call out to him, but her breath grew shallow as she strained to catch every sound. Mite became anxious and hesitant to move, but with a deep exhale, she closed her eyes, embracing the darkness.

What had appeared like a mystery became clear. The shifting shadows started to take on a familiar silhouette, and through the chaos, she could see his eyes, a calm within a storm. When she opened her eyes, there he stood. Mercury wasn't just her closest colleague; he was also her best friend. Mite inched forward, and his golden arms embraced her, both aware that she didn't need to call out for him to be there.

Although fatigued, she began to vent, "You know, he and I used to be quite close, Mercury. Not as close as Juliet has gotten to him, but close nevertheless. We used to be a team. There was romance between us, and maybe I am jealous because he has found a new interest. I can't help that I do care for him and am concerned for his well being. I've made sure that everything I do aligns with the goal of world peace and bent over backward to fulfill his plans. I've been there from the beginning, no matter the cost. Then this—this bitch comes in like she owns the damn organization! I just want to spend the day not thinking about Juliet's fucking face, but she seems to be everywhere and on everyone's lips. I'm exhausted."

"I understand." Mercury said, his golden arms comforting her as best as they could.

Time trickled past in that embrace, but the sounds of footsteps and chatter grew louder. Word had spread among the other High Guardians about the captured Marked One, and individual disagreements turned into a unified quarrel. The corridors echoed with distress as the crowd moved throughout. Mite and Mercury joined the other High Guardians, making their way to the Grand Hall. The golden and black figure led the charge, using his charisma to calm the irate High Guardians and bring them back to composure.

As the room settled into tranquility, the wooden doors creaked open. "Enim Amicitia," every voice intoned as they turned to face the same point.

"Pacem," both Juliet and the Overseer responded in unnerving synchrony, causing discomfort to ripple through the room.

Mercury yielded his position of authority as the Overseer made his way to the front, eyeing the foreigner and her attire with suspicion. She wore an outfit too gaudy, even for his golden tastes, and he knew that others would share his sentiment. He squeezed into his chair, notebook in hand, and waited for the hearing to commence.

Two soldiers dragged in Udiah, his bruised and battered body struggling to maintain balance. His tattered clothes were still stained with blood, as the soldiers had nothing to offer him. Udiah's face bore a fresh cut, and Mercury took note of these details, as neither he nor the others could bear to look at the Marked One for too long.

The Overseer stood up from his throne and looked down towards the defeated Marked One. All others rose to their feet in respect, but turned their heads to observe the colorless face of Udiah's judge. With the High Guardians split in their opinions, it was his that mattered most. The Overseer walked towards Udiah and met him face to face. As he did, the old man caught a glimpse of Juliet and frowned in disbelief. The reds and purples from the man's wounds bounced off the Overseer's skin. It was as if an empathic connection was made through the closed distance. This was until the Overseer broke his focus to follow Udiah's line of sight.

"Do you know each other?" He asked just loud enough for the injured man to hear.

Udiah wavered between protecting himself and her, but concluded, "What does it matter who I am, or she, or you? The Amicitia Licentiam is an agreement that declares peace for all, but it leaves some out. What about those exceptions that are like me, who get removed from their homes due to a king's short temper? Do I not have the chance to live elsewhere? Does my exile result in a living hell? What world peace is this?"

Mercury watched as the Overseer's hand closed into a fist. The other High Guardians shifted with awkwardness. Juliet looked them both over but stood rigid. Udiah's words resonated in the room. Half a minute passed before everyone started sitting back down, and as the Overseer made his way back to his chair, he peered at Juliet.

As the last chair was filled, Mercury led the conversation, "Udiah, the accusation against you is that of treason against the Amicitia Licentiam. How do you plead?"

"Not Guilty." Barked back the Marked One.

An awkward pause filled the air as Mercury wrote into his notebook. Meanwhile, Mite made sure to see the faces of everyone in the room and their reactions as they grew more uncomfortable with the silence. She made sure to observe the faces of The Overseer, Mercury,

Juliet, and all the other High Guardians. Mite's eyes shifted to Hari, who conveyed both his disapproval and signaled for her to refrain from taking action with a simple and subtle shake of his head. Mite wondered what he meant by it but responded with a slight shrug as she continued her survey. Her surveying rested on Vladsan's fearful expression as he rose from his chair.

"Marked One, we found you trespassing in territory that has been appropriated by the Grand Organization. The reason why it is illegal to be on these lands is because you were exiled by one of the kingdoms, the Calcite to be exact, and you have failed to obey the laws in place towards exiles and foreigners." What would have been a confident low tone came off as tentative, and it was recognized by all who were close with Vladsan.

Udiah's rebuttal was fierce and more towards the Overseer than Vladsan, "I have been saying this, where do we go? There is nowhere for us Marked Ones to go, the Grand Organization owns everything I know."

"That's an excuse!" Bemus shouted, his voice shrill.

The room erupted into another shouting match, with personal insults being hurled around. Juliet watched the commotion and then turned to the Overseer, who appeared shocked that his High Guardians had become unprofessional. Mercury's commanding voice brought the room to silence once again.

The Overseer made his way to his feet, and unlike the energy of all others, he remained humble as he said, "From my understanding, Udiah, you and the Marked Ones seek asylum and a second chance at life."

Hearing his concerns heard, Udiah and Juliet both looked at the Overseer wide eyed, as though he was connected to their hearts and listening to their internal thoughts. Udiah stuttered in disbelief, "Y-yes! That's what I— we are asking for,"

The Overseer smiled at his reaction, "Very well. So long as you and the Marked Ones swear fealty to the Amicitia Licentiam, you may enter into a rehabilitation program and have that second chance."

Udiah choked on what felt like a prison sentence. His happiness withdrew as if he was smacked in the face harder than the beating he already had. He was awestruck and at a loss for words. Mercury scratched his head as the High Guardians reunified in glory and acceptance of the Overseer's wisdom. The Marked Ones had no other options.

Juliet scoffed in disbelief as well, and under her breath she beckoned towards The Overseer, "What?"

"This is your chance to redeem yourselves, to prove that you are worthy of the trust and forgiveness bestowed upon you. You have been granted a second chance to acquire your part of our World Peace by joining with us as a unified dependent nation. But make no mistake, separation from the Amicitia Licentiam or the Grand Organization will not be tolerated." With that final warning, the Overseer left the room in a hushed silence, his words echoing in the ears of everyone present.

Chapter 5.3

"Let me understand this. The Marked Ones are forbidden from ever having their independence, there is no penalty for the Calcite's mass exile, and the one path available for all of us is to sign the Amicitia Licentiam?" The mature, pale male exhaled, his breath forming a misty cloud in the frigid air.

Ara's eyes shifted down as his wings slumped, "That is nothing but the whole truth, Grand Emperor."

"Damn," Sothis muttered, closing his eyes and pinching the bridge of his nose. "I knew something like this would happen. The Overseer is altogether incompetent and unfit for this position he wishes to claim."

Ara continued with disgust in his voice. "The Marked Ones are being directed to these reformation camps to unlearn their beliefs."

Sothis threw his hands up in exasperation. "This is ridiculous! I'll verify with Mite, but I appreciate you informing me of this, Ara."

The Wingman seized the opportunity to express his doubts. "You're going to trust her? I mean, I know she's a Wintersun, but she is also a High Guardian. With all due respect, she has made the Grand Organization her home. I'm almost certain that she would choose to protect her love for him rather than to consider betrayal."

Sothis looked around the room before acknowledging his doubt. "You may be right, but I must give her the opportunity to save herself. As you said, she is a Wintersun, which is a bond that means more than you can imagine. The reason why I even accepted her becoming a High Guardian was due to the fact that I knew it would prove useful to have someone trustworthy close to the Overseer."

"What if she doesn't take this opportunity?" Ara asked with a slight inclination of his head. Without trying to hide the disappointment he felt at that option, his wings dropped even more, almost dragging on the floor. "It could prove disastrous. She might prove herself to be playing both sides, and feeding the Overseer information of our movements. I know you care for her, but I must object to having her in our conspiracy."

Sothis pondered the idea but dismissed it with a shake of his head. "I can't have her put to the sword. I won't do that."

"I'm not requesting her death. I couldn't even imagine trying to hurt you in that way. There can be alternatives though. I doubt that she will come to see our side with just one conversation. Have her imprisoned for her own sake. Try to convince her then of the irrational actions of his love. If she never sees beyond her childlike fondness for the tyrant, then just leave her there until the war ends. Imagine if you refuse this route and the Overseer does find out she's crossed him." Ara couldn't avoid the frustration in his voice but he knew that the point of Mite would be a sore spot in their conversation. "She might come to hate you for a while, but she will stay alive."

Sothis was silent for a few seconds, his face twisting into a grimace at the thought. "Then we'll deal with it when the time comes. Let's prepare now. We will begin mobilization of our warriors and strike soon. Prepare your allies."

Ara nodded and turned to leave. A dimpled smile coated his face as he bounced out of the front door. His wings expanded and the ground left his feet as he soared towards the abandoned church.

Sothis lifted a hand to run down his face, a sigh escaping him. His hand dropped back to his side as his searching found a spot to settle on, "I hope she takes this opportunity." He muttered to himself. "The madness of the Overseer must not continue, it is not peace he is seeking, but control."

Sothis then glanced towards a nearby window to watch the Wingman as he began to disappear in the distance and thought out loud. "I hope we can face this coming storm, the last time the realms faced such a conflict the lands ran red with crimson blood, he might not see it, hells be damned he might indeed have good intentions, but he is walking the path of a mad tyrant." He stood up. A mix of dread and resolve dwelled in his spirit as he walked to his chambers. He remained quiet while wishing to escape the ill omens that he felt from the red hues of the sunset.

Ara had a confident smile as he continued to soar through the darkening skies. "With this, the rebellion is bound to become a true threat to the madman. We just might have a chance at freedom."

As the Hawke King touched the decrepit grounds of the old church he was received by a loyal entourage of soldiers that waited for the news of his meeting with the Wintersun royal. The first of the men walked closer to Ara and gave a respectful bow.

"I reckon your meeting had some success, my lord." The soldier said.

"Indeed, we must start the mobilization of the men. Call all our allies. Tell them that it's time to end the Grand Organization, and reduce it to ashes for the true freedom of the people of our world." Ara said, filled with renewed confidence and vigor.

"Of course, my lord." The soldier bent forward in another respectful bow, though it was a brief one. He soon straightened himself once again. "It will be done."

"Excellent." The smile on Ara's face grew with each exchanged word. "I know you will, but do inform me as soon as you receive any word back from them."

"As you wish, my lord." The soldier nodded his head, though remained where he was. He didn't appear to be offended by the reminder. "Is there anything else, my lord?"

"For now. You may go." Ara motioned his hand as he spoke, a gesture to accompany the dismissal.

The soldier gave one final bow, but before he made his way off he looked towards the old church and waved towards the multitude of youth who were glued to the window that separated them.

Ara watched as the soldier paced off, another burst of energy shooting through him. His hands rested on his hips, even his wings were a little jittery. He fought to contain his excitement. "If all goes well, we will have the freedom we deserve." He said to himself.

The remaining men looked to the Hawke King, a few murmurs passing through them, on the level of confidence and energy about the rebellion. They were used to serving their king and were glad to have a good one. However, this wasn't about them, but the Marked Ones. Their possible freedom was a cause to fight for, and to put their all into. The soldiers remained confident as Ara's positive energy radiated to and through them.

Chapter 5.4

As the next few days passed, the Overseer tried to keep himself busy with such tedious work that could have been handled by any of the High Guardians. Some rumors sturred that he was compensating for the times he was absent minded while others claimed that he felt guilty for the controversial decision about Udiah and those exiled. The truth was that he and Juliet started spending less time together. The reunification of the Marked Ones back into the Amicitia Licentiam had put a strain on their relationship.

"Treason," he thought out loud. "Is it treason if she does not serve any king or queen? Could she be betraying me by destroying what I have worked so hard to create? She has to be one of those migrants then. Futuo!"

He tried to focus on the archives he had already spent hours on, but the overwhelming anxiety tightened his arms and shoulders. The wrinkled papers between his fingers crackled like fire to his ears.

Every one of his senses went numb until the obstruction of frantic knocking at the door. "Overseer! Overseer! Open up! Now!"

He recognized Mercury's voice and shifted his gaze with a deliberate slowness. With the crushed papers littered around his feet, the Overseer looked to see the door burst open before he could lift and wave his hand. The golden man looked different somehow. He appeared out of breath and panicked, which was something the Overseer had never seen. Was Mercury. . . crying?

"What is it, Mercury? What's wrong?" His voice reflected a growing concern.

"They are dead! So many of them. So many dead. The Calcite! Our people! Why didn't you listen, you. . . you idiot!"

Mercury had never ever called him another name before, much less shown complete lack of respect. The Overseer knew this had to be urgent and grabbed his saber. "What are you talking about? Show some respect!" His concern was evident despite his shouting. "And stop crying. You are making a fool of yourself."

The golden man slumped to the ground and sulked. "If we had shown up sooner."

The Overseer waited for Mercury to regain his composure before asking, his voice shaking with fear. "Do you mind telling me what this is all about?"

"Come with me, Overseer. Since you refused to believe us, I will show you what has come of the betrayal of your closest allies." His grim facial features were displayed and his body suffused with grief as he walked away.

He decided to follow Mercury who stormed out of the castle. The Overseer caught up without much effort, but the High Guardian continued to move without hesitation, as fast as he could towards the East. What seemed to the Overseer as a casual walk was not far from a full sprint to the golden man. Still, Mercury's legs carried him further than ever before. Beads of sweat rolled down and dripped from his golden chin. His chest burned as if he lacked cardio training, yet he persisted.

The two had been on the road for a little over two hours before the Overseer grew impatient. "Enough with the mystery. Can you explain while we walk?"

Mercury stared him in the eye as they rounded the bend and spoke a single word. "Look."

The heavy door had been broken down, leaving shattered splinters clinging to the hinges like broken memories. The stench of death wafted out, assaulting their senses before they even stepped inside. The courtyard was a scene of horror, with bodies littering the area in various states of disarray. Some hung over the railings, their limbs twisted in unnatural angles, while others were in random piles. The air was thick with the metallic tang of blood, and with each step they took, they could feel the stomach curdling squelch of it beneath their feet.

"So, it seems as though some of these bodies are the actual soldiers that threw out and branded the Marked Ones. Also, we have another huge problem." He pointed to the Calcite Emperor who was hanging upside down and headless from the archway entrance.

The Overseer staggered and fell to his knees. The blood splattered and decorated his red reflecting skin. His hands dug into the ground below as he tried to breathe. His mind kept working meanwhile. Rigor mortis was apparent but the bodies were not yet bloated. The blood was still somewhat wet while still sticky. He still needed more information to infer if this was done within the day. Footsteps? As Mercury continued to mourn, the Overseer moved to his feet.

"Silence." He whispered just loud enough for Mercury's golden eyes to divert his way.

A faint sloshing pattern echoed behind the walls and caught both of their attention. They moved together towards the noise and cornered it within the confines of one small building. The two entered with their swords drawn and anticipated a close combat brawl. Mercury pushed the doors in and began clearing the home with the Overseer protecting his flank. The last door was closed. The floorboard creaked. The Overseer and Mercury looked at each other, and within a single breath, they breached into a small child's bedroom. To their dismay they found a Calcite girl around the age of seven gawking at them. As soon as the child saw them, she began to cry and yell for her mother who was sprawled out on the opposite side of the room.

"Don't you touch her!" the woman's weak bark signified she was not going to last much longer.

The Overseer recoiled as if a snake had hissed at him. The lesson had been learned: leaders of the new world are no match for a mother's love. When he looked closer at the mother, he saw the same familiar facial features beneath the filth. He had to know who they were.

"Excuse me, ma'am. Is there anyone I can reach out to whom you can trust? You and your girl need help."

The little girl's voice rose just above a whisper as she began, "My aunt—"

"Hush child," the mother interjected to silence the child. "No, Overseer, we can handle ourselves."

"Well, where are you two from?" He stepped forward and lowered himself to get closer; his curiosity piqued.

"We are from nowhere," the mother said, wincing in obvious pain.

"Mommy, tell him. He already knows. I don't know how, but I can tell he already knows! I can feel it!" The little girl grew more hopeful as the conversation persisted.

The mother gave a deep exhale, her glare piercing into the Overseer's eyes, seeking reassurance. With a subtle nod from him, she began recounting the events. "We have relatives spread all over. They all fled the Calcite when the economic changes became too great to bear. Workers weren't getting paid and families began to starve. We were told, this is a sacrifice we all have to make as members of the kingdom. The funny thing is, we went along with it at first. We believed the king and the nobles were being truthful when they were in fact feasting in their halls. Then the children started to become sick from this random plague. Very few could afford to buy medicine. That was a pain that was too great for some of us to bear. When anyone spoke out against the king or any of the nobles they were beaten, jailed, exiled, or even executed. It was hell."

As she spoke with a set of creased brows, her lips parted to release the torrent of words, he caught a glint of silver from her tongue.

"I even lost my sister and niece. When things got worse, she tried to help us here and there when she could, but she spoke up and they were both exiled. She told us she wanted us to think about leaving as well. She wanted us to join a small home outside of the kingdom not too far away, but they were branded as traitors. I was scared to go. Some foreign soldiers just decided to fight for them I guess. I wanted to leave with her, but I was too late. To them we were the same guilty Calcite. I lost my loved ones in vain trying to stay on the right side. So now I have nobody left. . . I. . . have. . . nothing. . ." The mother began to shake, then collapsed with bloody foam pouring from her mouth while the child wailed.

Mercury wretched and broadcasted a reminder. "This is what has become of your disbelief, Overseer. Now this child is without a home or anyone to care for her."

The golden man scooped up the girl and looked at the translucent man one more time. After shaking his head in disappointment, he walked off with the grieving child in his arms in search of other survivors. The Overseer grew numb again. He sat in the pool of blood with the silver tongued corpse, dumbfounded.

Chapter 5.5

"Hush, little one. Everything will be ok." His golden lips tightened as his footsteps cleared the red floor outside the castle gates.

The attack on the helpless citizens had left him in such a fury that his mind had gone blank. Along the path, he saw a recent opening in the bushes with a few broken branches and started into the forest in hot pursuit of the perpetrators. Mercury slowed his pace and began his hunt in silence. As he crept over fallen trees and under low hanging branches, he heard the sound of laughter ahead and saw a flickering torchlight.

"This is it." Mercury whispered to himself. "They must be punished."

He placed the child on her feet and lifted a finger to his lips. She nodded with tears still rolling down and turned to hide behind the very first tree. They shared a smile, which at first felt forced, but then gave each a boost of hope.

As soon as he caught up to the first rogue, he could see the man was covered in blood and was accompanied by two other hooded figures. Judging by their accents, he recognized two of the men from the Blood Moon, but the third figure walked in silence.

As swift as lightning, Mercury threw his dagger into the blood covered man's back and drew his sword. By the time the two remaining men understood what had just happened, Mercury had pressed the second man through and pinned him to a tree. As he set upon the third man with his bare hands, the hooded figure dropped his cloak. To the High Guardian's surprise it was one of the ferocious Carnelians.

The man-beast snarled and drew his blade, but the golden man was faster, disarming the rogue without effort by punching him in the face and twisting his hairy arm until the blade dropped and clanged against some rocks below.

A brawl between Mercury and the rogue fighter ensued. The two took their fight to the ground as his gold hands gripped the beast's neck. It was unfortunate for the High Guardian, but the Carnelian gained a moment of victory by throwing dirt in his golden eyes. A blind Mercury swung, but made no connection, and soon felt a sharp pain in his skull. The Carnelian had struck him and was now mounting. The rogue began to slug his fists into Mercury, creating a mess of gold and red below him. Just as the beast was about to drop the final blow, a familiar saber pierced his chest, spraying blood in Mercury's face.

"You damn fool. What were you thinking rolling around with a Carnelian?" The rogue's body leaned and fell off Mercury, revealing the Overseer standing before them.

He laughed and laid back in the dirt, winded from the altercation. "I have no idea, but you have excellent timing."

The Overseer blew a sigh of relief before offering his hand. "Come now, we have no time for pleasantries. I want information."

Mercury extended his hand and allowed the Overseer to lift him to his feet. After inspecting his sore skin and superficial cuts, the golden man started moving to the rogue pinned at the tree.

The Overseer moved past him and slapped the man so hard the birds flew from the trees around them. As the man came to, he began struggling and wincing in pain as he realized he had been impaled.

"Listen to me and listen to me good you piece of shit. I want answers and I want them now," the Overseer seethed. "If you cooperate I can ease your passing, but if you lie to me I will prolong your suffering with great intensity. I will know if you are deceiving me, so do not test my patience."

The Overseer turned to remove the dagger from the first rogue's back and, within an instant, held it to the pinned man's throat. "Tell me why you attacked the castle. Now!"

The man spat blood at him which lit a fire in the Overseer's eyes. He plunged the dagger into the man's thigh and twisted it back and forth. "Answer me now!"

Mercury tried to step in, but his protests fell on deaf ears.

The pinned man lost his composure and began to explain. "We had to send a message. We needed to make a scene that people would talk about for years to come. This is your fault, after all."

The Overseer continued. "How so? Speak, before your other leg tastes this metal!"

"It is the Grand Organization. You put these filthy pigs in power and protect them with your laws, but your legislation protects the royalty. The poor are left to suffer in the streets! You do not allow the people to protest against their tyrants, and look at what it has become. Do you hear us now, Overseer? We were outcasts from the nearby kingdoms. We found no support from our lands; we found support with each other. They starved us, and beat us, and killed us and you let it happen. In the name of the kings? Fuck the kings!" The rogue spit up more blood, and allowed it to drip onto the ground. "The king can rot in hell for what he has done to his people and so can you for protecting him! I guess Juliet was right all along."

The Overseer stepped back in horror as the dying man began to choke on his laugh.

"That's right, Overseer. She is one of us, and has been all along. You two were so close and she kept you nice and busy while we got all our preparations squared away, and the best part is, this is just the beginning!"

Mercury tried to console the Overseer but he glared at the rogue with rage and with one mighty punch, the Overseer cut the tree and the man in half. Panting and furious, he turned around to see another hooded figure standing beside a tree.

"I was trying to warn you."

The Overseer knew that voice from somewhere but could not place it. A part of him knew it had to be Juliet, but his heart could not accept it. "Warn me about what? That you were planning to murder innocent refugees? That you were just a decoy? That you wished me dead? Tell me, Juliet, what did you plan to tell me?" The hooded figure smirked and licked their lips, showing off their silver tongue. "I wish I could have told you how bad it was. I wanted to tell you how the king treated us but I could never find the words." The hooded figure appeared to be crying; tears dripped off her chin.

Mercury whispered to the Overseer, "Do not fall for this again. She is evil and you know it."

The hooded figure pointed at Mercury. "Shut your mouth! You do not know what I have endured. . . I was just like the other refugees at the church. I starved, I was beaten, and I saw my lover killed for voicing his opinion of the king. I too have suffered, but you never stepped in. I did what I had to do to allow this message to be heard."

The figure stood up straight and began to chuckle as she performed a mocking curtsy. "Please forgive me, my lord," she said as the silver tongue parted her lips yet again.

The Overseer stood motionless, enraged and overwhelmed with the circumstances, but Mercury grabbed his sword and made toward the mysterious rogue. The chuckling turned to laughter as the hooded figure turned to vanish into the woods. The laughter echoed in the trees, but the cloaked woman was gone.

The Overseer started after her, but Mercury stopped him. "There has been enough blood shed tonight. Let us return to the castle and regroup. We need a plan." The translucent man surrendered a nod and stormed back to the road he had come in on, and Mercury followed in his footsteps.

Chapter 6.1

"We used to be divided." A golden pair of lips parted.

Mercury affixed the High Guardian insignia to his chest, ensuring it sat perpendicular to the marble floor. He then examined the Overseer's uniform for any variations. After one last inspection, he released a breath of relief before proceeding with his story.

"The Emerald Empire, as we know it today, used to be a land full of war and destruction. Our ancestors would exchange leaders faster than generations could mature. Even the policies would shift from pacifistic to combative and back within a lifetime. It was chaos. However, with our differences, we viewed the dragons as divine. When the draconic took over, we put our differences aside and came together with the faith that our new rulers had our best interest in mind. Unlike the other nations, we became a collection of people that found peace despite our differences in culture and beliefs. Sure, we've had quite a few enemies along the way, but this unity proves that if we can succeed

as a nation, then we can do the same on a scale that's even more grand."

"Grand, you say?" The Overseer touched his thumb to his chin while soaking in every word he heard, but fixated on the last.

Mercury nodded, "I know some of the obstacles will be those who remain xenophobic to the other races, such as the Alexandrites, but I see it as a challenging opportunity. This treaty, the Amicitia Licentiam, will be able to end all wars by unifying all the kingdoms and empires. Imagine all the good we can do with this organization."

"Let it be a Grand Organization indeed." The Overseer smiled in agreement with Mercury's vision. However, just as quick as his lips curled up, they soon turned downward. "What if there are those who wish to wage war instead? Does violence not beget violence? As idealistic as this plan may be, will there not be suffering involved for true world peace to be attained?"

Mercury turned away for a moment to press his thumb and chin together. "This much is true my friend but, be that as it may, sometimes the sacrifice is worth it. Intellectuals will understand, and those that are lacking reason will need to conform or pay the price for not being adaptable."

"What you are uttering is blasphemous at the very least." The Overseer refuted. *"If peace is obtained through the reckoning of others then it was never peace in the first place. Good intentions do not justify the actions of what is to be obtained. Peace shall be granted by peaceful means."*

The quip from the golden figure was firm and quick. "You will see for yourself, I promise. The moment you face a crossroads as our new leader, you will be seen as a hypocrite. Even then, know that I will be by your side."

"Time will reveal the truth." The Overseer's confidence rivaled Mercury's, but the golden brows lowered and his cheeks relaxed.

The parchment that lay between them seemed to radiate an aura of impending greatness. Golden eyes observed as the first signature was inscribed, and those shining fingers moved over to join in the marks below his.

"Ah, the Emerald Empire is the first nation to join the Grand Organization, and I am her representative. Since the ritual was already complete with draconic blood, Great Overseer, what are your plans from here?"

After being motionless for some time, the Overseer revealed his thoughts, "Let us travel to the smaller lands between the larger ones and work our way up. Those nations will be more susceptible to our terms and conditions being that they are already threatened by rivaling neighbors. Just a few more rituals and I'll be powerful enough to defend them all."

Mercury squinted his eyes and gave a quizzical head tilt but, before he could utter a word, the Overseer strolled away with childlike enthusiasm. After a moment to himself, he broke his train of thought and looked over to the document once again. Just as he examined his uniform earlier, his golden eyes surveyed the Amicitia Licentiam for any errors or loopholes.

His thoughts spilled from his lips. "No, this agreement is foolproof, but the blood rituals still confound me. If his power can outperform this countermeasure, how can we prevail against what now haunts my soul? I fear as though I've made a grave error that I can't justify, yet it all hinges on the slimmest of possibilities. Still, I wonder, what if?"

Chapter 6.2

In a silent journey, Mercury, the Overseer, and the child made their way to the castle. The evening's events had shaken the Overseer, and Mercury found himself at a loss for comforting words. He, too, grappled with a complex mix of emotions. Towards the end, he felt compelled to voice his thoughts. "Do you see now, Overseer? It's become clear that she's been preoccupying you all this time for her own selfish reasons."

The Overseer responded. "I'm not a fumbling idiot. I recognize what has happened but, I can't help think—"

"Think what?" Mercury's eyes narrowed, along with his patience.

The Overseer continued, "I've been thinking about motives. What if she did all of this to save her own people? What if the Marked Ones are backed into a corner that they put themselves in due to their beliefs? As if they could control the mental illness that is destroying them, let alone recognize it."

"By slaughtering the innocent? Seems the most ineffective way, Overseer," Mercury seethed as they came to a halt.

"No, but you know the saying, Mercury, to make an omelet, you have to break a few eggs, don't you?"

"Hypocrite," Mercury retorted, his sharp words more of an accusation than a query.

This time the Overseer's eyes turned cold. The lack of respect was concerning, but he was curious enough to dive into it before shutting it down. Mercury turned his body towards him and lifted his chin. The defiance riddled his core and left him doubting the loyalty of his golden friend for the very first time.

The metallic lips remained stiff as they parted, "I'm certain the evidence doesn't convince you: the blood by your hands, the bodies on the ground, and even her speaking to us in the woods."

The Overseer interrupted his list, "We don't know that was Juliet. For all we know it could have been an imposter created as a part in tonight's tragic play."

"The one being played is you, Overseer."

The little girl who was with their company uttered some sounds that distracted them from their conflict. Her face twisted in discomfort causing Mercury to reach into his bag for a snack. She snatched it up and devoured it with delight. The two adults on either side of her exchanged looks one last time before making their way back to the main gates.

The guards welcomed them in and the entire town marveled with interest in the child they brought. The barber inspected her hair and started gathering creams and brushes. The grocer handed her a basket full of healthy treats. The tailor snuck in measurements to be able to provide her a unique wardrobe. The case manager gathered her name and date of birth for recordkeeping. Claire was welcomed into the society with open arms, and the Overseer looked over with pride towards Mercury who agreed with a nod that this was how everything is meant to be.

The child was approached by the Overseer afterwards who spoke towards the crowd about her future residency, "She has been through a horrific tragedy. I will watch over her until we find a permanent home. Meanwhile, I welcome all of you to come visit her often. Thank you all for your hospitality."

The crowd erupted in celebration and initiated a festival in honor of Claire and the Overseer. As they entered one of the opulent chambers of the castle, he gestured with a sweeping motion towards the room's luxurious furnishings, each piece chosen to cater to her tastes. Amelia, the dedicated servant, bustled about the space, adjusting curtains, fluffing pillows, and arranging decor with symmetry. Claire watched with a growing sense of appreciation as the room transformed before her eyes, tailored to her every whim and desire.

It was then that Claire spoke to where Amelia turned to listen, "I don't know which one I am more sad about, my aunt dying or that my mom and sister had to leave. I think that even though I am supposed to feel lucky right now, I am the most unlucky."

"Survivor's Guilt." The servant's voice rang from near the closet. Claire's head tilted with a confused scrunch before Amelia explained, "You feel as if you shouldn't be alive because everyone else close to you is gone. Like, what makes you special? Don't dread too much about that feeling. It'll pass with time. Until then, help me pick out something for you to wear after your bath."

Claire swallowed her response and made her way to the closet. She saw a cute periwinkle dress and pressed her palm on it. "This reminds me of the flowers my aunt would take me to go see. She said they were my sister's favorite so they became mine as well."

With Claire now in Amelia's capable hands, the Overseer convened a meeting, summoning a small selection of trusted High

Guardians. Vladsan, recognizing the urgency of the situation, hastened to join the gathering, his presence adding weight to the gravity of the discussion. Each member of the group prepared themselves for the topic ahead.

Troubled by the recent events, the Overseer began with a question. "Who is to blame for what happened at the Calcite Empire?" As he pondered this question, Mercury wanted to keep his thoughts to himself, but as he was about to voice his opinion, Bemus spoke up, "Overseer, I suggest you place the blame on the Marked Ones. Their adherence to a barbaric ideology is the root of all these troubles. If they would abandon these beliefs, we could achieve peace among all the nations. Their disposition to cause a migrant crisis and rebel from their flag to then attack the Calcite castle and create orphans are their doing. We respect you for protecting that child, but her parents should still be with her."

Mercury struggled to restrain his anger at Bemus' accusatory tone and words, but the discussion between the High Guardians then shifted toward Udiah and his actions. The Overseer commanded their attention, breaking through the heated exchange, "We must address the escalating migrant crisis. On one hand, we are obligated to protect all people and offer the Marked Ones sanctuary if they swear allegiance to the Grand Organization, perhaps even setting aside a section of land for them to call their own. On the other hand, we cannot ignore the fact that they attacked the Calcite castle, resulting in the Emperor's death. The window for negotiations has closed. This act is a clear violation of the Amicitia Licentium and constitutes an act of war. The Grand Organization, along with its High Guardians, will arrest all Marked Ones for conspiracy and treason, punishable by life imprisonment or death."

With this heavy decision made, the Overseer, Mercury, and the High Guardians embarked on their journey to Zeller castle. The clatter of their horses' hooves echoed on the cobblestone streets as they left the Grand Organization's main castle behind. The journey was shrouded in an eerie silence, with a noticeable sense of foreboding permeating the atmosphere.

As they rode through the town, the Overseer noticed that people glared at him with expressions ranging from anger to disappointment. News of the recent Calcite incident had spread far and wide, and it was clear that the populace was displeased with his actions. He had also ordered the church's destruction, and this was not received well with the common folk.

Mercury rode up next to him, his expression grave. "Lord, the news has spread to every corner of the realm. People are unhappy about what transpired at the Calcite castle. We must not tarry here; it's best to proceed to reassure our allies now."

The Overseer understood the urgency of Mercury's words. They needed to reach the Zeller Dynasty as soon as possible and address the situation before further unrest took root. Spurring their horses forward, the Overseer couldn't shake the unsettling feeling that had settled over him. It was as if the entire world had turned against him.

Approaching Zeller castle, the imposing structure loomed ahead. The massive stone walls, the imposing towers, and the banners bearing the Zeller crest created an intimidating sight. They dismounted from their horses, and the Overseer straightened his attire, trying to put on a confident facade. He couldn't afford to show any weakness in front of Victor. With Mercury and the High Guardians by his side, he made his way through the grand entrance. The meeting with Victor promised to be a pivotal moment, one that could shape the future of the realm.

Chapter 6.3

The Overseer's steps echoed through the grand corridor leading to the same Zeller Hall he had felt he was at just days ago. Inside, representatives from each kingdom neighboring the Zeller Dynasty gathered: the leaders of the Diamond Mortem Dynasty, the Spinelle

Kingdom, the Garner Kingdom, and the Emerald Empire. Even Mite representing the Wintersun Dynasty stood with them. The Overseer couldn't help but feel a sensation of falsa memoria as he entered the room, but this time, the atmosphere was different. All eyes fixated on him, and for the first time since the inception of the Grand Organization, he felt at the mercy of others.

A hush fell over the room, and Victor Zeller, the host and a powerful figure in the region, rose to speak. "Please, have a seat," he said, motioning to a chair at the massive round table. The Overseer obliged, his face a mixture of curiosity and concern.

Victor continued, "We must begin now, as time is of the essence. Given the delicate nature of the situation, I will act as interim Overseer for this specific occasion."

The Overseer's brow furrowed in disbelief. "What's the meaning of this?" he growled, the frustration clear in his voice.

But his calm voice answered in contrast to his anger, "Well, sir, due to your close involvement in our investigation and your reluctance to charge Juliet, we've decided to suspend your authority for this matter. The consensus among us is unanimous."

Annoyance simmered within the Overseer. He felt the urge to unleash his formidable power and take control, but then his eyes met Mercury's, who urged him to maintain his composure for the sake of peace. "Fine," he grumbled.

Victor continued, unfazed by the Overseer's discontent. "As you're all aware, against popular demand, Juliet has been pardoned by the Overseer for any accusations of treason."

Azrael, a High Guardian, interjected, "Perhaps it's best to set aside the matter of Juliet for now and address the issue at hand."

A few nods of agreement prompted Victor to proceed, "As I'm sure you all know, an attack has occurred at the Calcite Empire. Our investigations confirm that no more than a few survivors remain. The Overseer and Mercury attended the site. What did you discover?"

Mercury took a step forward. "We found devastation, Grand Emperor. The rebels had razed the Calcite castle and killed everyone inside. We hunted down and neutralized several of the rebels before returning."

Murmurs of discontent and shock rippled through the room. Victor explored further, "Did you recognize any of the attackers?"

The Overseer, looking grim, shook his head, his silence met with disapproving scowls from the leaders assembled.

"Tell us more," Victor urged. "Do you understand why this attack occurred?"

The Overseer raised his voice, frustration evident. "The rebels claimed they needed to send a message and thus declared war against the Grand Organization."

Discontent murmurs grew into heated arguments among the leaders. Victor intervened, "Enough! Proceed, Overseer. Your treaty promised protection from such incidents."

Mercury, irritated by the Overseer's reluctance to take action against Juliet, shot him a glare, but the Overseer remained resolute. "The Marked Ones had the opportunity to negotiate peace with us. At the moment we hold one of their elders, Udiah, in custody and intend to make an example of him to deter any who threaten world peace."

Victor scoffed, "A waste of time, in my opinion. Is it not true that your recent companion was seen near the gathering place of the Marked Ones before the attack?"

Frustration welled up within the Overseer, and he pondered how Victor obtained this information. "I've heard the allegations, but she denies ever being there."

With an arched brow, Victor responded, "So you're accepting denial as sufficient evidence?"

The leaders, and even some of the High Guardians, grew heated in their conflict. Victor's voice cut through the commotion, "Silence! Perhaps we should ask Juliet herself!"

The Overseer was baffled, and then his crystal eyes fell upon the auburn haired woman, who stood waiting in the doorway, her presence poised to alter the course of the conversation.

Chapter 6.4

"What would this council have to ask little ol' me?" Juliet said with a cunning smile, her demeanor defiant.

Victor, frowning, wasted no time in questioning her. "Where were you the night of the Calcite attack?"

"What Calcite attack?" Juliet feigned innocence.

"Do not play coy with me, she-devil. Everybody knows about the castle where hundreds of people were murdered." He snapped.

"Yes, I know of it, but what about it? There were several instances of the Calcite Empire warring with its people." Juliet retorted, her smile undeterred.

The Overseer, feeling the tension rise from Victor's aggressive approach, exploded, "There will be no trial! You will not execute this woman because a tragedy has occurred. Use your brains and let us conduct ourselves with some sense of diplomacy!"

However, this outburst served to divide the room further. Mite, frowning, distanced herself from the Overseer, and several High Guardians followed her. "Sir, with all due respect, you need to choose a side or this is all going to go sideways over some whore."

The Overseer's scowl met Mite's. "You should bite your tongue and yield from your misguided insults." His attention shifted back to the table. Talks of a split in power were brewing as national leaders began to fight over who should presume leadership. "Victor, end this madness before we go too far. . ."

"It is too late, my friend," Victor's face was as rigid as a stone wall. "It was you who took it too far. Your passion for World Peace was great. I almost believed that you could accomplish such a crazy idea. You were so close, but then you fell for a murderer."

"But she is innocent!" The Overseer objected, his step carried the weight of every defense he could fathom.

The Grand Emperor's stone cold face softened, but his voice remained firm. "You do not know that, Overseer, you feel that. It is a sentiment that is not shared, the migrant situation has sat at your desk for quite some time and you ignored it. To be honest, if I was in your position I may have done it as well, but I never sought to rule the world, just my people. You fought for the position you made, and you convinced most of us you could persevere through all struggles. Overseer, you trusted the wrong woman, and now look at the destruction it is bringing."

The Overseer surveyed the room, witnessing leaders at each other's throats and smaller alliances being made between them. After some time a voice cut through the noise. "Overseer!"

Turning, the Overseer saw Mercury pointing at Juliet and Mite, embroiled in a physical fight, pulling hair and clawing at each other. Juliet's claws ripped through Mite's snow-like cheek as the red haired woman received an uppercut through her nose. The Zeller guard intervened with haste, separating the two bloody combatants just as Vincent arrived, accompanied by a cadre of servants tasked with cleaning up the aftermath of the explosive event.

Through heavy breathing, Mite looked at the Overseer and said through gritted teeth, "Pick a side, the Grand Organization or this bitch that you call your woman. You can not have both!"

His crystal eyes glanced towards Mite and then at Juliet, but Juliet wouldn't wait another moment and ran out into the hallway. He looked at Mite and said, "This is not over," before chasing after Juliet.

Mercury shook his head, astonished, and mused, "Indeed, this is far from over. In fact it has just begun."

Mite, in a rage, screamed, "I have done everything for peace, but their actions scream lies! That's it, I'm done, I choose war!"

The Wintersun supporters cheered, taking off their Grand Organization symbols and dumping them on the table. The Wingmen howled and whooped at the idea of adventure and conquest. Mite, the supporting representatives, and about half of the former High Guardians all left the Zeller castle without another word. Victor, Mercury, and the rest left behind looked into each other's intense eyes that were all filled with apprehension.

The Overseer reached Juliet in the hallway, grabbing her by the arm, "Where are you going?"

"Anywhere but here!" sobbed Juliet, shaken by the meeting and her fight with Mite. "How could you pick them over me? They don't love you like I do. I have been by your side all this time, and you don't believe me. It isn't fair! How am I supposed to prove myself to you?"

The Overseer sighed, his frustration and confusion adding to the thick air. He searched Juliet's eyes for any hint of dishonesty before hugging her and whispering, "I believe you. Just go back to the castle and stay in my chambers. Nobody should bother you there. I have to finish this treasonous business; then I will meet you at the castle. Okay?"

Juliet nodded and kissed him on the cheek as he wiped a tear from hers. "Thank you. I know it'll be okay. I will see you soon."

Juliet continued down the hallway, leaving the Overseer standing there, torn between duty and personal conviction. He turned to return to the Zeller Hall, a storm of chaos awaiting him inside.

Chapter 6.5

Juliet's childhood memories were etched with the bitter taste of betrayal and the searing pain of branding irons. It was a time when the world felt like it was conspiring against her, marking her as an outcast even among her own people. As a Marked One in the Calcite Empire, she bore the mass of a stigma that branded not just her flesh but her very existence as inhuman and treacherous. The memory unfolded like a dark tapestry in her mind.

The Calcite soldiers, clad in cold, imposing armor, their faces hardened with disdain, took pleasure in their merciless task. The air was thick with tension as these independent thinkers were rounded up, their expressions a mix of fear and resignation. Juliet, just a child at the time, clutched at the fabric of her tattered clothes, eyes wide with terror.

The branding ceremony was a ritual of dehumanization. The sizzle of hot irons meeting flesh echoed through the air, accompanied by agonized screams that seemed to tear through the very fabric of reality. The Marked Ones were marked twice, not just in a physical sense, but also cast into a category of pariahs, condemned by the society they once called home.

The brand, a grotesque symbol of their supposed treachery, was seared onto the inside of their left wrist. Juliet still remembered the acrid scent of burnt flesh, the cruel permanence of the mark ensuring that they were forever branded as outsiders. The pain was not just physical; it cut deep into the soul, leaving scars that ran far beyond the surface.

As the branded ones were herded towards the outskirts, Juliet glimpsed a flicker of hope. Perhaps, beyond the borders of the Calcite Empire, there would be compassion, understanding, a chance at redemption. However, that hope was extinguished as they approached neighboring nations seeking refuge.

The once proud Calcite civilians, now broken and humiliated, approached each nation with desperation in their eyes. But the responses were uniform—a cold rejection, an unwillingness to harbor those tainted by the Calcite's prejudice. The alliance for world peace formed among the nations, united with the Calcite Empire, and became a barrier with no middle ground for the very people seeking safety and peace.

Juliet recalled the shame that clung to her, the dehumanizing glares from those who should have been saviors. It wasn't just the Calcite who saw them as less than human; the alliance that had sworn to stand against tyranny had turned a blind eye to their suffering. It was a betrayal that cut deeper than any branding iron.

The Marked Ones, with nowhere to turn, were left to navigate a world that deemed them monsters. They became wanderers, exiles in a land that should have offered sanctuary. Juliet, with each step, carried the weight of a branded past and the bitter taste of abandonment.

These memories haunted Juliet, shaping her understanding of a world that had forsaken her. They fueled her defiance and fueled her determination to break free from the chains of prejudice. As she faced the present turmoil, the echoes of her childhood resonated, a constant reminder of a world that needed to change.

Chapter 7.1

The Zeller Hall buzzed with activity as the Overseer entered, frustration etched across his face. Victor, orchestrator of the recent turmoil, occupied the head of the table surrounded by maps and war plans, his demeanor confident.

"What transpired, Victor? I advised against any drastic measures!" The Overseer's voice carried a mixture of urgency and irritation.

Victor peered up from his war plans, meeting his crystal eyes with a hint of disdain. "A minor setback. We are cleansing the Grand Organization of those who were never committed. If they chose to abandon our cause, then so be it."

"Abandon? What are you talking about?" The confusion was evident.

A condescending exhale escaped Victor's lips. "Did you not notice Mite and the others leaving?"

The Overseer's eyes widened. "No. I was. . . preoccupied. You chose to not join them?"

Victor grunted, dismissing the oversight. "I wanted to wake you up, not kill your project. Either way, they've left. Mite is spearheading a rebellion against you. I thought you two were inseparable. What happened?"

"We were close, and that subsided, to no fault from either of us. Victor, what's our course of action now?" The Overseer's concern lingered.

Victor leaned back, laying out the dire situation. "The Wintersuns, Hawkes, and Kristos have a massive army against us. They must be planning an assault at the Northeastern border near Eldoria Rift, expecting to reach our castle walls by sundown tomorrow. Towns in their path are being evacuated, but the potential damage could be catastrophic. The Wintersuns are ruthless, adopting a scorched earth policy. Our best option is to meet them there and force a confrontation. Our troops await your orders. Azrael?"

Azrael, who had been observing from under his hood, decided to speak. "Overseer, without laying blame, you must recognize your share of responsibility for this crisis. Perhaps a diplomatic effort might avert further catastrophe, if they are still amenable to dialogue. It's time to understand the burden of your choices."

Victor turned to the Overseer, awaiting his decision. The room fell into a contemplative silence as he grappled with Azrael's words. After a thoughtful pause, he stood and addressed both leaders. "Deploy ten percent of our troops to the rift's edge. Keep ninety percent in reserve, ensuring our elite forces are positioned. I will engage Sothis and attempt to bring an end to this turmoil. You have your orders; let's go."

As the leaders exited the Zeller Hall, Azrael pulled Mercury aside. "In fact, sir, we were hoping for your active participation at this crucial juncture. The Zeller and the Diamond Mortem stand united with the Grand Organization, despite our recent disagreements. We cannot afford to let peace crumble over this dispute. The defectors have returned to their kingdoms to prepare for war. Will you join us?"

Accepting Azrael's invitation, Mercury gathered his belongings. "Of course. Let's relocate this conversation to the Diamond Mortem castle for further strategizing."

Azrael nodded, "Agreed. We wouldn't want the Zeller castle to endure any more unnecessary bloodshed."

Mercury rolled his eyes. "I will join you soon. I need to muster what remains of the High Guardians and seek reinforcements for the Overseer. See you there." With those words, the golden man turned to exit, leaving behind an empty room full of anticipation for impending war and the realization that the Grand Organization stood at the brink of collapse.

Chapter 7.2

The Overseer departed the Zeller castle, a rush of urgency propelling him toward the Eldoria Rift. Passing through empty homes and untended fields, he saw the quiet devastation the impending war could wreak upon the land. The sight fueled his determination to reach the rift soon, knowing the repercussions of an imminent conflict.

The familiar landscape began to shift as he approached the rift's edge. His pace slowed, an unseen force draining his magical abilities. As the Overseer reached the destination, he sensed a daunting presence, a force he attributed to the combined might of the Wintersuns. His steps became deliberate, measured, as if he treaded on unfamiliar ground despite his familiarity with the area.

A bellow escaped his throat, "Call for the Grand Emperor, Sothis!" Hawke scouts, hidden in the shadows, revealed themselves and darted towards the Wintersun camp. The Overseer found a spot near a small village, the echoes of Victor's warnings playing in his mind. He decided to build a fire—an old fashioned method, a choice dictated by the inability to ignite it with his magic. He did not want to appear weakened before the inevitable confrontation.

As the flames flickered to life, illuminating the darkening shadows of the setting sun, he sensed the approach of Sothis and his retinue. They descended from the opposite side of the valley, and the Overseer, with practiced ease, greeted them with open arms. Sothis, however, declined the invitation to sit, choosing to stand with an air of defiance. "We prefer to stand," he retorted.

"I have come to parley with you regarding the war." His sword plunged into the ground, a symbolic gesture mirrored by the Wintersun.

"There is not much to discuss. We are now at war and there is no stopping this. We have had enough of you as our leader and we do not trust your childish Grand Organization or the treaty you have authored." Sothis' response was a resolute refusal, his eyes reflecting an unyielding determination. The Overseer felt a pang of frustration but maintained his composure.

"Call off this war. There are too many lives that will be lost over a matter that can be settled between us leaders. There must be another way." he implored, attempting to sway Sothis' resolve, but Sothis remained steadfast and dismissed any chance of reconciliation. The translucent man's stomach tightened, frustration mounting. Negotiations proved futile, and Sothis turned away, leaving the Overseer in the unsettling aftermath of failure.

The next morning arrived with a relentless downpour, a fitting backdrop for the impending clash. Both armies, obscured by the precipitation, massed at attention. Fires sizzled in the rain, and the earth turned to mud beneath the feet of soldiers on both sides. Sothis rallied his troops, the noise of their cheers cutting through the marching slush, while the Overseer stood silent and pensive, knowing the inevitable bloodshed loomed.

Mercury approached, inquiring about readiness. His pair of crystal eyes fell into a deep sadness, expressing a reluctance to engage in fratricidal conflict. Determined, he issued a somber order: "no prisoners, no mercy." The gravity of his words resonated across the camp, setting the grim tone for death.

As the horn sounded and feet thundered, the Overseer stood firm at the front. Descending into the valley, his voice thundered across the battlefield, calling out Sothis. The advancing army paused, their confusion evident. An eerie silence fell over the valley, a moment of uncertain prediction.

"Sothis Ra! Show yourself!" he shouted, demanding a final parley. Sothis emerged, flanked by his soldiers, ready to confront the Overseer.

Sothis appeared at the front of his army with haste and shouted back "What do you want?"

He pleaded once more, "Sothis, heed my words. This is madness. I do not wish to fight you. I do not wish for all this death. Call for a truce. Call off this war. It is not worth it."

"Ah, Overseer, is that fear I sense?" Sothis scoffed at the persistence.

He shook his head, "No. Sothis, sadness. You have been a good friend to me. I do not wish anyone to die today."

The Wintersun Grand Emperor yawned and stretched, "I will not perish, just you. My army will be victorious and we will be deposing you and your Amicitia Licentiam."

"Very well," he gave a woeful bellow as he drew his sword, which made each soldier raise their weapons. "Then what about this? Strike me down if I am the one to blame. We will duel without powers. I do not wish to see thousands of dead littering this valley."

Sothis considered the odds of winning a duel with the Overseer and agreed. "Indeed, there is one death that needs to happen. . ." Sothis' guards surrounded the Overseer and sheathed their weapons. He could feel the power radiating from the Wintersun army, being so close to so many of them. He knew this would be a tough fight without his powers, but everything was uncertain and this duel would be the tipping point.

Both leaders moved to a cleared space, their troops watching with bated breath. Unlike his sword, Sothis wielded a two handed glaive, and he was determined to keep his distance. Both fighters took a right step forward in unison, and circled each other in opposite directions. The soldiers watched as their leaders began to fight, knowing they were to witness a climactic battle never before seen in history.

With grace, the Overseer's sword slipped towards the pole arm, but Sothis blocked the jab with ease. He judged his distance, knowing he had a reach disadvantage, but speed made up for it. The blunt edge of Sothis' pole arm whipped through the air towards his semi transparent neck, just to be casted back by the sword. They continued this pattern for some time, trading blows at different angles to warm up before the real fight began. Within a second, Sothis performed a back sweep from his right leg, which caught the Overseer off guard, and slashed his weapon across his mandible.

The Overseer's free hand shot up to his jaw and light streaked across his skin and fizzled out. A blood drop crashed onto the ground below and Sothis laughed as his opponent acknowledged all abilities were nullified in the Wintersun presence.

"You're nothing but a mortal when standing next to me," Sothis boasted. He continued, "At the end of today, you will be nothing but a myth."

"Silence!" the Overseer barked as he lunged towards Sothis again. The other man backed up to parry the blade, his pale knuckle crashing into the bridge of the other's opaque nose.

As he recoiled, Sothis laughed again. "You're nothing but a fool with powers. Strip those powers away and you're a peasant."

"I will be ridiculed no longer." A blend of white lights danced around his skin again for a moment before dissolving. They clashed once more, clanking metal against metal until the Overseer whipped his sword like a saber and sliced the metacarpals of Sothis's left hand.

Sothis shrieked in agony and rushed his enemy to knock him off balance. The Overseer retaliated and swung low into Sothis' right tibia. Each of them were on one knee for a moment and with a forceful move, the Overseer and Sothis both swung and knocked each other's weapons out of their hands. As they rose again they began trading punches, Sothis' eye swelling as a cut on the Overseer's jaw opened up. It didn't take many more punches for him to realize that Sothis had lost peripheral vision. As Sothis' eyes closed, the translucent man drew the dagger that was on his enemy's belt and tossed it up into his neck, the tip piercing the trachea.

In a final, desperate move, a semi transparent fist collided into the temple of the frost-skinned man, leaving Sothis incapacitated. They both fell, but one rose, symbolizing the temporary victory within the valley's muddied grounds. The Overseer, bloodied and battered, stood amid the rain and the echoes of a battlefield that had just tasted its first drops of fraternal bloodshed.

Chapter 7.3

Days later, the Overseer and Victor hurried towards a gathering of soldiers clustered around a figure. As they approached, Azrael stood in the midst of the crowd, his expression twisted with anger.

The crowd opened up as the two approached and Azrael welcomed them with open arms, "Never have I seen a man fight with such fury! That was remarkable. I applaud you for your victory, but this is far from over. A messenger from the opposing camp flew overhead while you walked back. Chaos has taken control of the opposing army and they are not honoring your deal with Sothis. They are still out for blood. Furthermore, I think you need to see something. . ."

The Overseer let out an exasperated sigh, steadied himself on a nearby chair, stood up, and followed Azrael just outside the camp to where more than a few soldiers were singing and neglecting their duties. His sharp eyes caught a golden flash of a hand as the latest round of "cheers" were clinked. Azrael faced his palm down, signaling him to remain stealthy and follow him.

They crept closer until the verbage became clear. Amid the typical banter of drunken soldiers, one voice stood out—Mercury's. He boasted while plopping down into a chair, "Ah yes, although it is sad to hear that the great Sothis Wintersun was slain, I would have given my left arm to see them fight to the death! I suppose it may be a tad my fault though. I may have antagonized Sothis that he could become the new Overseer."

The creases etched deep into his forehead to where his brows almost touched. His lips pressed together to form a thin line while his jaw clenched, creating a slight tension in his facial muscles. A subtle grimace appeared at the corners of his mouth, betraying the pain he was trying to conceal. Despite his efforts to maintain composure, his eyes glistened with a hint of anguish, mirroring the discomfort he felt within. "How could he say things like that? Mercury has been my most trusted aide for years."

Azrael shook his head. "He has been boasting like this for weeks. I was there when he planted the idea in Sothis' head. He is not a true friend, but I thought you deserved to hear his hubris firsthand."

After another drink, Mercury snickered, "A fool and his whore! Anybody could do it. However, even if Sothis did kill him, I would just avenge the Overseer and take his place. I pretty much do his job for him anyways."

His whisper grew harsh towards Azrael, yet still quiet enough to not be overheard. "Why did you not say something sooner? A true friend would have spoken up."

"Overseer, would you have believed me? You still do not believe us about Juliet. A lover is one thing, but a close friend is a different matter when questioning loyalty. The best way we knew you would believe us would be to show you in person." Azrael reasoned, hoping his new companion would appreciate the method that was needed to show this betrayal.

But his thoughts stopped at a particular word. "We?"

"Mercury parlayed with Victor, Sothis, and I after your meeting with us regarding Juliet. When you left after her, you convinced Sothis to adopt this foolish plot. He said that any one of us could fulfill the role of the Overseer with his aide, and spoke about how gold is better than silver. Listen, we all have a right to voice our concerns, but this is a mutiny. The Zeller and The Diamond Mortem signed the Amicitia Licentiam agreement because we believe in a future without wars. Let this be the one to end them all."

"I see." He fell silent and listened to Mercury's boastful rant for a few more minutes.

The golden man was so drunk, he needed no encouragement as he continued. "I have seen less stable hands that would make a better Overseer. Hell, any of you could do his job. All he does is sulk and worry about uniting everyone under one banner. I do all the work! In fact, I will be the new Overseer after today. It will be just a title change since I am the driving force behind the Grand Organization's success."

"Is that so?" The Overseer emerged from the shadows. Ale spilled everywhere as soldiers dropped their steins and scrambled to stand at attention in his presence. Mercury's eyes widened as his throat tightened. "I trusted you, Mercury. You were my best friend. How could you do this to me? You turned my allies away, ignited a rebellion, and now you wish to take my place?"

"Why shouldn't I?" Mercury interjected, attempting to gain composure while he stood.

He squinted at Mercury, a mixture of hurt and accusation evident in his crystal eyes. "Why, Mercury? After all we've been through, all the battles we've fought together, how could you betray me like this?"

Mercury met those crystal eyes, his expression betraying a hint of sadness. "I didn't betray you. I was trying to protect you. Juliet has manipulated you, and I couldn't stand by and watch her use you like this."

The Overseer's jaw clenched, his fists tightening at his sides. "Again with the accusations of manipulation? She's never given anyone a reason to doubt her loyalty."

"You will always choose her, won't you?" Mercury's voice was filled with bitterness. "You would always choose Juliet over me, your friend of years. I've seen it time and time again. You'll believe her lies over my truths, just because of your feelings for her. That's okay. I went out of my way for you to discover her. I supported you in making those arrangements, but I have feelings too. You've casted Mite, myself, and many others out of your trusted circle because of her. Your decisions are your own, but they have affected me to the point where I can not tolerate the disrespect any longer."

"Mercury. . ." His expression softened, a pained realization dawning in his eyes.

But Mercury continued, the alcohol within him motivating anger to surface. With a sudden shift, Mercury let his rage be known. "I could do what you do in my sleep! Without me, you wouldn't be here, sitting as the head of the Grand Organization that I built with my own hands! This was my idea, and your accomplishments are built on the foundation of my blood, sweat, and tears. Nothing would be done without me!"

What once was an apologetic look from the colorful man turned into a stone-like stare as Mercury continued. His words reverberated in the tense silence, each syllable charged with raw emotion. "You think you can just dismiss me, cast me aside like I'm nothing? I've been by your side through everything, facing dangers and challenges that you couldn't even imagine because you stole what makes you powerful. And this is how you repay me? By siding with her, someone who ripped you away from me? You belong to me! It was I that authored the Amicitia Licentiam, I draft your policies, I arrange your meetings, I run the operations, I plan the day to day, I organize the High Guardians, I record the meetings, I enforce the rules, I am your spy when you want to stalk that silver tongued bitch that pushed Mite away from your side. You're blinded by your infatuation with her to see the truth! But mark my words, you'll regret this. You'll regret turning your back on the one person who's always been there for you when you needed it the most so Overseer, screw you—"

Mercury was cut off mid sentence as the Overseer plunged his blade into his golden gut. "—and your whore." The blood, thick and crimson, cascaded down in small streams, painting a masterpiece upon his semi transparent hand and the hilt of his sword. Each drop seemed to linger, suspended in time for a fleeting moment before succumbing to the inevitable pull of gravity. As they trickled downward, they traced complex patterns, weaving a tale of violence and sacrifice.

With a swift motion, the Overseer dismissed Mercury from his blade, and soldiers gathered around his motionless golden form. Above, the sight of blood upon the semi transparent hand and sword served as a stark reminder of the price of leadership, the sacrifices made in the name of this so-called 'Peace.' "Take heed. I am the Overseer. Disloyalty, usurpation. . . these are not tolerated under my rule. Nor will I ever be defeated. Resume your duties. I've had my fill of this nonsense."

Azrael revealed himself soon after, "Well, I suppose that is one way to deal with things. I understand the need to rule with an iron fist sometimes, but I didn't think that snake had any teeth."

"Teeth or not, I did not want his words to drip poison into anyone else's ears. I have lost two friends today. I do not wish to lose any more." The Overseer's eyes matched the coldness in his voice.

"Noted. We do need to prepare for the War with the Wintersun. I do not think they will pull any punches while the wound is still fresh."

"Agreed." They departed, leaving the soldiers to attend to the grave, and joined back with Victor, ready to face the impending storm. The echoes of loyalty and betrayal resonated in the air, marking the ominous prelude to the approaching conflict.

Chapter 7.4

Azrael and the Overseer returned to the camp, the distant sounds of clashing swords echoing through the air. Soldiers scrambled, gathering their gear in a frenzied dance of preparation. Approaching a nearby soldier, they asked, "What is happening?"

An officer drew their attention with his finger, pointing down into the valley. "Sir, a Wintersun emissary came over and demanded to fight you. A few High Guardians took soldiers to the front lines, but they appear to be losing."

Two High Guardians were locked in combat with a soldier unfamiliar to the Overseer. Ignoring Azrael's protests, he rushed down into the valley, pondering who this Wintersun soldier was.

As he neared, he recognized a second figure standing to the side– Mite.

The High Guardians executed a synchronized attack, their swords weaving through the air in a mesmerizing display of skill. The mysterious Wintersun warrior defended with graceful expertise, holding their ground against the relentless assault.

The translucent man, watching the intense skirmish, couldn't ignore the pressing question of why Mite was there.

"Mite! What is the meaning of this?" The words escaped the Overseer's lips before he realized the repercussions, and he regretted each of them. Both High Guardians turned their attention to Mite distracted from the ongoing battle, and in that very brief moment, the Wintersun warrior beheaded them with a single stroke.

"Damn it!" He cursed at the force of his guilt. Moving closer, he gathered himself before addressing the warrior. "Who are you? It is no small feat to match, let alone defeat a High Guardian, or two for that matter."

The fighter turned to face him. "I am Chaos."

It was then that the Overseer grasped the whole of Azrael's words, "Chaos has taken control." It was not that the Wintersun army fell into disarray, but instead that this individual was their interim Grand Emperor. "What do you want, Chaos?"

Chaos grunted and faced the Overseer with her sword still drawn. "I am here to seek justice for the murder of the Grand Emperor, Sothis."

He stepped forward, his voice firm yet coated with an edge of desperation. "That was not murder. It was a duel—a desperate attempt to avoid unnecessary bloodshed. Something you have no regard for," he declared, his glare unwavering.

Drawing his weapon, he readied himself for what seemed like an inevitable confrontation. "Chaos, I do not wish to add to the violence. I seek peace. Please, return to your camp and convey my plea to end this senseless conflict to your comrades—"

But his entreaty was met with a menacing laugh from Chaos, cutting through his words like a blade through silk. She scoffed, her voice dripping with contempt. "Did you not witness my victory over your precious High Guardians? I cannot be killed, for I am the most skilled fighter in the entire Wintersun Dynasty!"

She stood as a paradox of physicality, towering over most with her impressive stature yet possessing delicate and feminine features that soften her imposing presence. Her broad shoulders and muscular frame suggested immense strength, but it was her gentle eyes, full lips, and graceful movements that imposed an intimate grace.

The Overseer reflected on his unsuccessful appeal to Sothis, recognizing that Chaos, much like her predecessor, would never consider thoughts of peace. Despite this realization, he harbored no desire for further violence. Instead, he yearned for an alternative path, a resolution that did not culminate in bloodshed.

At that moment, Victor emerged behind him, accompanied by a small gathering of soldiers. "Are you alright?" he inquired, not out of concern but out of compassion, aware that they found themselves embroiled in yet another unwanted situation.

The Overseer directed his attention back to Mite. "And why are you here, Mite?"

Her jet black eyes were devoid of emotion. "I am trying to ensure that Chaos doesn't harm anyone else besides you, though it was your esteemed High Guardians who initiated this recent skirmish."

He observed a flicker of discomfort in her expression. Perhaps she doesn't mean that, he hoped. "So, you have come to confront me as well?"

"No. I'm here to observe. I could never—" Mite's voice trailed off. "It's decision time. Will you fight or flee?"

Chaos' harsh words cut through the air like the icy winds around her, "It matters not how formidable you and your lackeys may be. I shall leave an indelible mark upon your illusion of governance. Wintersun, attack!" With that command, the Wintersun soldiers surged forward. The Overseer, Victor, and their companions braced themselves, but were puzzled as the Wintersun soldiers bypassed them. It soon became apparent that their objective was not to engage in direct combat, but to target the surrounding area. The small outposts and cottages behind them were now in peril, prompting the leaders to call for their protection.

The Zeller soldiers moved to counter the threat, but found themselves outnumbered and outmaneuvered. As the Overseer moved to aid Victor and the others, Chaos launched herself at him. He deflected her attack with his sword, shouting, "Cease this madness!"

Chaos gave a menacing smile and taunted him, "Stop me, then."

The Overseer continued to engage Chaos in combat while the Zeller soldiers attempted to confront the Wintersun forces, but their efforts proved futile. The Wintersun outnumbered them three to one, leaving no opportunity to call for reinforcements. As the situation deteriorated, soldiers from the base camp rushed into the valley to lend assistance. Amidst the chaos, Chaos seized an opening and attempted to strike the translucent man's midsection with a second, shorter blade dipped in poison. However, her attack was countered by a forceful kick to her rib cage from the opposite side.

A tall, muscular figure adorned in sleek ebony armor surged forward, pushing Chaos away and placing himself between her and the Overseer. As Chaos regained her footing, the man spoke, addressing them both. "This battle is mine to bear. I am Thaw, champion and general of the Zeller military."

The Overseer, recognizing Thaw's capability, redirected his focus, joining Victor in quelling the pillaging and dispatching several adversaries.

Meanwhile, Thaw approached Chaos in stoic silence, unsheathing his highland sword with a determined smile. Without uttering a word, he braced himself for the confrontation. Chaos emitted a deafening roar, sending shockwaves through the valley, before lunging forward with astonishing speed, unleashing a barrage of strikes that Thaw evaded with quick succession. With each evasion, Chaos' frustration intensified, her attacks growing more ferocious. Yet, Thaw remained composed, sidestepping her onslaught. Despite her relentless assault, Thaw maintained his calm demeanor, parrying her blows with little effort.

Thaw countered with his own flurry of strikes, but Chaos parried each blow with expert precision. Their duel continued until it became evident that the Wintersun duo did not have the upper hand. With that, Mite dashed through the crowd, brandishing her sword. With remarkable agility, she leaped onto Chaos' back, launching an aerial assault against Thaw. However, Thaw remained unbothered, and just as elegant as the two women attacking him, rolled to the side to evade her attack. Drawing a second sword, he broke the tense silence with a resolute declaration: "Good, a real fight."

Mite and Chaos launched a coordinated assault on Thaw, who defended himself with his dual longswords. Despite their relentless attack, Thaw managed to push them back and initiate his own offensive. With rapid swings, he slashed at both Chaos and Mite, landing a hit on the front of Chaos' thigh, eliciting a cry of pain. Meanwhile, Mite circled behind Thaw and jabbed him in the side, finding a gap in his defenses. As Chaos aimed a massive overhead strike, Thaw blocked it with an agile 'X' pattern defense using both swords. Seizing the opportunity, Mite launched another attack, but Thaw kicked her in the chest, sending her tumbling to the ground. He then evaded Chaos' next strike and countered by slicing her sword arm.

Growling in frustration, Chaos switched arms to compensate for her injury, while Mite regrouped and joined Chaos in another frontal assault on Thaw. Despite their relentless attacks, Thaw demonstrated incredible swordsmanship, dodging, parrying, and returning blows with ease. Inspired by his skill, the troops cheered, but Thaw's defense faltered for a moment when Chaos' struck with a poisoned dagger grazed across his nose, causing him visible pain. However, undeterred, Thaw continued to defend himself.

    As Mite attempted to flank him again, Thaw pressed forward, engaging Chaos in a fierce exchange of blows. In the midst of the melee, one of Thaw's swords pierced Mite's stomach, causing her to stagger back to defend herself. Seizing the opportunity, Thaw leapt into the air in a backflip, swinging both swords to disrupt Mite's advance and causing her to stumble. Capitalizing on her momentary disorientation, Thaw delivered a powerful elbow to her temple, rendering her unconscious for the time being.

    Chaos issued a challenge to Thaw, proposing a duel to allow Mite time to recover. With determination in her eyes, she readied her blades as Thaw accepted her challenge. Despite his natural size advantage, Chaos relied on her speed and agility to evade Thaw's attacks, but struggled to land a decisive blow.

    Recognizing Chaos' strategy, Thaw adjusted his approach to counter her elusive movements. In addition to his swordplay, he incorporated knee and elbow strikes, frustrating Chaos' efforts. In a retaliatory move, Chaos hurled her dagger to distract Thaw, then aimed for an opening behind his knee. However, Thaw adjusted his stance with perfect timing to minimize the impact, delivering a powerful kick to her chest that sent her tumbling to the ground once again.

Mite reappeared behind Chaos, her presence evoking a sense of anger and determination. Declaring her intention to end the bloodshed and protect the Wintersun, she engaged Thaw in battle. Despite her agile dodges, Chaos was unable to prevent Thaw from kicking her away. Undeterred, Mite drew her blades and launched a fierce counterattack against Thaw, proving to be a formidable opponent.

As Mite and Thaw clashed in battle, The Overseer noticed their conflict and called for Victor to join him in intervening. However, before they could reach them, their view was obstructed by a towering Wintersun soldier, standing over nine feet tall and weighing over five hundred pounds. Charging towards them with immense force, the behemoth plowed through soldiers left and right, creating mayhem in his wake.

Reacting out of natural instinct, The translucent man executed a deft flip over the brute's back, positioning himself at the perfect angle. Victor attempted a similar maneuver, aiming a kick at his massive chest, but the Grand Emperor was overpowered, and forced onto his back. Armed with a battle axe featuring massive edges, the giant posed a formidable challenge, prompting the Overseer and Victor to recognize the necessity of a combined effort to overcome this formidable opponent and halt the conflict between Thaw and Mite.

Meanwhile, Chaos managed to rise to her feet. In her resolve, she retrieved her sword and steadied herself, preparing to reenter the fray. Lunging forward, she aimed a strike at the distracted Thaw, but instead her attack was blocked by his swift swordplay. Seizing the opportunity, Thaw delivered a well placed strike to Mite's chest, then grabbed Chaos by the neck and exerted pressure. Despite her weakened state, Chaos attempted to retaliate, but Thaw deflected her blade with his gauntlet, using her momentum to thrust her towards Mite's weapon.

Both women reacted with shock and disbelief as Chaos collided with Mite's blade. Mite, in a moment of horror, covered her mouth with her hand as Chaos' eyes rolled back in her head. With a smirk, Thaw released the Wintersun fighter and redirected his blade towards Mite, who realized, too late, the fatal error she had made.

The Wintersuns' morale dropped as Victor's blade met the edge of the giant's battle axe. He knew this fight could not last long, but he also knew that if he did not focus then he would be in trouble. A massive fist then connected with Victor's face, disabling him, and the translucent man knew he needed to act fast. He slipped around the outside of the brute's next arm extension, and met the backside of its elbow with his. He kicked down on the giant's hips to throw him off his stance and stabbed his sword up into his armpit. This produced some blood, but the Overseer knew it wasn't enough. He backed up to reset himself, knowing now how to end the fight.

Mite retreated, evading Thaw's onslaught in a desperate attempt to fend him off. Although she managed to inflict a few cuts on his arms and legs with her daggers, Thaw showed off his defensive skill by blocking each of her critical strikes. With her options dwindling, she plotted a final lethal move. Seizing an opening, she ducked beneath Thaw's swing and thrust her dagger towards the back of his leg, aiming to penetrate deep into his flesh. In a quick motion, she spun around, aiming for his kidney, finding a gap in his armor, and blood began to flow from his wound. As she prepared for another attack aimed at his throat, a glimmer of silver flashed before her eyes. To her surprise, Thaw stood calm before her, wiping the blood from his blade before tending to his injuries.

As Mite observed this, she couldn't shake the surreal sight of Thaw seeming to wipe off blood while more poured all over him. As she observed Thaw's futile efforts, a chill ran down Mite's spine, a sense of unease settling in the pit of her stomach. In that moment of surreal clarity, she reached for her forehead, seeking reassurance in the familiar touch of her own flesh. But to her horror, her fingers found nothing but empty air. In a sudden rush of panic, she realized that her forehead was missing, a gaping void where once there had been solid bone and smooth skin. Her vision blurred, the sky above tinted with shades of a bloody white and blue. As her consciousness faded, her severed head lay upon the ground, while Thaw resumed the battle, indifferent to her fate, determined to continue fighting as if Mite were inconsequential.

Victor recovered from the force of the blow, and adapted to the Overseer's strategy. Together, they launched a relentless assault on the giant, striking until they found weaknesses in his defenses. As their coordinated efforts wore the brute down, a semi transparent fist delivered the decisive blow, piercing through the brute's skull with a final, fatal strike.

The brute dropped, collapsing to the ground with a thunderous thud that echoed through the battlefield. Victor staggered back, his chest heaving as he struggled to regain his breath. But amidst the discord of clashing steel and desperate shouts, the clear-skinned man's senses honed in on a different kind of silence; a void where the relentless clash of swords had once been.

As he looked away from the fallen brute, the Overseer's heart clenched in his chest as he beheld the sight before him. Mite lay motionless on the blood soaked earth, her once vibrant spirit extinguished, her form now limp and lifeless. With a surge of desperate urgency, he pushed through the throng of battling soldiers, his every step a desperate race against time.

As he reached Mite's side, it was as if he shattered into a million pieces. He knelt beside her, his hands trembling as they reached out to touch her still form. But there was no warmth beneath his fingertips, no flicker of life in her vacant gaze. Tears welled in his eyes, blurring his vision as he struggled to comprehend the enormity of his loss.

In that moment, amidst the carnage of war, the opaque-skinned man felt emptiness wash over him; a gaping void that threatened to consume him whole. For Mite was more than just a soldier; she was a trusted High Guardian, a companion, a friend, someone he loved, and above all a beacon of hope in the darkest of times. And now, with her life snuffed out by the cruel hand of fate, the Overseer could do nothing but cradle her lifeless form in his arms and weep for all that had been lost.

As the tides of war shifted and the last remnants of the Wintersun forces were vanquished, he remained kneeling beside Mite's body, his heart heavy with grief. For in that moment, he knew that the world would never be the same without her by his side.

Chapter 7.5

Far from the chaotic battle, a Hawk scout perched atop a rocky outcrop, his keen eyes scanning the horizon through a polished glass. With the chaos of battle subsiding and the dust of conflict settling, he observed the grim outcome with a heavy heart. With a sense of urgency, he descended from his vantage point, his boots pounding against the earth as he raced back to deliver his report.

Breathless, the scout approached the king's tent, his heart pounding in his chest. "Sir, may I enter?" he called out with urgency.

Ara's voice echoed from within the tent, granting permission. "Yes, make it fast."

With a nod, the scout straightened his attire and entered the tent, his eyes meeting the king's. "Sir, I witnessed the fall of both our champions. There is no movement among the troops at this time."

Ara's brow furrowed in frustration at the news. "Damn," he muttered, his tone reeled with disappointment. "I held hope for Mite. It seems this Overseer is not the paragon of mercy he claims to be. Summon my soldiers."

"Right away, sir!" the scout responded, exiting the tent to carry out his orders. As he circled the camp, he raised his voice to summon each of the alliance's top men.

With reluctance, the leaders gathered at the commander's tent, their expressions etched with concern and apprehension. They had heard whispers of the devastating outcome from their own scouts, and the news hung heavy in the air.

As they assembled before Ara, he wasted no time in addressing them, his voice firm with resolve. "There is no room for error in the coming battle," he declared, his words cutting through the tense silence.

"We will strike hard and fast, showing no mercy to our foes. There is no time for further deliberation. Just action. Understood?"

Each soldier nodded in unsmiling agreement, their determination mirrored in their eyes. "Good," Ara affirmed. "Now, let us move with purpose. The next phase of our campaign awaits."

With that, the men dispersed, returning to their respective camps to gather their troops for the impending conflict. The ominous drums of war beat in the distance, signaling the onset of yet another segment in the ongoing struggle for supremacy.

Meanwhile, the Overseer cradled the shattered remnants of Mite's head in his trembling hands, a solitary tear tracing a path down his weathered cheek. Amidst the chaotic storm of soldiers surging past him into the heart of the Wintersun homeland, nothing else seemed to hold significance. "Dammit," he whispered, his voice choking with sorrow. "Why couldn't she have listened? We were friends for so long. If circumstances were different, perhaps. . ." His words trailed off into a bitter lament, swallowed by the clamor of battle raging around them.

With utmost care and tenderness, he placed the fragment of Mite's scalp back onto her forehead, his heart heavy with grief at the sight of her lifeless form. The once vibrant High Guardian now lay still before him, her eyes closed in a final, peaceful slumber. "Rest in peace, Mite," he murmured, his voice heavy with grief and regret. His crystal eyes turning towards the High Guardians standing vigil around him, their resolve a stark contrast to his own anguish, the man who was often colorful felt a profound sense of loss weighing upon his shoulders.

As his eyes followed the clash unfolding in the Wintersun capital, where the frenzied clash of opposing forces rent the air with the sounds of steel meeting steel, a wave of despair washed over him. Consumed by sorrow, he retreated into the sanctuary of the command tent, seeking solace amidst the familiar confines of his makeshift headquarters. Inside, Victor and Azrael awaited him, their expressions a mix of concern and reproach.

Azrael's voice cut through the heavy silence like a dagger, his words dripping with scorn. "You are running out of friends to kill, Overseer," he hissed, unyielding to any sympathy that was expected.

Victor shook his head in dissent. "Enough. Mite was still a remarkable individual. Despite her change in allegiance, she remained a friend. Let the man mourn her loss, and then we must focus on the task ahead."

Azrael decided to accept the advice without protest. "Very well."

Turning to the Overseer, Victor's tone softened, though his words carried a hint of admonition. "However, you must understand the consequences of your actions. Mite had unyielding love for you, evident to everyone but yourself, it seems. With her passing, along with the turmoil surrounding Juliet and Mercury's demise, we find ourselves embroiled in conflict. You must gather yourself and lead the Grand Organization with resolve."

His voice trembled with emotion, tears threatening to spill. "I don't know if I can, Victor. I feel overwhelmed, and everything is happening so fast."

Placing a reassuring hand on his shoulder, Victor offered words of solace. "We both understand the pain of losing something. You will find the strength to overcome this, but now is not the time for sorrow."

With a slow nod, he was sluggish as he approached the war map, composing himself as he formulated a strategy. "We must continue to confront the enemy head on. Their army's size and strength have dwindled since Sothis' death. The strongest of the Wintersun either defected or fell. Though I never desired this battle, our superior numbers and might will prevail."

Azrael's agreement was serious. "Indeed, in life, one seldom gets the battles they wish for. But we must face what comes our way."

He gave his final orders with determination. "Inform the generals to crush the enemy without mercy. Spare no prisoners. I require sleep; I will be in my tent."

Victor and Azrael nodded in acknowledgment before departing the command tent together. Alone in his quarters, the Overseer sank onto his cot with a heavy heart. "Oh, Mite. Why did you have to depart from my side? We could have accomplished so much together. I had envisioned a future filled with endless possibilities." A solitary tear traced down his cheek, its path stinging against the wound inflicted by Sothis. It was a harsh reminder of his shortcomings. Ignoring the pain, he succumbed to sleep, bracing himself for the inevitable continuation of the battle come morning.

Upon awakening, the translucent man was healed from his powers returning in the absence of the Wintersun's magic nullification. Even so, his head pounded like sliding rocks from a cliffside. Rising from his cot, he stretched his weary limbs and reached for his sword. Opening the flaps of his tent, he was blinded by the morning sun. After blinking away the sleep from his eyes, a messenger darted towards him. "Overseer, Overseer! Grand Emperor Zeller demands your presence in the command tent at once."

Acknowledging the urgency in the messenger's tone, the Overseer replied, "Thank you. I will make my way there soon." Before departing, he seized the opportunity to grab some abandoned breakfast and a cup of coffee from a nearby table. Hastening his steps, he reached the command tent, where Victor and Azrael awaited.

"Good morning," Victor greeted with a chuckle. "We were beginning to wonder if you planned to sleep through the rest of the war and skip your victory speech!"

He waved off Victor's jest with a tired smile. "I took the rest I needed, but it appears Azrael could use a century of hibernation."

Victor erupted into laughter, slapping Azrael on the back. "Looks like the Overseer is back in form! Let us proceed with our planning."

Azrael grumbled unintelligible words as he unfurled the war map onto the table. Victor gestured towards the highlighted areas and launched into his report. "While you were resting, our troops engaged in fierce combat throughout the night until just an hour ago. Both sides agreed to a temporary ceasefire to recuperate. For every casualty inflicted by the Wintersuns, we managed to eliminate ten of their soldiers. Furthermore, we've bolstered our ranks with reinforcements from the Mortem. About one in every five fallen soldiers is salvageable, but the Wintersuns have caught on and are now burning their deceased. We anticipate securing the entirety of the Wintersun capital by tomorrow morning. What are your orders once we achieve total victory?"

The translucent man pondered for a moment before responding. "Given your unwavering loyalty, I've decided to annex their territory. You and Azrael will divide the spoils and resources obtained from our conquest."

Victor and Azrael exchanged triumphant smiles. "Agreed. Let's teach these rebels a lesson they won't forget!"

In the ensuing weeks, the Grand Organization's forces surged northward, quelling any remnants of resistance. By the end of the first week, rebel forces had been eradicated from the central region. By the second week's conclusion, the Wintersuns had lost control of their remaining territories to the Grand Organization. As week three drew to a close, the Overseer convened a meeting at his castle. Seated in his customary position, he surveyed the diminished gathering. About half of the High Guardians remained, their loyalty tested and proven.

His crystal eyes lingered like forgotten sentinels, guarding the vacant seat once occupied by Mite, now echoing with the silence of her absence. His introspection was interrupted by the arrival of Victor and Azrael. "High Guardians, report," he commanded, snapping back to the present.

Commander Vladsan of the Northern Sanction was the first to deliver his report. "Sir, there are no rebel forces remaining within the borders of the central sanction. Our defenses have been bolstered to repel any potential counterattacks. Not a single intruder will breach the castle walls without our permission."

"Excellent. Next," he prompted, his voice carrying not a hint of interest.

Hari from the Eastern Sanction rose from his seat and offered a respectful bow. "Sir, I am grateful for the opportunity to continue serving at this esteemed table. According to my intelligence, the rebels have suffered significant losses. It appears they are operating at less than half their original strength. Our forces have claimed over sixty percent of their territory and continue to advance towards their remaining strongholds with each passing day."

"Very promising. Next." He leaned forward, his crystal eyes gleaming with a mixture of irritation and expectation as he awaited the next item to be presented..

An eerie silence fell over the Grand Hall as the Overseer surveyed each High Guardian seated at the table. It became apparent that many were either absent or lacking leadership. Scourge of the Southern Sanction was back in his homeland, gathering support, while Azrael had delegated leadership of his troops to Darakon of the Western Sanction.

Victor's voice cut through the tense atmosphere. "Overseer, we still have the matter of Juliet to address. She has vanished without a trace, and our search efforts have yielded nothing. Shall we continue our pursuit?"

The Overseer paused, his brow furrowing with concern as he deliberated. "No more searching," he declared after a moment, his voice carrying a note of finality. "We have more pressing matters at hand. If she wishes to remain hidden, so be it. Our priority now is to recover from this Wintersun rebellion."

Victor and Azrael exchanged glances, their expressions masking their unease. They nodded in agreement, though their smiles held a hint of suspicion. "As you command," Victor replied, his tone betraying a sense of reservation.

With that, the Overseer rose from his seat, signaling the end of the meeting. As he departed, a nagging doubt gnawed at the back of his mind. Where could Juliet be? And why did she choose to disappear now, of all times?

Alone in his chambers, the Overseer's thoughts churned with dread as he prepared for bed. The influence of the ongoing war coupled with Juliet's mysterious absence clouded his mind. Perhaps he should have relinquished his position long ago, he mused, a pang of self doubt creeping into his thoughts. But no, he dismissed the notion. He was the Overseer, after all— flawless, untouchable.

Despite his efforts to push aside his concerns, sleep eluded him. Still restless, he tossed and turned, his mind plagued by doubts and uncertainties. Exhaustion claimed him, and he succumbed to a fitful slumber, haunted by the specter of doubt that lingered in the depths of his subconscious.

Chapter 8.1

The Western sanction became a theater of relentless conflict, where the skies darkened with the smoke of burning villages and the land quivered under the weight of marching armies. Amidst the chaos, the Marked Ones found themselves cornered, their backs against the proverbial wall as they faced the onslaught of Azrael's Diamond Mortem.

With determination, Azrael led his forces deep into the heart of Hawke territory, launching a relentless campaign that left devastation in its wake. The once mighty Empire found itself teetering on the brink of extinction as the Diamond Mortem's advance knew no bounds. In the span of a mere two weeks, the Hawkes were pushed to be decimated and their territory overrun.

As the dust settled and control over the conquered lands was consolidated, Azrael faced a critical decision. Half of the Diamond Mortem's army remained behind to fortify the acquired territory, ensuring its borders remained impregnable against any potential threats.

Meanwhile, the other half set out to reinforce the Zeller forces in their ongoing struggle against the Kristos.

Led by Victor, the Zeller and their reinforcements faced fierce resistance from the rebel troops. Despite their ferocity, the rebels were no match for the seasoned warriors of the Diamond Mortem, who dispatched them within a fortnight. With the Kristos' territory annexed into the Central sanction, the Overseer turned his attention to the remaining Marked Ones, intent on stamping out the last remnants of resistance.

United under the banner of the Grand Organization of the Amicitia Licentiam, the forces commanded by Azrael, the Overseer, and Victor presented a formidable front, rejuvenating the public's confidence in their leadership. As they marched onward, their resolve unshakable and their determination unwavering, they vowed to bring an end to the age of rebellion and usher in a new era of peace and stability.

After the final clash of swords had ceased and the echoes of battle faded, the Overseer returned to his castle, knowing that the true test lay ahead: facing the scrutiny of the other kingdoms. With the war's end drawing near, emissaries and leaders from every corner of the realm began to converge upon the High Guardian's castle.

In anticipation of the summit, the translucent man spared no expense in preparing lavish chambers to ensure the comfort and hospitality of each arriving dignitary. As the last king's carriage rolled into the courtyard, the Overseer dispatched messengers to gather the royal leaders for the impending meeting.

As he awaited the gathering, he couldn't help but lament the absence of Mercury, now a traitor to their cause. The burden of orchestrating the summit, coupled with his myriad other responsibilities, frustrated him to new lengths. However, he concluded to seek out a new assistant to aid him in his duties before making his way to the Grand Hall.

As he entered the room, the Overseer's survey swept across the assembled leaders, each awaiting his address. Questions hung heavy in the air, but he paid them little heed as he made his way to the head of the table. With a commanding gesture, he signaled for silence.

"I understand there are many questions weighing on your minds," he began, his voice firm and authoritative. "Allow me to address some of them before we proceed. Yes, the rumors you've heard are true. A rebellion did indeed erupt across each sanction, plunging our lands into conflict. However, I am pleased to inform you that, with the combined efforts of myself, Azrael of the Diamond Mortem, and Victor of the Zeller, the rebellion has been quelled. You need not fear invasion or further unrest."

His words sparked murmurs among the leaders, each grappling with the implications of his revelation. Some voiced their shock at the news, expressing their frustration at not being informed earlier. Others cast blame upon Juliet, questioning her role in the uprising.

Raising his hand once more, the Overseer quelled the rising clamor. "I am aware that many of you are concerned about Juliet," he continued.

Bemus shouted, "Hear hear! Never in our kingdom has a woman caused so much trouble!"

While some in the room chuckled, his crystal eyes fixed a stern stare on the man and retorted, "I doubt that! Regardless, she will face consequences once we apprehend her. Your cooperation in locating her will be crucial. I encourage all of you to provide any information on her whereabouts so that she may be held accountable for her actions."

Hari of the Emerald Empire rose from his seat, his voice filled with indignation. "And what then? Will she be pardoned yet again? We cannot allow this cycle of injustice to persist. Wars have been waged over less, but few times has a conflict been instigated by a woman. It is an affront to our sovereignty! Who will be the next victim of her deceit? What of the smaller kingdoms, like the Fushsites or the Garner? Will they suffer the same fate as the Calcites? Or will they too be disregarded, forced to take up arms against us, just as the Wintersuns did?"

The Overseer raised his hand once more, signaling for silence. "No, that will not happen. The incident in the Calcite Empire has been addressed. Yes, we underestimated the Marked Ones' capacity to foment rebellion. However, that mistake will not be repeated."

The crowd murmured among themselves before falling silent again, but he continued with a firmness in his voice. "I can assure you all that order has been restored and will remain so. The rebellion has been quelled, and the realm is no longer under threat. The Marked Ones have been defeated, and unity reigns once more."

The ruler of the Onyx Empire rose to his feet, his voice resolute. "Do not evade the issue, Overseer. Despite our unity, this war still occurred. Your association with that woman has caused untold suffering. We demand answers. What fate awaits Juliet?"

The Overseer slammed his hands onto the table and stood up. "I will address this matter," he declared, his tone commanding. "There will be no further questioning on the subject." Regaining his composure, he sat back down. "I will not tolerate any threat to this land, whether from friend or foe."

The Grand Hall buzzed with whispers and disbelief. "Enough!" His complexion grew into an irate mix of reds. "If you doubt my resolve, then I will step down from my position if this issue is not resolved soon."

The King of the Spinelles interjected, "And how do you define 'soon,' Overseer?"

He scowled back at the Spinelle royalty and replied, "Give me a couple of weeks, and you will all have answers, whether you like them or not." The crowd of representatives grumbled in disdain, which further fueled his frustration. "Do the rest of you intend to rebel as well? Have you no trust? I have unified this land. I have brought prosperity to many nations and protected you from evil! This disbelief and disloyalty offends me to the greatest degree. I have made a single mistake, and now you wish to condemn me?"

The Grand Hall fell silent as the leaders contemplated the Overseer's impassioned words. He continued, still firm in his effort, "I will not tolerate this grumbling and bickering. I will set the record straight. No substantial evidence has been brought to my attention. I will not condemn anyone, not someone close to me based on hearsay. I will resolve this confusion within a fortnight. Now, unless anyone else has any further questions, this meeting is adjourned."

His crystal eyes glanced over and he gave a slight nod to the High Guardians present, signaling it was time to escort the leaders to their chambers. Left alone, his body sank into a chair, his mind swirling with frustration and uncertainty. How can I make it clear to everyone it wasn't her? He pondered, feeling the rush of the war and Juliet's mysterious disappearance bearing down on him.

Hours ticked by in solitude before he rose from his seat and trudged back to his chambers. Unsure of how to confront the issue of Juliet's absence, he drew a bath, hoping the warm water would ease his troubled mind. As he submerged himself, his thoughts continued to churn, the turmoil of the recent events gnawing at him like a persistent ache.

"A fortnight. . . you idiot," he muttered to himself, his frustration apparent even in the dim candlelight of the chamber. Yet, no matter how hard he tried to push the matter aside, it continued to gnaw at his thoughts, refusing to be ignored. A sharp knock pierced the silence, jolting him from his contemplation. "Who is it? Do not come in. I am not receiving visitors at this time," he called out, his tone curt and unwelcoming.

"It is I, Hari," came the voice from beyond the door.

"What is it?" The Overseer's curiosity got the better of his sorrow for that moment.

"The High Guardians wish to meet with you." He said, dreading an emotional outburst.

"Very well, tell them we will convene in two hours' time." He closed his eyes and sighed as the sound of receding footsteps signaled his solitude once more. What could they want after that last meeting? he wondered. Regardless, I need to unwind and be ready. He lingered in the warm water for a while before pulling the plug. As he dried off, he muttered, "It has to be about Juliet. . . Will they never let me have a minute to think?"

He got dressed and opted for a short walk to calm his nerves and clear his mind. In time, he found himself back at the Grand Hall, where he knew the High Guardians awaited him. With a deep breath, he pushed open the doors and entered.

Chapter 8.2

The Overseer strode into the Grand Hall, greeted by the sight of the five High Guardians with the highest seniority seated around the table. Anticipating an explanation for the emergency meeting, he made his way to the head of the table, his expression neutral. As he settled into his seat, Darakon rose and bowed. "Enim Amicitia."

"Pacem. We apologize for the suddenness of this meeting. We won't take much of your time," Darakon began.

"Proceed," his face showcasing exhaustion carried into the abrupt command.

Darakon continued, "First, with your blessing, we would like to replenish our ranks of High Guardians. We've been shorthanded since the rebellion, and now, with peace more vital than ever, we seek to appoint new leaders to fill the vacancies left by our fallen comrades, Mercury and Mite. May they rest in the grace of Omnibenevolence."

The weary man nodded and added under his breath, "and Omnipotence."

"We have all decided to put forward Ervikson of the Spinelle Kingdom as the apprentice assistant. His intel and leadership were invaluable during the war, making him a prime candidate for the role of organization and documentation. If it is acceptable to you, we would like to promote him without delay," Darakon concluded.

He nodded once more, his expression tense as Darakon continued.

"Very good. And at last, we have the main reason for this meeting," Darakon said, drawing his attention.

He lacked energy, but mustered as much as he could build for this moment. While arching a skeptical eyebrow, his opaque face leaned forward changing shades with light. "Go on," he encouraged, his tone calm yet curious.

"It concerns Juliet," Darakon announced in his usual blunt tone.

Although he did not move, annoyance flashed across his colorful face.

"Most of us were present at the summit and heard your directives. However, we felt the need to debrief you on the situation," Darakon continued. "Every single one of us received multiple complaints as we escorted the leaders back to their rooms. It appears that the general opinion of the majority of the leaders from the allied kingdoms is that we should execute Juliet or jail her for life at the very least. We understand your feelings on the matter and that you plan to deal with the situation soon, but we need you to know that we are on the verge of another rebellion. The allied leaders are not as complacent as they appeared to be during the summit. If you are going to do something, you need to do it post haste. We fear that you do not have the fortnight you are requesting. Left unchecked, we fear this rebellion will be as large as the last one, crippling everything you've built. There have been whispers throughout the entire South Sanction about favoritism for the traitor Juliet."

The Overseer's fist came down hard on the ancient stone table, the resounding thud echoing through the Grand Hall. "We have no proof that she is a traitor! Why doesn't anyone recognize that?" he bellowed.

Darakon gave a nod out of respect before speaking again. "Sir, we recognize that, so we have put our minds together and have come up with the idea of a trial, at least for the sake of testing Juliet's loyalty in front of the public. I'm sure that would calm down the vast majority."

The Overseer pinched his nose but remained silent for a minute, contemplating the proposal. "A test? What type of test?" he considered, his voice softer now, laced with curiosity.

"Sir, we do not have that answer but wished to present the idea to you. The fate of the Grand Organization may depend on the test, but you could construct something so significant and prove to everyone that they were, in fact, misled," Darakon's sincere tone was obvious.

The Overseer gave a deliberate and slow nod, his mind racing with possibilities. "A test. . . Yes, some sort of proof that there was no correlation between her and the attack on the Calcite Empire," he murmured to himself, the gravity of the decision pressing upon him.

Darakon resumed his seat without another word, his focus fixed on the Overseer. The room fell into a heavy silence as the translucent man pondered the gravity of the situation. After a moment of reflection, he addressed the assembled High Guardians. "Was there anything else?"

The High Guardians shook their heads in unison, signaling that they had nothing further to add. Darakon rose once more, his demeanor respectful yet resolute. "No, sir. We would follow you into the underworld and back, regardless of your choices. We are your loyal servants. All we ask is that you consider our suggestions and remember that bringing peace and order to the world should be your top priority."

"Thank you, Darakon," he responded with a nod of acknowledgement. "I can assure you all that it is. If any of you see Juliet, you need to bring her back here at once. If she resists, tell her that her life is in danger, and I demand her safety within my castle walls. You are not to take no for an answer. You are all dismissed. Oh, and congratulations, Ervikson," he added as an afterthought, acknowledging the Spinelle's recent promotion.

His voice met the creek of the door opening with uncanny timing. In from the dappled light of the hallways, a figure emerged, exuding an aura of wild elegance. He moved with the grace of woodland creatures, his every step a dance in harmony with nature. Adorned in raveled jewelry crafted from polished wood, shimmering stones, and delicate feathers, he seemed to embody the very spirit of a forest. Antlers crowned his noble brow, a testament to his kinship with majestic creatures of the woods. His eyes, the color of moss in the morning sun, sparkled with ancient wisdom and untamed magic. Each piece of jewelry seemed to tell a story, a tribute to the natural world and its boundless beauty. As he raised his hand to greet the Overseer just as the sun greets the world at dawn, the sunlight itself seemed to bow in reverence to this handsome male antlered druid, High Guardian of the Spinelle Kingdom, and a symbol of its enduring splendor.

Ervikson then smiled from ear to ear, his expression a combination of gratitude and determination. With that, the High Guardians filed out of the Grand Hall, leaving the Overseer alone with his thoughts. Frustrated and weary, he made his way back to his chambers, hoping that rest would rejuvenate both his mind and his creativity.

As he settled into bed with a copy of the Amicitia Licentiam in hand, the impending decision danced across his mind. Thoughts of Juliet and the precarious balance between her innocence and the stability of the Grand Organization plagued his thoughts. Could he afford to gamble the world's integrity for the sake of one woman? Or was there a way to reconcile both ideals?

As the Overseer drifted into the realm of sleep, his mind became a battleground of twisted imaginings.

In the depths of his subconscious, he found himself wandering through the shadowy corridors of his castle, the air heavy with a thick sense of foreboding. In an instant, he stumbled upon a figure cloaked in darkness, their features obscured by the depths of their hood. His heart quickened with a mixture of fear and curiosity as he approached, his footsteps echoing in the silent hallways.

With each step closer, the figure seemed to grow taller, looming over him with an aura of menace. The Overseer felt a knot tighten in his chest as he struggled to make out the identity of the mysterious intruder. As he reached out to grasp the hood and reveal the face hidden within, a sense of dread washed over him like a tidal wave.

In a flash of surreal horror, the hood fell away to reveal the face of Juliet, twisted and contorted into a grotesque mockery of her former self. Her eyes bore into his with an intensity that sent a chill down his spine, and her lips curled into a malevolent smirk that seemed to mock his every fear.

Frozen in place, the Overseer could do nothing but watch in horror as Juliet's form shifted and morphed before his eyes, her features twisting and distorting into nightmarish shapes. The air around him grew thick with a suffocating darkness, swallowing him whole as he was consumed by the suffocating weight of his own terror.

With a start, he awoke from his nightmare, his body drenched in a cold sweat and his heart pounding in his chest. For a moment, he lay there in the silence of his chambers, grappling with the remnants of the haunting vision that still lingered in the recesses of his mind. It was a nightmarish reminder of the darkness that lurked within him, a darkness that threatened to consume him whole if he dared to let it take hold.

When dawn broke, he rose from his bed feeling more exhausted than when he had retired the night before. Dragging himself down to the dining hall, he slumped into his seat and waited for the servants to bring him sustenance. As he sipped his coffee and nibbled on his breakfast, a hollow laugh escaped his lips. It was a bitter sound, filled with the bitter realization that he was trapped in a never ending cycle of turmoil. Yet, amidst the despair, a flicker of determination sparked within him. He knew that he could not allow himself to be consumed by his fears. With a newfound resolve, he began to formulate a plan, a glimmer of hope cutting through the darkness that had enveloped his mind.

Chapter 8.3

The Overseer's footsteps echoed through the empty corridors as he hurried to Darakon's quarters. He rapped on the door, his mind racing with the urgency of his plan. Inside, he could hear the faint sound of movement, signaling Darakon's presence. "'Hurry, Darakon," he called out, unable to contain his impatience. "I know you're awake. Open the door. I have a solution to our predicament."

After a while, the door creaked open, revealing Darakon's tired visage. "Indeed," he greeted with weariness in his voice. "Though the morning brings a sense of calm."

But he brushed past Darakon, his focus unwavering. "Enough pleasantries," he said, almost stumbling over his own words. "We have urgent matters to attend to. Has there been any sign of Juliet?"

Darakon shook his head in humble silence. "No, sir. Our search has been relentless, but she remains elusive."

His colorful brows flexed in frustration. "We cannot afford to let her slip through our grasp again," he declared. "We need to find her, and we need to find her now."

Just then, Amelia came charging down the hallway, her hurried steps echoing against the stone walls. She skidded to a stop a few feet away from them, avoiding collision with the two men who stood before her by mere inches. "Overseer, Darakon," she gasped, her breath coming in short bursts. "We've found Juliet. She's been spotted conversing with patrons in the market. What are your orders?"

The colors on his skin darkened at the news. "You will detain her and bring her to me," he commanded.

Amelia swallowed a nervous gulp and nodded, her eyes wide with apprehension. "Yes, my Overseer."

"Good," the Overseer was blunt and bold. "Now, gather a few High Guardians and get the job done. You have your orders. Go!"

With a short bow, Amelia turned on her heel and sprinted off down the corridor. Darakon regarded his leader with a blend of curiosity and concern. "What is this plan you have concocted?" he inquired, his voice laced with uncertainty.

However, he turned to Darakon with a smirk playing on his lips. "You will see soon. You will all see. But first, Darakon, I need you to secure one of those Marked Ones for me. I won't tolerate another rebellion, and this is a crucial part of the test. You have until Juliet is in my court again, so I suggest you move now."

Darakon nodded in acknowledgment, then opened the door and departed without another word.

The Overseer heard an uproar echoing through the castle's courtyard. Shouts and taunts filled the air, directed at someone with such passion that it caught his attention. Peering out the window, he beheld a distressing sight: Juliet, struggling against her restraints as she was dragged along. Concern pricked at him. Descending to the courtyard with elegant swiftness, he hurried to meet her. Meanwhile, Juliet's voice rang out amidst the chaos, defiant and fiery, as she rebutted every insult thrown her way.

She fought against her captors with fervor, resistant to returning to the castle. Juliet's anger was more than apparent, yet upon catching sight of the Overseer, her demeanor shifted to one of distress. "My dear," she exclaimed, her tone softening quicker than her earlier retorts. "I've missed you! What are these people doing to me?"

"You say you've missed me, but it is you that has been missing. Where have you been?" His authority was firm and unyielding as he leveled his eyes with Juliet's.

"My people come first, and it is them who I have been with. I apologize if that troubles you, but I have been fighting to take care of them ever since I was a child." As Juliet spoke, memories flooded her mind, vivid images of the struggles and hardships she endured to protect them flashing before her eyes. This was the final step to ensure their safety in a world filled with danger.

As the Overseer's sword sliced through the bonds that held Juliet captive, a collective gasp rippled through the courtyard. The onlookers, a mix of soldiers, servants, and citizens, watched in stunned silence as Juliet's hands were freed and she stood before them, her defiance unyielding despite the hostile glares.

With a swift motion, he sheathed his sword and gestured for Juliet to follow him. As they made their way through the courtyard, whispers followed in their wake, the murmurs of disapproval mingling with the rustle of clothing and the shuffle of feet.

Juliet's eyes remained steady, her chin held high in the midst of the accusatory scowling directed her way. She knew she had enemies among these people, those who resented her presence and questioned her loyalty. But she refused to let their judgment sway her resolve.

As they reached the entrance to the castle, the Overseer turned to Juliet with a determined expression. "We will get you cleaned up," his tone provoking no argument. "And then we will talk more about everything you've had to go through."

Juliet nodded, a flicker of gratitude in her eyes as she followed the Overseer into the castle. Though the courtyard had been filled with tension and hostility, she knew that she had trust in him, someone who saw beyond the accusations and stood by her side in defiance of their shared adversaries. She could almost feel her mother's hand on her shoulder, supporting this moment.

As they entered, Amelia awaited with towels and clothes bundled together standing next to one of the castle guards. The Overseer directed Juliet to follow her for the prepared bath. "Amelia will be assisting you. Come back to the front of the castle as soon as you are finished."

Juliet smiled, and with a determined stride, she followed the guard and Amelia into the castle, leaving the courtyard behind her.

As she disappeared from view, the Overseer turned his attention to Darakon, who stood just out of sight with a hooded figure bound on the rump of his horse. A sense of satisfaction washed over him as he saw the pieces of his plan falling into place.

"Excellent," he thought to himself, a glimmer of hope in his eyes. "Everything is falling into place."

With a subtle whistle, he summoned two soldiers who approached him with military accuracy. They gave a crisp salute and awaited his command.

"I want you two to assist Darakon at the gates with our new guest," the Overseer instructed, his voice firm and authoritative. "Afterward, I want you to go into town and fetch a few prisoners. Dress them all in identical robes and have them lined up in the courtyard. You have no more than one hour. I suggest you go now."

The soldiers saluted once more before hastening off to carry out their orders. The Overseer watched them go, expectancy building within him. "Soon," he convinced himself, "everything will be revealed, and they will see her as I see her. All will know that Juliet is innocent."

Chapter 8.4

As the soldiers returned from town, their boots kicked up dust from the dirt road, signaling their arrival to the castle courtyard. The Overseer, standing tall and imposing, awaited their return with hopefulness. His glances swept over the soldiers as they approached, acknowledging their diligence with a nod of approval.

In their custody were two prisoners, their hands bound behind their backs and expressions wrought with fear. The Overseer's eyes glinted with satisfaction as he observed the successful execution of his orders. He extended his hand in gratitude, clasping the soldiers' forearms in a firm shake.

"Thank you," he said, his voice carrying a tone of appreciation. "Your efficiency is commendable."

With a quick salute, the soldiers stepped aside, allowing the prisoners to be lined up as instructed. Meanwhile, from the entrance of the castle emerged Juliet, her presence commanding attention as she stepped into the sunlight. Her appearance was transformed, her features softened by the bath she had just taken, yet her resolve remained unyielding.

His crystal eyes lingered on her for a second, a flicker of admiration passing through his eyes before he refocused on the task at hand. With Juliet's arrival, he felt a renewed sense of purpose, knowing that together they would confront the challenges ahead.

He guided her away from the bustling courtyard, seeking a moment of privacy amidst the gathering in front of the castle. Leaning in close, he spoke in a hushed tone, his words laden with longing. "I have missed you, you know," he confessed with crystal eyes searching hers for a flicker of understanding.

A playful giggle escaped Juliet's lips at his words, her eyes dancing with mischief. "Oh, you naughty thing!" she teased, a hint of affection in her voice. "What am I helping you with?" she inquired, her curiosity piqued by his secretive demeanor.

The Overseer's expression darkened as he shifted the conversation to more serious matters. "We have captured several prisoners of war," he explained, his tone grave with the responsibility. "And I need your help to decide what to do with them."

A look of discomfort crossed Juliet's features as she withdrew from his embrace, her reluctance evident in her stance. "You know I hate such things," she admitted, her voice filled with sorrow. "I cannot bear to inflict punishments fit for those criminals," she added, her empathy for their plight evident in her words.

While intertwining his fingers with hers, he sought safety in her touch before approaching the grim topic. "Now, I was thinking we should execute them all," he began, his voice heavy with the burden of his decision. "But I just need your second opinion, because I feel like I may be unfair," he confessed, his eyes searching hers for reassurance.

Juliet's grim nod mirrored the pressure of the situation as she followed him to where the prisoners stood in silence. The crowd stood around them in anticipation, hoping to see fairness in the judging of the three accused. Stepping forward, she approached the lineup, her resolve unwavering despite the heaviness in her heart. With a determined gesture, she flipped back the hood of the first prisoner, the muscles throughout her face frozen in suspense as she awaited the Overseer's explanation.

"He murdered a woman who was pregnant with her first child," his voice was coated with anger and sorrow. Juliet's features tightened with empathy for the innocent life lost, but she nodded, understanding the seriousness of the crime and supporting the execution.

The courtyard agreed in a silent sheer, a contrast to their frustration in Juliet just moments prior. Moving down the line, she continued to unveil the face of the next prisoner, the revelation a testament to the atrocities committed. Though her heart ached with her task, she remained confident in her posture, to show everyone that she was deserving of her voice.

As Juliet removed the hood of the second prisoner, she awaited the Overseer's explanation with scrunched brows, her eyes probing for details. "And him?" she inquired, her voice steady despite her anxiety.

"He was caught stealing," the Overseer replied, his tone laced with disappointment. "In normal circumstances, this would be corrected with a prison sentence, but this is his third offense," he added, his crystal eyes fixed on Juliet as he awaited her judgment. Around them, the assembled crowd watched with bated breath, their murmurs fading into an anticipatory silence.

With a thoughtful expression, Juliet considered the severity of the prisoner's transgressions, her mind racing with the implications of her decision. Though the offense was not as grave as the first, she recognized the importance of upholding the law and maintaining order within the Grand Organization. With a determined nod, she sided with the initial verdict, signaling for the prisoner to be executed.

There was a ripple of reaction from the onlookers, a mixture of both support and disagreement as they acknowledged Juliet's tough decision. Despite the dissenting opinions, they respected her unwavering commitment to justice, recognizing that she possessed the emotional strength to enforce the law without compromise.

As Juliet moved to reveal the identity of the third prisoner, a thick tension hung in the air, the anticipation of the crowd felt tangible as all eyes were on her. With a steady hand, she pulled back the hood, her heart pounding in her chest as she braced herself for what lay beneath.

As the features of the third prisoner came into view, Juliet's eyes widened in shock, her breath catching in her throat at the sight before her. The third prisoner was none other than her mother. The Overseer watched, his own curiosity flared by her reaction, knowing that this moment would be pivotal in shaping her perception of justice and her role as a leader.

"And what did she do?" Juliet's voice trembled as she posed the question, her focus fixed on the prisoner with a mixture of apprehension and disbelief. Her mother stared back, unmoving, without any hint of recognition towards Juliet to not reveal her true identity. It was safer this way, for if anyone should be saved, it would be her daughter.

The Overseer held his breath, awaiting Juliet's judgment, knowing that her decision would not just determine the fate of the prisoner but also solidify her standing among the people. This was the final test, the opportunity of truth that would define her innocence, eliminate all doubt, and earn her the respect of those gathered before her.

Darakon spoke this time, the cold tone of his words caused a few to shiver with a tingling sensation, each passing second felt longer than the last. "She is guilty of exile," he announced, "a Marked One who attacked the Calcite Empire."

Juliet paused as she processed the accusation. She beckoned her lover over to the last prisoner, a sense of unease settling in her stomach. "Perhaps they do not all need to be executed," she suggested, her voice carrying uncertainty for the first time. "I mean, the attack was horrendous, but do we have evidence that it was the Marked Ones that attacked?"

Darakon's response was swift and resolute, his tone unwavering as he reinforced their stance on loyalty and allegiance. "Yes, Juliet, we do not tolerate any separation from the Grand Organization," he affirmed, speaking for every person that now questioned Juliet's hesitation. "Failure to abide by the Amicitia Licentiam is treason. Of course, we are also defending your honor in doing so. We will not tolerate slander against the Overseer or his company."

She stammered, her voice faltering as she addressed Darakon. "Well, I am not comfortable with that," she admitted, the emotion of reluctance filling and replacing her confidence. "I would rather you pardon this Marked One."

As the truth was revealed, the Overseer's heart sank with a mixture of disbelief and horror. The realization that Juliet would defend the woman before her shook him to the core. Her plea for mercy echoed through the courtyard, drawing skeptical glances from those around her. As he approached the third prisoner, a tense hush fell over the crowd. With a swift and decisive wave of his hand, the throat of Juliet's mother was opened, and that familiar crimson liquid spewed down her neck. A wave of shock was sent through the witnesses and left Juliet frozen in fear. The auburn haired woman struggled to find her voice, her tear streaked face a portrait of anxiety.

As the Overseer turned to face Juliet, his expression hardened with a cold, unwavering conclusion. The glint of his hand caught the flickering light, casting an eerie glow over the courtyard as he cleaned the blood from its surface. His question cut through the tense silence, dripping with disgust and accusation, leaving Juliet speechless and vulnerable under his piercing glare. "Why do you cry for a criminal?"

Tears welled in Juliet's eyes as she struggled to find the words to respond, her mind reeling with conflicting emotions. "I. . . I do not know," her voice no more than a whisper, "I don't think it was fair."

His scoff echoed through the courtyard, causing Darakon to smirk, a break from his typical character.

"Why else would you defend a prisoner?" the questions continued, his voice laced with contempt. "You could have defended the murderer or the thief, but you did not ask to see their evidence. You cared about the Marked One. Even more so when I slit her throat."

The Overseer's words pierced through Juliet's numbness, shattering the void within her. In that moment, she realized the full extent of his cunning; he was unyielding, not manipulatable. She had been nothing but a pawn in his grand scheme, a pawn that had mistaken itself for a queen. Her critical failure now sealed the fate of everyone she loved. It was as if the last thread connecting her to hope snapped like the stalk of that last leaf, plunging her into the abyss of despair.

Juliet's hand moved, devoid of emotion, as if controlled by some unseen force. With an eerie calmness, she reached for the hilt of the Overseer's sword, her fingers closing around it with unnatural precision. Gripping the weapon, she stepped forward with a hollow determination, her movements betraying no hint of the turmoil raging within her.

As the blade descended towards the translucent man, there was a vast pause, a moment of suspended expectation. But he remained unmoved, his expression an inscrutable mask. There was no flinch, no sign of pain or surprise. It was as though her strike was nothing more than a mere gesture in the face of his unyielding resolve.

As he stood there, his eyes locked with hers, he couldn't help but feel a profound sense of sadness at the realization of what she had become. She, who had once held such promise, had now succumbed to the darkness within her, willing to stoop to any depths to achieve her own ends. For at this time, he understood that Juliet was no longer the person he had once known. The Overseer's disappointment radiated from him, and the crowd around them began to worry.

His skin began to shimmer and shift, transforming into a breathtaking kaleidoscope of colors that danced and swirled across his form in a mesmerizing display. People scattered in fear, their eyes wide with disbelief at the mystical sight before them. But Juliet stood resolute, her gaze unwavering as she faced her lover head on. She knew what was coming, and she accepted her fate with a sense of grim determination. In an instant, a blinding light erupted from the Overseer, its brilliance illuminating the entire courtyard with an intensity that was almost unbearable. Juliet closed her eyes, her heart pounding in her chest as she braced herself for the inevitable. And then, in an instant, the light consumed her, swallowing her whole and erasing her from existence with a finality that sent shivers down the spines of all who witnessed it. As the light subsided, there was nothing left of Juliet but a lingering sense of loss and the haunting memory of her goal.

Chapter 8.5

On the third day after the unsettling events unfolded, a gentle rap echoed through the chambers, drawing the Overseer's attention away from the view beyond the windowpane.

"Overseer, please let me in," Victor's voice carried a soft urgency.

Without a word, his translucent hand was waved, a silent command that unlocked the door with subtle magic. The Grand Emperor entered the room, his presence a soothing balm amidst the turmoil that churned within.

Victor's eyes scanned his relaxed appearance, taking note of the weariness etched into every line of his face. With a knowing look, he spoke in hushed tones, acknowledging the struggle that waged within the Overseer's soul.

"That rough, huh?" Victor's words held a shared sentiment born from years of his own past companionships.

The Overseer remained silent, his gaze fixed upon the shifting tapestry of clouds that decorated the sky. In the midst of turmoil and uncertainty, he found solace in the silent audience of a trusted friend.

"I understand the burden you carry, my friend," As Victor settled into the room, he approached the conversation with a gentle yet probing tone. "But you cannot shoulder it alone. I am here for you."

Gratitude flickered in the Overseer's eyes before being replaced by the emotional anchor gifted from recent events. "I appreciate your support, Victor, but there are matters that require my attention. Matters that demand resolution."

"Listen well," Victor began, his shoulders slumped forward as he approached the Overseer. "I understand you had a great deal of feelings for her, but sometimes we become consumed with the wrong things. I would be a liar if I said I have not had my eyes fixed on a woman before."

His jaw clenched at Victor's words, his crystal eyes locked on some distant point beyond the window. The Grand Emperor's attempt to lighten the mood with a hearty laugh fell flat against the brooding silence. Sensing the need for a change in approach, he reached out to clap the Overseer on the back in a gesture of support. But before Victor's hand could make contact, an aggressive burst of cinnamon-colored dust surged from his opaque skin, sending him gliding across the room with a startled yelp. He landed with a thud against the far wall, his breath knocked from his lungs.

"Shit!" the Overseer muttered, his concern evident as he rushed to Victor's side. "Are you okay?"

Victor waved off his friend's concern, pushing himself into a sitting position. "I've had worse," he managed, though the wince that accompanied his words betrayed the pain he was trying to downplay. "Just caught me off guard, is all."

Tears welled in his crystal eyes, their shimmering trails carving a path down his hanging eyelids. "Victor, I am sorry," he choked out, his voice thick with emotion. If not for his position, he would have been condemned for assaulting royalty. "I have been under so much pressure. I have no idea what to do, I am losing control."

With a gentle hand on the translucent man's shoulder, he offered words of forgiveness and compassion. "I know, I know," his voice still soft and reassuring. "Listen, if you need a break, I can take your place. You don't have to carry this burden alone."

His eyes flashed with a mix of gratitude and defiance, "I appreciate the offer—"

"Not like that," Victor interjected, his palms out towards him in surrender. "I would never seek the throne out from under you. I wish to ease your burden as Mercury would do, acting as interim Overseer in your place. It would be a temporary leave of absence. Stay for a week or two and get some rest and relaxation."

The Overseer raised his finger to his lips. "Just for a week?" he inquired after a brief pause, seeking clarification.

"Or two," Victor affirmed with a warm smile. "Look at all you have accomplished and the bridges you have crossed. You deserve the time off. Get yourself sorted and come back to your unified Grand Organization. It is your dream coming to fruition."

Relief passed over the Overseer's features as he contemplated the proposal. "I think you are right, Victor," he admitted through a sigh. "I do deserve a break. I am going to pack a bag tonight and head out."

Once the decision was made, the Overseer wasted no time in preparing for his much needed recess. He summoned one of his most trusted servants, Amelia, to assist him in the task.

In his closet, the Overseer was more than energetic as he selected his attire for the journey. He opted for practical yet elegant garments befitting his station: a tailored doublet of deep blue velvet adorned with intricate gold embroidery, paired with sturdy leather trousers and polished boots. Over his attire, he draped a luxurious cloak of rich crimson, its edges trimmed with fur to ward off the chill of the impending autumn weather.

Next, the Overseer turned his attention to his personal effects. He packed his belongings into a sturdy leather travel bag, ensuring that he had all the essentials for his journey. Among his possessions were a quill for recording his thoughts and observations, a small pouch of gold coins for any unforeseen expenses, and a vial of his best wine for emergencies.

As he packed, Claire stood nearby, ready to assist with any task the Overseer or Amelia required. The young girl's presence provided a sense of calm amidst the flurry of preparations, and he was grateful for her company.

Just as the sun began to set over the horizon, casting a warm glow across the castle walls, the Overseer donned his traveling cloak and slung his bag over his shoulder. With a sense of relief, he bid farewell to Claire, Victor, and his loyal servants and then set out on his journey, eager to leave behind the burdens of his duties and embrace the promise of adventure that awaited him beyond the castle walls.

Chapter 9.1

There was an air of expectation mixed with a hint of uncertainty among the members of the High Guardians. People were used to Mercury filling in for the Overseer for short durations of time. However, he was not Mercury, in fact, he was not even a High Guardian at all. For the first time, The protectors of the Amicitia Licentiam were ruled by the Grand Emperor of a Dynasty.

Victor set out to refute their fear of impending doom. He was never a tyrannical leader for the Zeller, and wanted to respect the current rules in place, even if he himself did not support them. He spent hours reviewing the laws he studied, but from the new perspective of the enforcer instead of the follower. He concluded that steering the Grand Organization by following a higher standard would honor his friend during his absence.

Darakon, his weathered face etched with lines of experience, approached Victor in his suspicion, "I'm not sure your reasoning for acquiring this position, but there are rumblings among the others about potential changes. Some are concerned that you may focus on compromising our readiness and take over. I want to remind you that although our numbers have dwindled, our interests are unified in supporting the Overseer and are prepared to defend the Amicitia Licentiam with our lives."

Victor listened, his expression thoughtful yet resolute. "I understand your concerns, Darakon, and I appreciate your honesty and loyalty. Rest assured, my commitment to the Grand Organization at this time is not one for selfish gain. I support maintaining our peaceful relations, and will fight alongside you in any war just as I have already proven to you."

Darakon nodded, his features relaxing as he absorbed Victor's words. "I see your point, Victor. And I trust your judgment. It's just. . . for those of us who have grown accustomed to a certain way of doing things, change can be unsettling. Do good and good will be done unto you." With those words, the High Guardian said his farewells and left the interim Overseer to his duties.

Victor crafted a comprehensive strategy aimed at addressing long standing issues and ushering in a new era of prosperity. One of

Victor's first priorities was to foster a culture of inclusivity and collaboration within the High Guardian's ranks. Recognizing the importance of harnessing the collective wisdom and talents of all members, regardless of rank or background, Victor initiated open forums and brainstorming sessions where ideas could be exchanged and debated. Through these collaborative efforts, Victor sought to tap into the Grand Organization's collective potential and inspire a sense of ownership and pride among its members.

    Ervikson was one of the High Guardians that worked hard on restoring the preparedness of the team. Right after learning his duties, he took on a training position to help teach the new, incoming recruits. By the end of the training session, the recruits were exhausted but exhilarated, their newfound skills and confidence evident in their every movement. Ervikson surveyed the group with pride, knowing that they were one step closer to fulfilling their potential as High Guardians.

    In particular, the interim Overseer saw a marked improvement in internal harmony and cohesion. With Juliet no longer a divisive figure within the organization, members rallied together with renewed purpose and solidarity. Victor's inclusive leadership style and commitment to consensus-building ensured that conflicts were addressed to completion, paving the way for a more harmonious environment.

In one instance, Bemus and Golnesa found themselves sharing a quiet moment in the courtyard, basking in the warmth of the afternoon sun. As they sat on a bench, their conversation turned to the recent changes within the organization, including the impressive leadership of Victor during the Overseer's absence.

"You know, Golnesa," Bemus began with a snarky smile, "I must say, I've been quite impressed with Victor's performance as interim Overseer."

Golnesa nodded in agreement, her eyes sparkling with admiration. "That's surprising coming from you, but it is remarkable how he took charge with such confidence."

As the week ended, Victor's efforts began to bear fruit. The Grand Organization, once plagued by internal strife and inefficiency due to the war, began to undergo a remarkable transformation under his leadership. Membership recovered and morale soared as the members witnessed a renewed sense of purpose throughout the hallways of the castle.

Chapter 9.2

The Overseer's heart raced as he made his way back to the castle. His footsteps echoed against the cobblestone path, each one a reminder of the uncertainty that gnawed at him with excitement.

The castle's shadows seemed to stretch out and greet him as he drew closer. The familiar sight of the imposing gates sent a shiver down his spine. What awaited him beyond those gates? Had everything remained as he left it, or had unforeseen challenges arisen in his absence?

There were no envoys sent to update him on the situation during his absence, leaving him to wonder if the absence of news was indeed a harbinger of peace or a precursor to greater turmoil. The uncertainty gnawed at him, feeding the flames of his anxiety with each passing moment.

With a deep breath, the Overseer readied himself for whatever awaited him beyond the castle walls. As he pushed open the castle gates and stepped into the familiar surroundings of his domain, he knew that whatever the future held, he would meet it with courage and conviction.

"Where is interim Overseer Victor Zeller?" he inquired, his voice carrying a note of urgency.

The servant paused in his sweeping, glancing up with a warm smile of recognition. "Welcome back, Overseer!" He greeted him with a large smile. "Enim Amicitia. He is in the Grand Hall with the High Guardians."

"Pacem," the Overseer replied with a nod of appreciation, his mind already racing with questions. What could be happening that Victor had organized the High Guardians? With a sense of determination, he set off towards the Grand Hall with a purposeful pace.

With a swift and decisive motion, he pushed the heavy doors wide open, the grandeur of the chamber unfolding before him in all its splendor. To his surprise, he found Victor and a few of the High

Guardians engaged in active conversation, their laughter echoing off the walls.

"I have returned," the Overseer declared, his voice cutting through the lighthearted atmosphere like a blade cutting through silk.

Victor's laughter filled the air like the tinkling of crystal chandeliers. "Ah, Overseer, your return is as needed as ever. We have been awaiting your return." He paused, allowing the time to settle. "We've gathered to discuss the progress and developments in your absence, and we're ready to share the successes we've achieved. Come, sit with us."

His self determined crisis dissipated as he took in the scene before him. With measured steps, he approached the head of the table, where Victor stood, a serene smile adorning his features. "Thank you, Victor," the Overseer began, his voice betraying a hint of uncertainty. "Forgive my abrupt entrance. I was under the impression that urgent matters required my immediate attention." He settled into his seat, a lingering sense of curiosity coloring his demeanor.

Victor chuckled as he placed a loose fist to his mouth. "No but, it seems your vacation did little to ease your anxiety, but perhaps a sip of ale will do the trick," he suggested, gesturing towards a stein placed on the table as an invitation. The Overseer gave a grateful nod, seizing the vessel and taking a deep swig from its contents. As the cool liquid coursed down his throat, he felt a sense of relaxation wash over him.

"Ah, now where were we?" Victor mused as he sought to steer the conversation back on track. "Yes, Ervikson was just going over the finalizing reports."

Pride filled the young man's lungs as he was prompted to speak. "It is with great pleasure that I report such news, Overseer. We have begun to enjoy a rare period of tranquility, with no signs of unrest, rebellions, migrants nor even Marked Ones in any corner of the earth. Our efforts to maintain order and stability have borne fruit, and it appears that we are indeed experiencing a state of world peace. It is a testament to the effectiveness of the Grand Organization and the Amicitia Licentiam."

The leaders both showed their appreciation and adjourned the meeting. As the last of the High Guardians left, Victor turned to the Overseer with a concerned expression etched on his face. The room felt empty with echoes of footsteps fading into the distance, as empty as Victor's tone. "Are you okay?" He searched the man's opaque face for any signs of distress. "I thought the whole point of getting away was to reduce your anxiety, and yet you have returned to us as a bundle of nerves."

Swirling the remnants of his drink in the stein as he pondered Victor's question, he began through near closed lips, "The truth is. . . I do not know how to allow myself to relax anymore." This confession was a rare glimpse of vulnerability, and Victor gifted an empathetic sigh. "However," he continued, "I did a lot of thinking while I was away."

Victor arched an eyebrow as a silent invitation for the Overseer to continue. "I think my time is passing," the uncertainty flowing from his colorful lips. "I can feel a darkness creeping over and within me. It nags at my waking thoughts and plagues my dreams."

With each word spoken, the warmth drained from Victor's face, leaving a stiff and cold response. He leaned forward to urge the Overseer to elaborate further.

"I believe I require an extended period of rest, and I will need your help to make it happen," his words trailing off into the quiet of the room.

Victor sat up in his chair, "We need to continue this conversation in a more private setting. Meet me in your chambers in one hour. You need time to unpack and settle. I will be up soon."

The Overseer acknowledged Victor's directive by biting his tongue. It was clear that they had much to discuss, and he was sure that this would be one of his last conversations with the Grand Emperor. Upon returning to his chambers, he went through his belongings, and as he finished, a gentle knock sounded at the door.

True to his word, Victor entered with a warm smile, settling into a comfortable chair and lighting a pipe. After a few seconds of quiet contemplation, the Overseer cleared his throat. "I have a solution that involves you keeping your current position."

Victor, expecting words of comfort, was surprised by the direction of the conversation. "Go on," he beckoned.

"You have demonstrated exceptional leadership and wisdom in maintaining the stability of the Grand Organization during my absence," the Overseer asserted. "Moreover, you have firsthand experience in building your dynasty from the ground up, which has endowed me with a deep understanding of the sacrifices and discipline demanded by kingship. Therefore, I am prepared to step down and allow you to take on the position of my successor."

Victor choked on his inhale halfway through, "Successor? I would not have even considered it, to be honest with you."

A chuckle escaped the Overseer's otherwise emotionless bearing. "Great leaders know more than what to do, but also when to do it. Omne ignotum pro magnifico est. When all things become known, and the mystery fades, nothing but faith, hope, and love remains."

Victor mulled it over. "Is it this lost love that's preventing you from carrying on?"

"There is no lost love." He corrected the Grand Emperor. "Just disappointment of what you expected to witness in a person. A fool confuses love for emotion, and I have proved that I was that fool. My loss was not in Juliet, Victor, but instead I realized with great sorrow that I did not show love to those that deserved it before I lost them."

Victor's jaw clenched as his eyes widened. His body froze in shock as he processed that the Overseer had sacrificed everyone he held close to him for this one goal. In his deadened inertness Victor offered some quick form of empathy, "Pride comes before the fall—"

"—I have no end, Victor." He shot back, "I am unending. Immortal. You were correct when you said I have no respite from my duties. However, if I am being honest, those decisions remain massive on my soul."

Victor failed to have a response for the first time in his many years.

The Overseer continued, "My sorrow will not yield. I have seen lives spawn into the world just to pass through, as if their contributions were insignificant in the void of time. As though their connections have no rippling effect through the wave of the living. I envy that peace, that ending I wish for when I may lay my head for good."

The Grand Emperor's forehead creased as he grew worried, "I hope you are not suggesting that you want to end your own life."

An empty laugh cracked through the air. "If it were so simple. I can not cease to exist, but I can be suspended in a form of hibernation, with your help."

"My help?" Victor asked, scoffing in disbelief.

The Overseer explained, "Although I am near all powerful, I can be separated. Split into three entities of mind, body, and spirit. This is no easy task, but if I can be isolated from myself, I shall gain the rest I seek."

The Grand Emperor pressed his thumb to his chin for a few seconds as he thought, "Are you sure you wish for this separation?"

A translucent hand rested on his shoulder, and a more calm demeanor presented itself from the Overseer's lips, "I wish for my soul to not be plagued by my mind, my heart to rest from the pain in my soul, and my mind to reflect on my mistakes, so that I may not make them again. Do not be saddened, for this will be my very own peace."

Both leaders sat in silence contemplating the harsh reality of this request. After what felt like hours, Victor muttered, "If I can fulfill this ritual, I will take on your role as you request, but I need to know everything."

The Overseer stood up with a weak smile and began to pace in front of Victor. "Of course, even being separated is just a transition in my state of being. I can still be brought back. It is important that you ensure that each piece stays apart from each other."

He stopped to draw his sword and display it for the Grand Emperor. "The Sword of the Lost Beloved."

Victor's furrowed brow exhibited confusion as the Overseer continued, "This weapon has tasted every type of blood known in this world. This will be where my heart will reside. Once you combine a drop of each and coat the edge with it, pierce my heart to bind them."

The Overseer placed the sword down at his feet. "Altogether, my mind must be stored into a medium that can hold its knowledge. I would recommend a book, for instance. Leave that blank slate open and above my head during this process so that it may fill with my memories. Afterwards, shut it and keep it closed, for if anyone reads it will awaken me."

"The last step, for my body, any open object will do. My sole request is that you honor it with your memory of me. Once the ritual of the mind and heart is complete, destroy my body and leave the remnants inside. I can be restored to my current self if both my mind opens and my heart tastes. My body needs to feel the air to connect to them." The Overseer peered into Victor's eyes, as if searching for any trace of deceit or malice lurking within. Yet, to his relief, there was no flicker of deception, no shadow of hidden agendas, rather the unwavering commitment of a trusted friend.

"I understand, Overseer," Victor replied, his voice resolute, but his frown and lowered eyes showed otherwise. "I will carry out your wishes to the best of my ability. This ritual of yours, though daunting, shall be executed with the utmost care and respect."

He leaned down to grab the sword and admired it, accepting it as a symbol for the task that was given to him. It seemed weightless, but the patterns were beautiful. The saber gleamed a mesmerizing display of contrasting colors. Half of its length shimmered with the crystalline brilliance of diamonds, catching and refracting the ambient light in a dazzling display of iridescence. In stark contrast, the other half of the blade was as dark as midnight, fashioned from the smooth, obsidian-like material. Its surface seemed to saturate the blade with an aura of mystery and depth. The transition between the two materials was seamless, a perfect balance of light and darkness, strength and elegance.

Chapter 9.3

With sweat dripping off his soaked brow, Victor wasted no time in calling upon Azrael, Vincent, and Darakon to gather in the Grand Hall. He considered the practicalities of his task, and it would hinge on having the right tools at his disposal. There was no time wasted in gathering the necessary supplies, as every move he made was deliberate to prepare for the meeting.

The Diamond Mortem's Grand Emperor was the first to arrive and speak, "I hope you don't plan to summon me often. I was busy taking care of things back home." A subtle scowl marred his features, his brows knitting together in frustration.

As the others entered behind Azrael, Victor's lips quivered as he attempted a smile, but it faltered as he greeted them, "Enim Amicitia."

"Pacem." They each responded through habit.

Victor was almost too paranoid as he set down a stack of vials on the stone table, the glass catching the soft light filtering through the windows. As he stepped back, he gestured towards the collection, ensuring that each member of the group had a clear view. "We need to fill these."

Azrael tilted his head to the side, "What?" He barked, his eyes darting around in search of clarification.

The interim Overseer exhaled once more before elaborating. His forehead became like dew from his nerves, "We need to fill each of these vials with blood. One species for each vial. I need to ask this of you, because it was asked of me by the Overseer. It is strange, I know, but I ask for your trust."

He then directed his attention to Azrael, "You are the leader of many, and I know you have the capability to take care of most of these faster than I could."

Then his focus shifted to Vincent, "You know our lands as well as I do, collect everything within our capacity."

Victor's eyes darted to Darakon after a brief hesitation, "I need you to take care of the rest. Everything in between the Zeller and Diamond Mortem. I will need to visit the war barren lands myself and acquire the Larimar, Hawke, and Wintersun's blood."

The individuals gathered looked at each other with uncertainty before Azrael asked a follow up question, "I understand what you're asking for, but the question I need is why? For what urgency are you demanding this of me? Why isn't the Overseer doing this himself if this is for him?"

Victor took a moment to consider Azrael's question, his brow crunching together as he weighed his response. However, even though his throat seemed to be as dry as the desert, he spoke with a calm and measured tone. "I understand your concerns, Azrael. The Overseer has entrusted me with a task I cannot go into detail with, but rest assured, his intentions are for the security of the benefit of the Grand Organization.

"Fine, you'll have them by the end of the month." Azrael's brows knitted together, a visible frown etching across his face as irritation coursed through him. With a sharp exhale, he pushed back his chair, the scrape against the floor causing arm hairs to stand. His movements were tense and purposeful as he rose to his feet, his jaw clenched and muscles tense. Without another word, he turned on his heel and strode towards the exit, his departure a silent declaration of his frustration.

Vincent, Darakon, and the others sighed and walked out right after. Victor felt a knot tightening in his stomach. His palms became clammy as he struggled to push the thought of preparing this ritual. With a deep breath to steady his nerves, Victor stood from his seat, his movements unsteady as he gathered his belongings.

With one last glance around the room, Victor squared his shoulders and walked out as if he was unsure of his own capabilities. As he stepped out into the crisp night air, the weight of the world seemed to bear down on him. "This is it." He whispered to himself, "this is the end of the Overseer."

Chapter 9.4

After a grueling six day-long journey, Victor arrived in the Northern Sanction, the landscape around him bearing the scars of conflict and turmoil. Weary from the road, he sought refuge in Jakarth, the once bustling city marking his first stop in this war-torn region.

As he entered the city gates, Victor's eyes scanned the streets, taking in the sights and sounds of Jakarth. The air was thick with tension, and the faces of the townsfolk bore the weight of the ongoing strife. Determined to gather intelligence and assess the situation firsthand, Victor made his way through the streets, his senses alert to any signs of danger.

Stopping at a local tavern, Victor mingled with the locals, concentrating on their whispers and murmurs. He learned of skirmishes on the outskirts of town, of villages razed to the ground, and of families torn apart by the ravages of battle. He had been speaking to townsfolk for several hours, but was met with confused looks and comments about how the Wintersun had not been seen since the war.

As the sun began to dip below the horizon, casting long shadows across the streets, Victor grew convinced that his best chance of finding valuable information lay in the cover of night, when the underside of the city emerged from the shadows. He ventured from the tavern into the alleyways, his footsteps matching the hastened beating of his heart.

It was on the final alley of the main street, its narrow confines shrouded in darkness, that Victor's keen ears caught the sound of a voice calling out to him. Intrigued, he paused in his tracks, his hand reaching for the hilt of his sword by natural instinct as he prepared to confront who awaited his attention.

"Lookin' for tem 'suns, are ye?" An older woman emerged from what seemed like mist, her form obscured by the swirling fog that clung to her like a shroud. She was hunched and stooped, her spine curved with age, and she moved with a slow, deliberate gait, her steps measured and careful. In one gnarled hand, she clutched a twisted cane, its wood gnarled and weathered, a testament to the countless years it had been in her possession.

"Who's asking?" Victor replied.

"Jus' an ol' lady who has mo' answers than questions these days." Her attire was as dark and mysterious as the night itself, a tattered cloak draped around her shoulders, its hem trailing along the damp cobblestones. Atop her head, a tangled mass of wild, unkempt hair framed her weathered features, strands of silver intermingling with streaks of midnight black. Despite her frail appearance, there was an undeniable air of power and authority that surrounded her, an aura of ancient wisdom and arcane knowledge that marked her as something more than mortal, similar but not quite the same as his own people.

Despite her weathered appearance, he sensed she might hold valuable information about the elusive and fragmented Wintersuns. "What do you want in exchange?" he asked through more skepticism than intrigue.

Her eyes gleamed with a sharp, piercing intensity, "Oh, I jus' would like a ride across town wit' ya. Me ol' knees ain't what they used to be, M'lord."

Victor forced a tired grunt and glanced back at his horse, a thoughtful expression crossing his face as he considered the older woman's predicament. Without a word, he retraced his steps to where his steed was tethered nearby. With practiced ease, he untied the reins and led the horse back to her side. "Allow me to assist you," he said as if he was speaking to his own grandmother, offering his hand to help her mount the horse. Once she was situated, he stepped back and gestured for her to hold onto the saddle horn for support.

"Let's ride on. I will tell ya' when to stop." The cobblestone pathways seemed to stretch forever before them, illuminated by nothing more than the flickering glow of torches. As they continued on their way, the sounds of the tavern faded into the distance, replaced by the steady rhythm of their footsteps and the rhythmic clip-clop of the horse's hooves.

The woman pulled on the reins, bringing the horse to a halt with a gentle but firm tug. The animal neighed as its hooves dug into the floor. Victor looked around but saw no more than a few boarded up shops, and then casted a questioning look in her direction.

"Are you sure?" He asked, but got no answer other than a finger pointed to one peculiar building that seemed to welcome him with its abysmal open front door. He looked back over his shoulder to inquire more just to see that the older woman had vanished. Perplexed, his instincts urged caution as he gripped the hilt of his sword.

As he gave a close listen, the eerie sounds of faint revelry and merriment reached his ears, emanating from a secluded spot behind one of the neglected storefronts. With a quick, decisive motion, Victor tethered his horse to a nearby post, ensuring its safety before proceeding.

With measured steps, he rounded the corner of the building, and entered the darkness. The musty scent of decay lingered in the air, adding to the creepy atmosphere of the abandoned structure. Each step seemed to protest under his weight, groaning and protesting as if it was unwilling to bear the burden of his journey. Victor found himself standing before a weathered wooden door, and with a hesitant hand, he pushed it open, revealing a vast, empty room.

The space was bathed in an ethereal green glow, filtered through the tattered curtains that hung from the windows. At the far end of the room, seated upon a high-backed chair, was the figure of an old woman, her form shrouded in the dim light. Her face was obscured by the shadows, but Victor could sense her focus on him as he approached. The air was heavy with an oppressive stillness, broken by the occasional creak of the floorboards beneath his feet.

As he drew closer, the old woman's features came into focus little by little, her wrinkled visage illuminated by the flickering candlelight. Her eyes, gleaming with a spiritual intensity, seemed to bore into his very soul, sending shivers down his spine.

With a voice that seemed to resonate from the depths of the earth itself, the old witch spoke, her words echoing through the silent chamber with a haunting intensity. "I am Madame Chaffa of the Larimar Kingdom. You are Victor Zeller, Grand Emperor of the largest Dynasty within the Grand Organization, Enim Amicitia."

"Pacem." He kept his posture low, almost as if he were trying to blend into the shadows.

Chaffa continued, "Now that we know each other, why are you here?"

"I came to prepare a ceremony so I may replace the current Overseer." Every sense was heightened, every nerve on edge. She was no more than a few feet away from him, yet he projected as if she was much further away.

Chaffa scoffed. "That is treason."

"Not if it is the natural flow of things." Chaffa's upper lip quivered in retaliation, but Victor continued. "The Overseer has grown tired of his current role and sent me on this journey himself."

Victor's words held a weighty promise, and she couldn't help but feel a glimmer of hope stirring within her. "Preparing to succeed the Overseer himself?" she echoed through clenched teeth.

Victor pushed his head down in a firm nod, his gaze steady. "Indeed. Our lands in the North boast the most resources and strength. With your cooperation, Chaffa, we can ensure peace as the Grand Organization intended. Your people will have the opportunity to rebuild, with the guidance of a leader who understands the nuances of power and justice." He paused, letting his words sink in. "I am that leader. Will you trust me?"

Chaffa's expression darkened. "The Zeller were complicit in the devastation of these homes due to that war." she pointed out, her tone cautious. "Why should I believe that you won't start another one? What assurance do I have that you won't break your word?" She crossed her arms in sharp regression, her posture tense as she weighed Victor's proposition.

Victor's shoulders relaxed into an almost defeated slouch. Neither apology, promise, nor note could make up for Jakarth's destruction, and he knew that the best way to respond was through his conviction. "When I fought alongside the Overseer during the war, we did not know how far it would go. The Wintersuns decided to pillage these lands and all we could do was react. We did everything we could, but I see today that we weren't even close to saving everyone. I cannot promise you certainty or assurance. However, I can tell you that I will earn your trust if you let me. Maddam Chaffa, Will you lend me your strength and your wisdom as we work together to heal the wounds of the past and build a better tomorrow?"

Chaffa remained defensive as she considered Victor's pitch, but took her time to understand and in the end twisted her lips in reluctant defeat, "What do you need from us?"

"Blood," Victor almost choked on the word as though his throat was filled with the crimson liquid.

Chaffa gave an instant shake of her head. "Too many lives were lost in a war we never chose to fight," she declared. "I refuse to sacrifice any more blood."

Victor countered to reassure the woman. "You're a wise leader, Chaffa," he remarked. "I don't seek lives. I just need a few drops of blood." With a gesture, he presented a handful of vials. "It may seem odd, but the Overseer is a being of magic. To perform the necessary ritual, I need potent magic, which can be derived from a sample of blood from each."

Chaffa chuckled at the misunderstanding, which was uncommon for her, but it did trigger a memory. "This is very similar to the first time I met the Overseer," she recalled. "He asked for just a drop of blood to bond with the document he called the Amicitia Licentiam. At the time, I didn't grasp the symbolism behind it, but now I understand that such blood might be the wellspring of his power."

Victor's expression softened as he listened to Chaffa's wisdom, a glimmer of ambition dawning in his eyes. "It seems we have a common thread between us," he remarked. "The Overseer's methods may be enigmatic at times, but there's often a deeper significance to his requests. If this blood does hold the key to his power, then our task becomes all the more vital."

Chaffa reached out for one of the vials Victor had presented. With practiced muscle memory, she withdrew a small needle from the folds of her cloak, careful not to prick herself until she was ready. Holding the vial steady with one hand, she pricked the tip of her finger with the needle, allowing a few drops of crimson blood to fall into the container.

Once satisfied with the amount collected, Chaffa set the vial aside and turned her attention to a dignified jewelry box that lay near her. Victor's eyes followed her gentle movements as an ear was removed from it. Chaffa's weathered lips moved in uncanny fashion, forming ancient words that seemed to hang in the air like a delicate mist. No louder than a whisper, her voice resonated with centuries of knowledge and power. Her hand closed into a fist, squeezing the ear as she chanted the incantation. As the spell was coming to a close, a few more drops of blood filled that vial.

"The blood of the Larimar." The old woman gave a final notion that the favor Victor sought was complete.

"Thank you!" The Grand Emperor couldn't help but feel a surge of gratitude and excitement coursing through him. The prospect of embarking on his mission filled him with a sense of purpose, propelling him forward and out of his chair.

With a grateful nod to Chaffa, Victor turned to leave, his footsteps quickening. But just as he reached the threshold, a sudden realization struck him like a bolt of lightning, causing him to pause in his tracks. "Before I go, I have one last question, Madame Chaffa. Where can I find the remaining Hawkes?"

Chaffa's expression turned somber as she considered Victor's question. Her eyes shifted to the floor for a moment before she met his face once more with a wholehearted smile. "In the mountains of course. East of here. Now go, and fulfill your duties. . . New Overseer."

With one vial filled and two remaining, Victor's determination surged as he swung onto his horse's back. Despite the temptation to rest at the local tavern for the night, the thrill of uncovering the Hawkes' whereabouts propelled him forward, urging him to press on with his quest. Reflecting on Chaffa's cryptic clues, he pondered, "She stated they would be found to the east. That's where I'll start."

With a resolute nod, he spurred his horse into action, the anticipation of what lay ahead speeding up his heartbeat. As his horse galloped eastward, the landscape blurred into a whirlwind of motion, each stride bringing him closer to his goal.

Victor rode all night to the east to try and find any trace of the Hawkes. When the sun peeked over the faraway mountains he knew that he needed to rest. He stopped near a trickling stream that was surrounded by lush green grass at the edge of a forest. "A perfect little spot," he thought out loud.

While his horse was grazing with content on what seemed like an endless feast in front of it, Victor went to the water's edge to wash his face. As he knelt down, he became lost in thought while looking into his reflection. Victor imagined what he would look like wearing the Grand Organizations colors instead of his own. But he thought it must be no different than his current position as Grand Emperor, he had already tested it for two weeks.

Victor could almost hear the cheers of his people supporting his growth when he snapped himself out of the dream. There were no cheers, there was no chanting, but strangest of all there was no sound. No birds or crickets chirping, no squirrels or field mice chittering, and even his horse appeared on edge. Anxiety melted his chest, and the Grand Emperor raced to mount his horse and started back on the road.

After a few steps, an arrow plunged into a nearby tree at the same level as Victor's head. Without hesitation, he spurred his horse to a full gallop. He knew he was being watched but for someone to take a shot at him spelled pure trouble.

Victor and his steed galloped full speed through the forest to elude their pursuers. Ducking branches, he tried to catch a glimpse of who was shooting at him. He squinted and he thought he could see a shadowy outline on horseback but then another arrow came whizzing straight for him. Without conscious thought he pulled the reins to make his horse turn right and dug his heels in, praying his horse still had enough energy to get away. As the horse started to slow its pace, he knew he didn't have much time to get ready before his attacker was going to be upon him.

He saw a low-hanging branch approaching almost too fast to notice, and he grabbed it to flip himself up onto it. Just a few seconds later, the shadowy figure emerged on the path in hot pursuit. As the attacker was riding below, Victor dropped down and grabbed it by its cloak, yanking it off its horse.

The figure let out a shocked exclamation as it was pulled off its mount, but was nimble enough to land on its feet. Victor was quicker. His sword was already at the figure's throat and he growled, "You have a lot of nerve coming after a Grand Emperor like that. Who are you?"

The figure did a backflip to increase the space between them and kicked Victor's sword to the side in the process. Victor drew two daggers from his belt and shouted, "Answer me! Who are you?" The figure stood silent for a moment before dashing for the tree line to escape. Victor gave chase. The cloaked figure made great strides and Victor began to fall behind. As the figure reached the tree line, Victor threw one of his daggers in an attempt to pin his assailant. However, he missed by an inch and snagged some of its cloak.

As part of the cloak tore away, Victor saw shimmering skin that looked like a bright bronze. Then, as quick as the figure had burst into his life, it was gone.

Victor listened to the receding sounds of branches breaking and leaves crunching as his assailant fled into the woods. He collected his sword and his dagger and held the scrap of cloak in his hand. The fabric seemed to absorb light as though it was creating some sort of void. Victor had never seen anything like it before aside from the Overseer's markings.

He summoned his horse with a sharp whistle, stowing the scrap into one of the saddlebags before settling back into the saddle. Guiding his steed into a brisk trot, Victor's mind buzzed with unanswered questions. Why had he been attacked as such? Was it a random act of violence, or did someone have knowledge of his quest? Was it Chaffa's men trying to thwart his mission?

As he pondered these mysteries during his ride, Victor decided to exercise greater caution going forward. Every shadow, every rustle of the wind would be met with heightened vigilance as he continued his journey.

As he reached the edge of the forest, Victor could see a small town in the distance. "Perfect, I could use a drink, and I bet you could too!" he said to his horse. He made his way into the center of town and hitched his horse outside the tavern. He was weary, but climbed the steps and paused to stretch his back before heading inside.

Once inside, he was greeted with the reaction he had become accustomed to. Everybody stopped mid-conversation and stared at him. After a moment, they returned to their conversations as if he no longer existed.

He went straight up to the bar and sat down on a small stool that groaned under his weight. The bartender was a heavy set grizzled old man with an eye patch who was cleaning a beer stein with what Victor hoped was a clean cloth. "What's your poison?" the barkeep asked.

"Murkwood ale, if you have it," His breath was shallow, exhausted from the trip.

The bartender laughed and replied, "Does this look like the city? As if we stocked up on high end ales and wines?"

Victor rolled his eyes and hissed under his breath, "Well, what do you have then?"

The barkeep, still chuckling, replied, "We have mead, whiskey, and water, but I wouldn't recommend the water."

Victor ordered a mead with some hesitation. The bartender walked away still chuckling and returned a moment later with a tall stein of mead. Victor looked down at the drink, which had unidentified particles floating in it and what appeared to be a dead bug in the foam. He picked out the black floaty and set it on the bar and took a sip while trying his best to hide his disgust. A bitter taste flooded his mouth that caused him to gag, but he swallowed it down and motioned for the bartender to come back over when he was finished with his other patrons.

The barkeep came back and asked, "It is no Murkwood Ale, but it sure hits the spot, don't it?"

Victor replied, "It sure does. . . Say, you look like the sort of guy who knows things. I am looking for some information."

The barkeep grinned a semi-toothless grin and said, "Information isn't free my friend. Maybe after you finish your second drink, we can talk," and walked away, leaving Victor with another full stein.

Victor shuddered as he lifted the stein to his lips again and took another swig. It burned his throat and stomach and he wondered if he had been served mead or horse piss. He downed the rest of his drink and called the barkeep back over. "Whiskey this time, please."

The bartender smiled and said, "Yes sir, right away!" As he was pouring Victor's third drink he said, "The whiskey we make here is the best in the area. Nobody wants mead after they taste this whiskey!"

Victor scoffed under his breath, "Or after they taste the mead."

"What was that?" The barkeep's smile faded and jaw tensed.

The Grand Emperor noticed the abrupt change and abandoned his thoughts to retract and change his comment, "I said it'll be tough to beat the mead. It was quite flavorful."

The bartender gave Victor the glass full of amber liquid and waited for him to drink it. The Grand Emperor smiled and shot the whiskey back, doing everything to try and not to let it touch his tongue. He choked back a cough as it slid down his throat. It tasted like something had crawled into the barrel and died. Victor let out an exaggerated sigh and smiled back at the barkeep. "Yep, it, without a doubt, beats the mead. Now I was wondering if I could get some information from you."

The bartender crossed his arms and asked, "You say I look like someone with information, but why? Because I work at a tavern? Because I am a barkeep? This isn't the Muse. I will have you know I just moved here a few weeks ago, and I don't know anything."

Victor whispered a curse into his hands as he covered his face. All that self-induced suffering for nothing.

The bartender roared with laughter. "Ah, I fooled you. Of course I know all sorts of things. I grew up here and have never been bothered to leave. What do you want to know?"

Victor composed himself and leaned in and asked, "Have you heard word of the Hawkes? Have there been any sightings in the area?"

The bartender thought for a moment and said, "Ahh, I think there was a strange sighting a few weeks back. Looked like a big group of them that were moving their camp around every few days till they were gone. Haven't heard from them since. I think they were headed northeast of here, towards the mountains. I bet you gold to guppies that was in all likelihood who you are looking for."

The Grand Emperor absorbed the information and held up a finger. "One more question."

The barkeep started to refill Victor's drink but he put his hand over his glass. "No more for me tonight. In fact, I wanted to know if you had any vacant beds?"

The man nodded and said, "Yes sir, we do. Fifty gold a night."

The Grand Emperor choked at the price. A high-end city inn was a simple twenty gold a night. Given his experience with the drinks he was hesitant to indulge the bartender any further, but he was very tired. "Fine," he said, and laid the gold on the counter.

The bartender grabbed a key from under the counter and told him, "It is the last door at the end of the hallway upstairs," motioning to a set of stairs off to the side of the bar.

Victor thanked him and made his way up. As he reached the last room of the hall he took a deep breath and braced himself for disappointment. He turned the key in the lock and opened the door. It let out a loud squeal from its hinges. In the room was just a straw bed and a side table.

Victor sighed and said to himself, "I don't know what I was expecting," and sat down on the bed.

But as soon as he sat, a mouse ran out from under the sheets. With visible disgust, he remade the bed, checking for any additional bedmates, and settled in for the night.

Chapter 9.5

The next morning, Victor awoke at the crack of dawn feeling well rested. He knew he had so much time before the Hawkes moved their camp again, so he flinged his clothes on and gathered his things before descending to the main floor of the tavern.

When he got downstairs, the front door burst open and a cloaked figure was rushing out. Victor dropped everything but his sword and ran to the door. He looked in all directions but could not see the cloaked figure anywhere. Then, he turned to demand answers from the bartender but the room was empty except for a young boy behind the bar. The lad was cleaning glasses with what Victor assumed was the same cloth from the previous night.

"Boy. Did you speak to that man?" The boy, frightened by the commotion, just nodded. Victor lowered his voice and feigned a kind and patient tone and continued. "It is very important that you remember what was said. What did the man in the cloak ask?"

The boy muttered, "They asked if, uhm, if I saw someone, uhm, like you here."

His eyes lowered into a suspicious squint, "Did you tell him I was here?"

The boy shook his head from side to side.

Victor continued, less disturbed but still uncomfortable, "Did they ask you anything else?"

The boy nodded and said, "He asked if anyone owned the horse outside."

Victor's face grew grim as he realized that last night he did not see any other horses outside. "What did you tell them?"

"I told them that it was our delivery horse. I think he was a horse thief and I didn't want him to take it. You have a beautiful horse, mister." The boy responded

"Yes, he is a fine steed. Anything else?" The boy shook his head again. "Fine. Here is a gold piece. You never saw me here, okay?"

The boy nodded again and went back to his chores. Victor picked up his things and went outside to check on his horse, which was taking a long drink from a trough and looked up when he heard him approaching. He whinnied and stamped the ground in excitement.

"Somebody is ready to get back on the road! Aren't you boy," Victor said as he patted the horse's neck and seated himself in the saddle, taking a deep breath. It was time to find the Hawkes.

Victor rode northeast for most of the day towards the mountains the bartender had told him about. As he reached the base of the mountains, he stopped for a rest. Victor pulled out a spyglass and scanned the peaks for any activity. After a few minutes of searching, he saw what he had hoped for: smoke rising up from a mountain a few peaks into the range, from what would have to be a bonfire. Victor collapsed his spyglass and began making his way through the mountains to the smoke.

Along the way, wildlife seemed to abound around him. He was watched at all times by mountain goats, mountain lions, and various creatures. As he drew closer to the smoke, the wildlife became scarcer. Noticing this, he rode on with determination. Fewer animals are found where there are more people, therefore there must be people up ahead, Victor thought.

As it happened, he was correct. Victor rode towards the camp with his hands in the air. In his peripheral vision, he saw guards and lookouts higher up the pass looking down at him. After passing a few tents, he heard a guard shout "Halt!"

Victor squeezed his horse with his legs to stop him and replied, "I mean no harm. I seek the leader of the Hawkes and I come in peace."

"What makes you think the Hawkes are here?" His voice was firm, his stance unyielding, as if daring Victor to challenge him.

"My best guess. Was I right?" There was a moment of silence and Victor felt like there were at least a dozen arrows pointed at him.

"What is your business here?" The voice was low, resonating with authority.

"I seek to speak to your leader," The Grand Emperor replied, keeping his tone respectful, though he felt a pang of indignation at being spoken down to by a mere guard.

This time a female voice rang out, "Regarding what?"

He paused before raising his voice to respond. "Regarding the governance of the entire realm."

There was another moment of silence. "You may enter, but if you do anything that raises suspicion you will be shot on sight. Do you understand?"

Victor replied, "Yes. Where do I need to go?"

The female voice replied again, "Come to the purple tent near the peak and we can speak there."

Victor believed he must be speaking to a queen, and looked up to see a young woman looking over the ledge. She had long, wavy black hair and a mischievous smile. She waved and disappeared.

Victor began riding through the village of tents as he made his way up the mountain. As he rode along, he noticed it was very quiet. At first, he thought it might be because an outsider was riding through their commune, but he realized that would be a much better alternative to reality. Victor scanned the campsite looking for children, but he could not find any outside. He heard no conversations, no laughter nor singing, and no work being done nor things being gathered. There was a stillness as he passed many tents. One tent had its flaps open and he looked inside and wished he had not. Inside the tent was the body of an older woman who had died and rotted so much that bone poked out through dry, leathery skin. Victor shuddered and carried on.

He saw similar scenes in other tents. Many had died and others appeared very ill. Any younger people seemed preoccupied with taking care of their elders.

Victor reached the purple tent, got down from his horse and hung his weapons on the saddle before entering. As he approached, a guard stopped him. "You cannot go in there."

Victor was confused. "But I was invited by the young lady with the long black hair."

The guard stepped aside, looked Victor in the eyes, and warned him, "Not many have been invited. Show respect. They will not hesitate to kill you." Victor nodded and entered the tent.

Once inside, he saw a young lady with black, wavy hair flowing down past her shoulders studying papers at a desk. He cleared his throat before speaking, "Your Highness."

The young woman whipped around and shouted, "Who let you in here? Guards!" Several guards rushed in, swords drawn. The young lady turned red and continued shouting. "You think I would let your kind speak to me? After all you have done? Did you not see the damage you have caused as you rode up here? Have you not seen the death and destruction you and that pig the Overseer have caused with your petty war?"

Victor remained silent and confused. The young lady continued, "Give me one good reason I shouldn't have your throat slit right now?"

A voice called out from behind them, "Because I would like to hear what he has to say." Another woman, identical to the first, stood between her and Victor. "Darling, he claims no harm and I think if we listen to what he has to say, we may have your chance for revenge yet."

The first young lady calmed down after a moment and waved the guards away.

Victor's chin raised, "Twins?"

The ladies looked up at Victor and answered in perfect unison, "You may call us twins. We were born at the same time, but we share one life."

Still confused at the sight of two women so identical, "What magic is this then?"

"We are not sisters." They said in unison, "We are the same individual, but split into two bodies."

Victor had never seen two people look the same, much less one person be in two places at the same time. "My name is Victor. What are your names?"

The lady from the cliffs said, "my name is Nora."

The lady he met after then answered, "my name is Nyla."

Victor bowed to each of them and motioned to a nearby table. The ladies nodded and the three of them sat down.

"Hurry up and say what you need to say, we have much to do," Nyla said with a frown.

Nora added, "Yes, I wish to hear more about what you said earlier about governance of the realm."

Victor cleared his throat and began by asking how they felt about the Overseer.

They frowned and glanced at each other before answering, "I am sure you have gathered that we hate him, but we harbor no such feelings for him. We do think, however, that he is not fit to be Overseer. He has made too many mistakes and no one man should have all of that power."

Victor nodded before answering. "Yes, that is a common sentiment held by many. You are not alone."

Nyla slammed her hands down on the table. "Not alone! Do you see any help out there? Even the Wintersun are not helping us at all. There has been no respite since we were cast out of our lands and spread to the wind! Sickness and mountain air have claimed many of our elders, supplies run low, we don't even have land to call home, and you say we are not alone?"

Victor waited for her to finish. She was seething but sat back down in a huff when Nora put her hand on her shoulder.

Nora picked up where Nyla had left off. "As you can see, Victor, our people have been devastated by the war. We have received no aid from any other nation. We are outcasts and nobody will help us because we rebelled as a nation against the Overseer."

Victor bit his lower lip, and Nora continued, "Now what are you proposing? I hope you did not come all this way just to ask us how we feel about the Overseer."

He looked at each of the girls and asked, "Are you both queens or is it just. . ." The girls waited for him to finish speaking, causing him to cut himself off and go red in the face.

Nora laughed. "Good try there. We are both in fact one queen. After our father passed away from sickness we assumed the throne. If you can call it that." She gestured to a large rickety looking chair at one end of the room.

Victor regained his composure. "I am sorry for your loss."

Nyla grew serious. "You should be." She returned to her relaxed demeanor. "Anyway, out with it already. What do you want?"

Victor leaned forward. "I am proposing that the Overseer should not be in power anymore."

Nora and Nyla looked at each other and laughed. "And how do you think that worked out for us last time?"

Nyla continued without Nora, "Yeah, do you think we are imbeciles? Have you seen the state of our camp?"

Victor held up a hand. "No, I do not mock you, Your Highnesses. It is planned that I take the mantle and I plan to make big changes. I have already spoken to your former king and father, Ara Hawke and he pledged to my cause." He hoped his lie had gone unnoticed.

The girls shared a glance before Nyla's tone grew harsh. "And what did he pledge? More men? We do not have any, and even if we did, we would not send them on a suicide mission."

Nora saw Victor shaking his head and put her hand on her sister's shoulder again. She asked, "The Hawkes pledge not to the Overseer even after defeat. What did you offer them?"

Victor answered with a sparkle in his eye, "I offered them a second chance. I told them that they would not be persecuted any further and that they could rebuild. I offer you the same thing. You can have a portion of your land back and you will not be wiped out forever."

The ladies looked at each other and sat in silence for a moment before asking in turn, beginning with Nora. "So what makes you any different from the current Overseer?"

"Yeah, how do we know you won't just abuse your powers like he did? Most of you men are all the same with your wars and your power struggles," Nyla added.

Victor nodded in agreement. "You are correct, there is not a lot of difference between him and I. We are both powerful men. However, I also understand how to share power."

The girls waited in silence for Victor to elaborate.

He continued, "I plan to hold a council that does not consist of just High Guardians. I wish for a world council. We will have delegates from all nations present at all meetings. There will be no surprises and no matter the size of the nation, everyone has an equal vote. I intend to institute a more democratic model on the global scale."

Nyla was impressed by Victor's last statement and sat back with her arms folded. Nora nodded and asked, "What do you need from us to make this all happen?"

Victor smiled and brought out his enchanted water bag and opened it, showing the ladies the contents. "This is blood from the Larimar Queen, Chaffa. I need blood from a Hawke. I will be using deep magic that requires the blood of each kingdom to end the Overseer."

The girls looked somewhat horrified and recoiled from the bag. "You want our blood?"

Victor nodded and replied, "I do not need much, in fact if you each contributed half of what you see, I am sure the blood within your veins is identical as well."

Again, they glanced at each other and shrugged before they each drew a dagger. Nora placed hers in her palm and made a small cut, but Nyla plunged her dagger into the table next to the water bag. "I swear, if anything bad comes from this, I will kill you myself."

Victor chuckled and stared into Nyla's eyes and said, "I wouldn't have it any other way." Nyla withdrew her dagger, never breaking eye contact, and made a small cut on her palm. The two ladies each let some blood flow into the bag until it looked like it had doubled in volume.

Nyla snapped her fingers and guards came in with some bandages for their hands.

Victor stood up and bowed again to each queen. "Thank you for your contribution. In a short time, you will reap the benefits. I promise you that. Before I go, I need to know. Have either of you heard anything from the Wintersun? They are the last people I must speak to."

Nora and Nyla both shook their heads.

A grateful expression softened Victor's features, his eyes lighting up with appreciation as he nodded. "I thought it best to ask. Thank you, my ladies."

Nora smiled and Nyla just dismissed Victor with a wave. He nodded, exited the tent, geared back up, and mounted his horse. As he made his way back down the mountain, he could not help but feel as though he was being watched. The guards and citizens were nowhere in sight, but Victor had an uneasy feeling as he exited the camp. He came off of the mountain and back to the valley he had come from. The entire trip was completed in silence and he did not see a single animal the entire way back.

Victor feared he was being followed and took off at full speed across the meadow in front of him. He looked back a few times but saw nothing but rolling fields of green grass with the mountains as a backdrop. Nevertheless, he continued at full speed away from the mountains.

He thought, Two down, one to go! We are so close. I will get you what you wish for. Now, where am I going to find those bloody Wintersun? He rode around the west side of the mountains so he could continue north. After a few hours, he stopped near a large cave to rest. It seemed peaceful enough with no signs of life anywhere near it.

The Grand Emperor lit a lantern and investigated the cave. Even inside it was quite barren and did not appear very deep. He brought his horse inside and set up a small fire to make some dinner. Once his stomach was full he set up a spot to sleep on the cave's floor next to his horse. Victor, feeling quite accomplished for having gotten two blood samples in one week, fell asleep within minutes.

Chapter 10.1

As nights bled into days, Victor searched almost every corner of the Northern Sanction for any sign of the Wintersun. He retraced his steps back through Jakarth, questioning locals and scouring the area for any clues, but his efforts proved fruitless.

He tapped into his entire spy the Grand Organization and asked almost anyone who would lend an ear. Days added up until the end of the month drew near. He began to lose hope. After his resounding success prior, he assumed that finding the Wintersun would be a piece of cake.

Victor chased down cold trail after cold trail every time he heard of a Wintersun boasting that they would return, or whenever he heard of a demonstration against the Overseer. All his efforts were in vain, regardless of how fast he arrived.

One day, one of Victor's spies met him in a busy tavern just inside the old border of the Wintersun kingdom. "Thank you for meeting with me, Grand Emperor Zeller. I trust the information I have for you will be useful."

Victor smiled and pounded back a much deserved Murkwood Ale. "Yes, Reese, I have always had good results from your intelligence. What do you have for me today?"

Reese leaned in so as not to be overheard and whispered in Victor's ear. "I heard that the reason you cannot find the leader of the Wintersun is because there is no leader. There is a power vacuum in the Wintersun dynasty and every time someone makes it to the top, they either go into hiding and are assassinated or try to lead and end up getting killed. Either way, it is not the best position for leadership these days."

Victor nodded while looking around the room to see if anyone was watching them. Satisfied that they were not being stalked, he whispered back, "That explains why I am having such a hell of a time finding them. I am not sure how I am going to get what I need from any of them if they won't stop killing each other. I mean, they would kill a Zeller even quicker than one of their own."

Reese chuckled and whispered back, "Right you are, milord, so whatever you are trying to get from them, I would suggest just taking it. I mean, the blighters would not be alive long enough to bear a grudge anyway before the next one offs him."

Victor contemplated Reese's words for quite some time before agreeing. He summoned the bartender to bring them two more pints. Halfway through their second round, Reese turned his face to the wall and hissed to Victor, "Don't look now, but we have company in the corner."

The Zeller Grand Emperor feigned laughter, grabbed his stein and pretended to drink, but used it as cover to look to the corner of the room. There sat the hooded figure that had been following him, silent and motionless as a sentinel. Both blending into the crowded tavern and sticking out like a sore thumb once noticed, the figure seemed to vanish as another patron walked between them.

Victor sighed and finished his drink. Reese, somewhat more alarmed, questioned his lack of concern. Victor waved his hand and said, "That bastard has been following me since the second day of my journey. We crossed blades once but they always seem to be one step ahead of me. They have some kind of magical cloak too. Look at this," he said as he reached into his bag and pulled out the scrap of cloth.

Reese's eyes grew wide as he yanked the cloth out of Victor's hands and held it up to the light before hiding it under the table. "Do you know what this is?" Victor shook his head. Reese became astonished, "This is fabric from the Shadow Empire. See how it absorbs the light? This is fabric from another plane of existence. This is pure magic!"

Victor looked at Reese and asked, "How do you know so much about it?"

Reese responded, "As far as anyone knows, three cloaks are known to have been brought to this world. One is in the hands of the Overseer, the second is in the hands of an efficient assassin from the Jade Empire, and the last one's whereabouts are unknown. These cloaks mask your identity and make you stealthier than most. You are near invisible in low light if you have one."

Victor recalled how difficult it was to see the cloaked rider in the forest when they first met and how he felt watched but could never find the source. "Is there a way to detect someone wearing this cloak?"

Reese shook his head and handed the scrap of cloth back. "No, Grand Emperor, I don't know of any way to counter the cloak's effects. The wearer is invisible if they want to be."

Victor gritted his teeth. He knew that whoever was following him had a reason, but he did not know what that could be. "Reese, has word spread about my travels?"

Reese thought for a moment before answering, "Somewhat, yes. Word has spread that a Zeller noble is combing the countryside, but nobody knows why."

Victor caught the bartender's eye and ordered another round. "That will have to do for now. Thank you for sharing what you know."

Reese clinked steins with Victor. "To our health and prosperity!"

A chuckle escaped Victor's lips before he uttered, "Indeed!" The two finished their drinks and went their separate ways.

Victor mulled over what Reese had told him about the cloak as he rode out of town. Once he was in the countryside, he turned his thoughts back to the mission at hand. He had to find a Wintersun to complete the ritual. His spies had told him that the rest of the High Guardians had finished their missions the week before, and Azrael was securing the other blood bags. Everything hinged on Victor finding the final piece.

He decided to ride to the old capital in the heart of what used to be Wintersun territory. It was almost the middle of the night when Victor arrived at the city limits. He knew the chances of finding lodging were slim to none. He decided to set up camp a few hundred feet off of the main road.

He spent a little time gathering up a few chunks of wood from a fallen tree and surveyed the area for a few minutes. Once he found a suitable spot, he started a small fire and tended to his horse. Exhausted, he cooked up one of his last pieces of meat and started thinking about how and where to replenish his stocks. He was starting to run out of gold.

Victor looked at his horse grazing nearby and chuckled, "Ironic isn't it, old boy? A king with more gold than he could ever spend starving to death out in the wilderness. A whole lot of good that gold does for me out here." His horse snorted as if he also found it humorous.

Victor chuckled again and added another log to the fire. He pulled off some of his gear and sat up against a nearby log. He pulled out a vial of blood and opened it. He said, "Speaking of irony, isn't it interesting that the one thing that keeps us alive is the same thing that will kill the Overseer?"

The horse snorted again and continued grazing.

Victor chuckled again and said, "Ah, yes, priorities. I suppose we both need to eat. Don't worry, I will get you some premium hay when we get back to the castle. You have been a good horse."

He gazed into the bag and swirled its contents. As he watched the blood spin, he noticed something out of place.

It took Victor a second to react. He capped the vial and drew his sword. Spinning around, he was quick enough to deflect a well-aimed strike meant for the back of his neck, from a sword that seemed to materialize from nowhere. He looked up to see the cloaked figure.

"You will not escape again," Victor growled.

The distorted voice answered, "I do not plan to."

The two traded blows as Victor's horse whinnied and brayed and kicked, trying to get loose from the tree where it was tied. The hooded figure continued, "You do not stand a chance, Zeller. There is nobody here to save you."

Victor shot back, "What do you want from me?" He took another wild swing at the cloaked figure's head but the figure just leaned backward and allowed the blade to pass before stepping back. "You have been following me for a month, you tried to take my life, and you have been interfering with my mission. You have no idea what I am even doing!"

The cloaked figure seemed to pause, and parried Victor's next blow, getting so close he could smell its rotten breath. "I do, in fact. I know you are collecting blood from every race and you still need the Wintersuns'. Why do you think you cannot find any? You see, it is my sole purpose to make sure that you fail by any means necessary. I am tired of meddling in your hunt and so I have decided to kill you."

The figure took a swipe at Victor's midriff with a dagger but he backed off to dodge the attack. "Why must I fail?" he asked while out of breath.

But the response did all but satisfy the inquiry, "Because you must." It unleashed another flurry of blows and plunged its dagger into Victor's sword arm. He yelled in pain and held his wounded shoulder. Whoever this was, they were very skilled.

The figure struck again and again, causing Victor to backpedal further until he was almost up against a tree. The figure thrust at his stomach but the Grand Emperor sidestepped and slashed at his foe, cutting into its back. It emitted a distorted cry of pain.

The sword pierced into the tree with such force that it became stuck. The assassin then pulled a second dagger from its cloak, and ran at Victor, slashing and swiping with its daggers, giving him multiple cuts and gashes all over his upper body.

Victor was overwhelmed by the speed of the blows and began to swing at random, trying to avoid exposing himself while landing a hit anywhere on his assailant. His sword connected with bone and the figure let out another shriek of pain and dropped one of its daggers as its arm hung limp at its side. "Even with one hand, I will kill you," it growled.

The Grand Emperor went on the offensive and tried to overwhelm the attacker with his two blades, but the figure was too fast. It dodged and weaved away from most of his strikes, and blocked the ones it could not escape.

Within a second, the figure knocked away Victor's sword and the two were left to fight with a single dagger each. They circled each other and took swipes from arm's length to try and find an opening to finish their opponent. The figure raised its dagger and unleashed a war cry, which startled Victor's horse. The animal kicked the figure with both hind feet, sending the person soaring through the air and crashing into a tree, where it crumpled to the ground.

Victor kicked away his opponent's dagger and grabbed the figure by the cloak. He tried to unmask the figure, but it responded with a flurry of blows, stunning him for a moment. The figure crawled towards its dagger, but Victor jumped on top of it and started wrestling it on the ground.

He raised his dagger over where the figure's heart should be and drove it down with both hands. The figure panicked and stopped the dagger with both its hands, allowing the blade to pierce both its palms to the hilt. It was pushing back, blood dripping down its arms.

The two were exhausted from fighting, but Victor had the upper hand. As the dagger inched closer to the figure's chest, it hissed, "Screw you! He deserves to kill the Overseer, not some noble that will be just as wretched. He will kill you and then he will kill him!"

Victor shouted back, "Who? Who is he?"

The figure just cackled, kicking at Victor and struggling some more.

"Tell me!" he screamed with flecks of spittle flown from his mouth, his voice hoarse with desperation.

Out of breath, the figure had managed to whisper, "Never."

"So be it." Victor put all his weight onto the dagger. In the silence of the night, all that could be heard was the sound of the blade ripping through the fabric followed by screams of pain. It was done, the dagger was embedded in the figure's chest.

Victor pulled it out and stabbed the body several more times to make sure the fight was over. He brushed dirt and blood off of his face and sat next to the figure for a moment to catch his breath. After he got his breathing under control, curiosity got the better of him and he pulled back the hood. To his astonishment, it was a young Wintersun boy.

Victor pulled the cloak off and stuffed it into his saddlebag. He grabbed the dead boy's wrist and opened it with his dagger. After he had collected enough blood to fill up his last vial, he carried the corpse into the woods a few hundred feet from his campsite and dumped it there. He noticed the boy had a small satchel with him and took it. By the fire, he went through its contents. Inside were bandages and some sort of tincture, which burned an ominous green color when thrown into the fire. There was also a note scrawled on a small piece of paper. All it said was:

Soon we will rule the land side by side. Grand Emperor Victor Zeller must be stopped at all costs.

-M.

Victor put the note back inside the bag and threw them both into the fire and watched them burn. He was elated that he had completed his mission, high on adrenaline from the fight, in pain from his wounds, and wary of the corpse he had just left in the woods. He decided that this was not the place to rest. He put out the fire, gathered his equipment, saddled up one more time, and started back to the Grand Organization's castle at full speed.

Chapter 10.2

Victor rode into the city almost two days later. He had stopped a few times to give his horse a break and to eat. Neither of them had slept and it was evident.

The horse walked to the stables and waited at its stall. Victor was near unconscious as he slid off and stumbled around a bit, opening the gate to let the horse back in.

He pulled his legs up the steps of the castle and called over Amelia. "Tell Grand Emperor Azrael I have returned and to meet me in my chambers."

The servant bowed and scurried away. Victor looked at the stairs leading to his chambers and sighed in exasperation. He scrawled a note to not disturb him and left it on the door. He flopped onto his bed still clothed and crashed into a deep sleep. A few hours later there was a loud knock.

Victor groaned and barked "Who dares?"

Azrael poked his head inside. "It is me, Victor. I came earlier but you looked like you needed at least a few hours of sleep."

Victor groaned, "I could use a fortnight of rest."

Azrael laughed and replied, "Well, my enchantments do not have time limits. I will take the final vials and keep it with the others. The Overseer can wait one more day. Rest and we will convene tomorrow for the ritual needed to lay him to rest. He told me everything that is required and I have gone ahead and gathered the remaining elements. You have nothing to worry about. You have done well and—"

Victor interrupted Azrael with very loud snoring which the leader of the Diamond Mortem Dynasty took as his cue to withdraw.

Victor slept the rest of the evening and much of the next morning before there was another loud knock at the door. "Rise and shine! Today is going to be a grand day!" He opened his eyes to see the Overseer standing in the doorway grinning.

"What time is it?" Victor mumbled.

The Overseer took on a shaming tone, "Why, young man, the day is half over! You best get out of bed and get some food into you!"

Victor sat up and rubbed his eyes. It felt like it had been ages since he'd gotten a full night's rest.

The Overseer couldn't contain his enthusiasm. "Get yourself cleaned up. I have had the servants prepare a feast to celebrate your success. I will see you downstairs within the hour." He disappeared without another word as he shut the door behind him.

Victor looked into a mirror and saw he was still covered in blood and grime from his journey. He touched his shoulder but it did not hurt at all. The wounds had all healed and there were nothing but scars. He changed into some clean clothes and headed downstairs to the dining hall, where he saw the Overseer, Azrael, and several High Guardians. They all cheered and raised their drinks when he entered.

"To the man of the hour," the Overseer shouted.

Victor smiled and took his seat. He made eye contact with Azrael and pointed to his shoulder. Azrael just winked. The lot ate and drank as Victor recounted the tales of his travels. After everyone had their fill and heard his story, they all decided to take a few hours to settle and would reconvene in the throne room.

The Overseer and Victor went for a walk together. They stopped near a brook and just watched as the water flowed by.

"Are you ready?" Victor asked out of the blue.

The Overseer didn't answer right away, he just kept staring at the water and smiled.

A few minutes later he decided at last, "See, my essence is like the water in this stream. It flows in a single direction and it is near infinite, but the truth is it is the same water. If you followed one drop it would go out to sea and be carried by the rains back to this stream's source. If the water stops flowing it becomes stagnant and polluted, but as long as it is always moving it stays fresh. I have been in this form for far too long and I am becoming stagnant. I am ready for whatever comes next."

He turned and started walking back, and Victor followed.

When they returned to the castle, the Overseer told Victor to get ready for the ceremony and headed towards the throne room. He returned to his chambers and sat in silence on his bed for a few minutes, looking in the mirror. "How does one get ready to put their Overseer to rest?" he muttered to himself.

He tried on a black cape but decided it was too gruesome. Instead, he settled on a fancy outfit with accents of royal blue and burgundy, and returned to the throne room where he was greeted by both the Overseer and Azrael. In the middle of the room was a large stone table surrounded by candles, and beside it was a small table with a shallow, carved-out slab adorned with various runes.

The Overseer climbed up onto the large slab and sat cross-legged in the middle with a smile on his face. Azrael flicked his wrist and closed the doors, sealing them shut with a ward.

Victor walked up to the Overseer and asked him one more time, "Are you sure?" He could see through the smile on the Overseer's face and looked at his very tired eyes.

The Overseer put his hands on Victor's shoulders and said, "I have never been more sure." The two looked into each other's eyes for a moment, sharing more emotions and understanding than words could ever describe.

Victor walked over to Azrael, who had emptied out all of the blood from the vials into the smaller slab. He handed Victor a dagger. "You are the final piece, Victor. Zeller blood is the last of the bloodlines."

Victor took a deep breath and cut open his palm and made a fist over the slab. As his blood dripped into the shallow pool it began to swirl and bubble and the runes on the side of the slab began to glow. Azrael wheeled over a cart with two objects on it. The Overseer explained as Azrael handed each item to Victor.

"I wish to be separated into mind, body, and soul. For this, we need three objects. The vase is going to represent my body. I received this priceless vase as a gift from the Emerald Empire and I have grown fond of it. My mind could never be contained, but this book will serve to share my thinking. It is an enchanted book that records history as it happens. It has focused on my life and the events around me. Also, the Blade of the Lost Beloved I gave you will carry my soul. May it strike with the purest of intentions as I attempted to in life. Azrael will take you through the rest."

The Overseer laid down on the large slab and opened his shirt. Azrael told Victor to dip his fingers in the blood and to drip it over the objects. As Victor dripped the blood onto the three totems, Azrael chanted incantations to form a bond between the three. Next, he instructed Victor to smear some blood on the Overseer's forehead, chest, and stomach. Azrael continued chanting to form the bond between the Overseer and the three objects. He placed the vase between the Overseer's legs and the book under his head. The final step was to bathe the sword in the mixed blood. Victor stirred the blood with the blade, coating it as best he could on both sides.

With blood dripping on the floor as he walked, Victor took his place at the Overseer's side and raised the sword over his heart. The Overseer looked at Victor, who was hesitating, and said, "You will do great. I know you will make a fantastic Overseer. This is the best thing that could happen for me and I cannot thank you enough. Give me peace."

Victor took a deep breath and plunged the blade into the Overseer's chest. During this, his eyes burned like purple fire and a bright light seemed to be emanating from within him that grew in intensity. While he was in pain, the Overseer could not stop smiling and was saying his goodbyes to the world before looking at Victor and mouthing the words "Thank you."

A single tear fell from Victor's eye as he watched the Overseer and whispered, "I will see you again soon. Either in this life or the next."

After a few more seconds, the bright light from within the Overseer became blinding as the room was lit with the intensity of the sun. Then, just as it had waxed, the light waned. Victor expected to see a bloody corpse on the slab but there was nothing more than the vase, the book, and the sword standing upright balanced on its tip. He reached out and took the sword. It seemed to have a slight purple hue to it now and he could feel power emanating from it.

He sheathed the sword and placed the book and the vase in a trophy case near the throne where they would not be disturbed. Victor opened the book to see what was written inside, but Azrael shut it.

He looked at Azrael who was trying to repress his grief, the Diamond Mortem Grand Emperor said through gritted teeth, "I would not advise that. That book is now imbued with his power."

Victor replied, "So?"

Azrael scoffed and replied, "So how do you release magic from any dark book holding spirits? You read it, you imbecile." He paused before continuing, "I am sorry. These events have been. . . trying for me."

Victor nodded and reassured Azrael, "I understand. It is okay. It has taken a toll on me as well." He locked the trophy case and the two of them stood for a moment in silence to honor the memory of their leader and their friend.

Azrael flicked his wrist again and opened the doors to the throne room, revealing a crowd of servants investigating the disturbance. He clapped his hands to gain everyone's attention. "The previous Overseer has seen fit to hand over the position to Victor Zeller. You will serve him as you served your previous lord. The last Overseer has been laid to rest and will be remembered for years to come. While he made mistakes, he was both a great leader and a good friend. A tad misguided at times, but he always tried to do what was right. However, today is not a day of mourning but one of celebration! Tonight, there will be a feast and all are welcome! Send word for every nation's leader to come and meet their new Overseer!"

The servants murmured amongst themselves for a moment before cheering and scurrying off to prepare for that night's feast.

Victor and Azrael parted ways and went to their chambers to reflect on the events that had just transpired and also to prepare for that night's feast. It was the beginning of a new era, and there would be speeches required.

Chapter 10.3

Victor stood tall with his chest puffed out as he looked at himself in a full-length mirror. He had put on a ceremonial outfit for that night's dinner and thought he looked impressive. He had chosen a white set of trousers and a purple vest over a white dress shirt. With the Blade of the Lost Beloved hanging at his side, he strode down the hall to Azrael's room, knocked on the door and waited.

Azrael opened the door and greeted Victor with a quick bow. Victor held up his hand, "No need for such formality. It does not suit me."

Azrael chuckled, smoothing out his new suit, almost flaunting it towards Victor as if he would have noticed any difference from the other black suits he always wore. He realized his effort was in vain, and shifted. "What do you need?"

Victor scrambled between his thoughts, "I just wanted to see if you were ready for tonight's dinner?"

Azrael put a hand on Victor's shoulder and looked him in the eye. "I am, but are you? You have quite the shoes to fill."

Victor grunted in admission and brushed Azrael's hand away. "I am ready," he said with a hint of dread in his voice. He continued, "The feast begins in a few hours. I will see you downstairs."

Azrael nodded and retreated into his room with the door still open. As he examined himself in a mirror he said, "You know, there will be a lot of questions. I hope you are prepared." When no rebuttal came, Azrael turned around to see Victor had already left. He shut the door and muttered, "Or I suppose I will be on question duty, since our new leader has yet to master the art of conversation."

Victor went outside for a walk. He returned to the brook where he and the previous Overseer had held their last conversation. He watched the water rush past for a few minutes. He drew the Blade of the Lost Beloved and squatted down and played with the water, drawing formless shapes with the tip of the sword.

The Zeller Grand Emperor looked from the water's surface up to the sky and said, "I wish you peace and prosperity wherever your essence has gone. I hope whatever is next is everything you hoped for. You will be missed." He sheathed the sword and returned to the castle. Leaders from various nations were arriving and Victor greeted a few as he climbed the steps.

Amelia walked over, interrupting those exchanges for an update. "The feast will be ready within the hour, Overseer."

Victor nodded and dismissed her. "Overseer," he muttered to himself. It would take some time to adjust to the new title. Victor stayed near the castle entrance and greeted his guests as they arrived. After about half an hour, the dinner bell rang out and everyone entered the dining hall.

Inside, many leaders and nobles were seated around large tables. All of the High Guardians sat at a table near the front of the hall with a large seat reserved for Victor and an empty chair beside it with Azrael's name on the place card.

Victor turned to address the entire hall. "Welcome everyone! Tonight we have gathered to both mourn and celebrate the passing of the last Overseer. We mourn his passing because he was a great leader, but we celebrate that he has seen fit to pass on his mantle and has found peace at last. I am sure there will be many questions, but for now we will honor his memory with this great feast!"

The gathering cheered and those with drinks already poured raised their glasses. Azrael took his seat next to Victor. He leaned over and whispered, "Excellent way to open the night. We may make an Overseer out of you yet."

Victor chuckled and thanked the servant that brought his food. The hall enjoyed a feast of pheasant and roast boar with fresh vegetables and barrels filled with many different drinks. Hearty conversation and laughter continued for hours. As the servants cleared the plates, they also brought out pitchers of premium liquors for further enjoyment. Leaders from faraway lands continued to arrive at the hall as more food was served.

He settled into his seat and loosened his belt. "I fear I may have over indulged!" Victor said to nobody in particular.

Azrael wiped his face and blew out a deep breath before sitting back as well. "I fear we both have, but a little gluttony is called for on nights such as this. I have an additional reason to celebrate."

Victor looked at his friend with interest.

Azrael continued, "I just received word this afternoon that my wife is expecting."

Victor's eyes grew wide. He grabbed his drink and stood up.

Before he could speak, Azrael pulled him back into his seat. "Not tonight. I do not want to draw attention away from his memory."

He paused for a second before patting Azrael on the back, "I understand. That is noble of you. Regardless, congratulations!"

The Grand Emperor of the Diamond Mortem Dynasty gave a rare and mystical smile, "Thank you. We expect him to arrive just before winter comes."

"That is fantastic news. I have not sired any children of my own. Perhaps you should groom him to take my place." Victor laughed at his own joke, "I am not immortal like he was and I will need peace someday as well."

Azrael scoffed and took a sip of his drink.

Victor raised an eyebrow and inquired, "You do not agree? I would think many would covet this position."

Azrael shook his head and asked, "May I speak my mind?"

Victor nodded. "Of course."

Azrael leaned over and said, "With all due respect, perhaps what the land needs is no Overseer at all. The leader tends to become a scapegoat for the land's problems and it is impossible to please everyone. The land grew and prospered on its own long before the Grand Organization, and I suspect it would carry on in the absence of an Overseer. Which begs the question, is an Overseer needed at all?"

Victor was surprised by Azrael's opinion and asked, "Do you think I should abdicate the throne then?"

"No, I do not. However, I do think that the last Overseer's mission was to unite the land under one banner. Perhaps your mission should be to make every nation self-sufficient so that mediation is not needed. There will be growing pains and injections of chaos, but does any one nation threaten the others? I believe that by deferring to a higher power shows weakness and dependence. If every nation was sovereign, then management would not be needed."

Victor retorted, "But what of war? Injustice? Poverty and plagues?"

Azrael scoffed again, "Did these also not come to pass under the rule of the last Overseer? Do you think yourself a much better leader than him? He was nigh-omnipotent according to his own words, and yet he could not bring the land into total submission, so how will you?" Azrael set down his drink before continuing. "Perhaps this conversation should be had at another time and when we both have not had as much to drink."

Victor agreed and finished his drink. "Azrael, your words sting but they also ring true. I will take your opinion into consideration as I have yet to define my purpose as Overseer. In the meantime, would you gather the book and the vase and bring them here? I do not trust the servants with such important things."

Azrael nodded. "Of course, my legs could use a stretch. I will be back in a few minutes." He stood up and made his way out of the dining hall.

Victor contemplated Azrael's idea of not having an Overseer in power at all and poked at some scraps on his plate.

Chapter 10.4

Azrael returned with the book and vase and placed them on a cart near Victor. He sat back down, but appeared uncomfortable.

Victor noticed the unusual behavior and inquired, "Is something wrong?"

Azrael shifted in his seat, "No, but I am concerned about having them out in the open."

Victor's eyebrows lifted in curiosity, his gaze sharpening as he leaned forward, "Why is that?"

"Because they are powerful, Victor." Azrael explained, "If anything happened to them, there would be catastrophic consequences."

Victor paused, then said, "Define catastrophic."

The Diamond Mortem Grand Emperor glanced at the book and vase before speaking. "To be honest, I have no idea. What I do know is that each of the three totems holds a part of him. This Overseer was very powerful. That kind of power needs to be held in check with discipline and self-control, but he is no longer with us. If his power were somehow released from any of the totems, it would be uncontrolled, raw, and I'm almost certain destructive to the planet. Without his consciousness, the thing keeping the powers contained within is the balance between the three totems. I have never completed the ritual we used to separate him before, so I have no idea what the consequences could be. This is uncharted territory."

Victor nodded in understanding and added, "So they need to be kept safe no matter what."

Azrael gave a slight and nervous nod as an answer.

Victor thought for a moment before asking, "So should we separate them? I had planned to display them in a glamorous shrine, but now I fear what may happen if they are all found together."

Azrael agreed. "That is a wise fear. If it were up to me, I would send the vase to the Emerald Empire. They take great care of their relics. He gave you the Blade of the Lost Beloved, so I believe the Zeller should continue to keep stewardship of the sword. As for the book, I would give that to the Shadow Empire. It contains more than just a record of events. His mind is contained within. The body and soul are pure as they are, but the mind can be corrupted. It is a powerful thing that, uncontrolled, can cause the greatest destruction. If you give it to the Shadow Empire, they can keep it in their dimension away from any potential malfeasance."

Victor stroked his chin, "I agree. I appreciate the way you think."

He looked over his shoulder at the two items for a moment, took a deep breath, and stood up, smoothing his shirt with his hands. He waited for the conversation to die down as various leaders and guests noticed him standing at the front of the room.

He cleared his throat. "Thank you all for coming here. We honor the last Overseer's memory with our celebration, but there is one more thing. The previous Overseer had a final request. He wished to be separated into mind, body, and soul. This has been done by imbuing each aspect of him into one of three totems; however, it should be known that this is temporary. He is immortal and will continue to live on through these enchanted objects. I believe it is in everyone's best interest to know that these totems are beyond dangerous. If his power were to be released," Victor paused for dramatic effect, "it would have catastrophic effects."

Victor looked back at Azrael for approval, but he sat with his arms crossed, expressionless.

The new Overseer continued. "As such, I have decided to bestow each totem to one of three different nations to guard them for the safety of the realm. They cannot be destroyed because the power inside will be released, so I have made my selections with careful consideration."

Victor turned around and picked up the vase. "This vase contains the essence of his body. I believe this will be safest in the hands of the Emerald Empire. Could their representative please step forward?"

Hari stood up and made his way to the front of the room. Victor handed him the vase. The man bowed out of respect and headed back to his seat, placing the vase on the table beside him.

Victor drew his sword and held it straight up. "This sword is the Blade of the Lost Beloved. It contains the essence of his soul. I have decided to bestow this to the Diamond Mortem." Azrael shot up in his seat in shock. Victor laid the sword across his palms, turned to the hooded man, and extended the blade to him.

Azrael looked around the room before standing up, whispering, "Are you sure?"

Victor was warm, but stern. "Yes, I am sure."

Azrael drew his own sword and placed it on the table. He then took the enchanted blade from Victor and placed it in his sheath before sitting down again.

Victor picked up the book and faced the room again. "Last but not least, this book contains the essence of his mind. This book is the most dangerous of them all. I believe it will be safest in the hands of the Shado—"

The doors to the dining hall busted open with a loud bang. Every person in the room turned and looked to see a figure covered in a ratty cloak. The figure tugged at the drawstring around his collar and the cloak fell to the ground. Gasps were heard from around the room.

A golden man stood before them adorned in full war paint. The High Guardians stood up, hands on their swords.

Victor called out from across the hall, "Mercury? I had speculated you were still alive. What is the meaning of this?"

Mercury laughed as he stepped forward. "Of course I am alive and well, I am the one who should be the Overseer. Yet it appears that you have beaten me to it despite my best efforts. I have to admit you bested my agent, but I thought I would have had a little more time."

The High Guardians all drew their swords and stood at the ready.

The man continued in spite of the threat, "You see, that bastard stole my idea and positioned himself as the head, and I swore that if it was the last thing I did, I would end him."

Victor held up his hand, motioning for Mercury to stop. "Many men died because of his war, but now is our chance to rebuild."

But the golden man continued walking into the hall. "You do not command me. I pledge my allegiance to no man."

One of the High Guardians, Ovidius, left the table and charged up to the man to arrest him, but Mercury drew his sword and offered the tip in their direction.

As the High Guardian reached him, Mercury attacked. Ovidius' sword met the other's to deflect the blow, but the man's swing was so powerful it shattered the High Guardian's blade. The golden man then drove his sword up under the Romanite's chin, piercing the top of his skull. He pulled it free, and spat on the body as it fell to the ground.

"That was rude. Now where was I? Ah yes, the important part. I hope you are all listening." The entire room was silent as the guests sat in their seats.

"You see, I was listening on the other side of that door, and I liked what I heard. It appears that there is a chance I can kill the Overseer once and for all by destroying his totems. Therefore, I will be taking them. By force, if necessary. Once that is done, everyone will know that I, Mercury, was the one who slayed the Overseer."

Mercury locked eyes with Victor and snapped his fingers. Just then, a host of armed Wintersun and Hawke soldiers stormed into the hall, weapons drawn. "You know, I should thank you for making this so easy. To be honest, I was not sure how to kill an immortal being, but you have made things rather convenient by dividing him up."

Victor glared at him and hissed, "I will not allow this."

Mercury chuckled and shot back, "You do not have a choice." He held up his hand and snapped his fingers again. The armed soldiers began to attack everyone in the hall. Guests burst from their seats in a panic as they rushed to defend themselves.

Victor shouted at Azrael, "Go! Now!"

Azrael hesitated for a moment, then fled out a nearby door. Victor grabbed Azrael's sword that was left behind from the table and made for the same exit.

A Wintersun soldier appeared in the doorway, but Victor was ready. He cut the soldier's head off with a quick swipe and rushed out the door with the book still in his hand. Mercury stood in the middle of the familiar room wet with blood from the guests being murdered around him and laughing.

He shouted after Victor, "Go ahead! Run! I will be right there!" as he plunged his sword into a fleeing guest.

The rest of the High Guardians leapt into action to try and end this new threat. They cleared the doorways at the front of the hall and defended them against the Wintersun soldiers as the surviving guests ran for their lives.

Mercury stopped when he caught sight of the vase that Victor had given the representative of the Emerald Empire. Somehow, in all the chaos, it remained upright on one of the tables. He walked over to it as the last of the guests were making their exit. He bent over to be eye level with the vase.

In a childlike manner, he poked it, causing it to tip over the side of the table, and said, "Oops!"

As the vase fell, Ervikson saw it and shouted, "Get down!"

Mercury cackled as the vase hit the floor and broke into a thousand pieces. As soon as it shattered, a blinding, white light filled the room and the sound of a thousand cannons going off rang out for a full minute. The High Guardians took cover as best they could and covered their ears. Meanwhile, the Wintersun continued their slaughter and remained exposed to the magic.

When the light and the sound faded, Ervikson looked around and was horrified. Those who did not find cover had their eyes burned out of their sockets and had blood running down the sides of their faces from their ears. Even a few of the High Guardians had fallen victim to the magical blast. There was fire throughout the Grand Hall and it was beginning to spread to the rest of the castle.

Ervikson called out, "Brothers! We fight for the last Overseer and the next! Let's end the Wintersun threat once and for all!"

The remaining High Guardians rallied, cheered, and rushed back to the fighting. Ervikson himself led the charge and began dispatching Wintersun soldiers, making his way towards Mercury. Although the Spinelle representative was wounded and tired, he continued to fight, slashing through Wintersun soldiers at all cost.

Ara Hawke appeared from around the corner and hovered his way towards Ervikson. The Wingman swung his wings side to side to clear the way, flinging tables and castle guests in the process. When he reached Ervikson, he reached out and grabbed the High Guardian by the head and the torso, lifting him over his head and pulling him apart, showering himself in blood.

The other High Guardians were horrified. They swarmed Ara and attacked from multiple angles. The Hawke King fought back with great determination, but over time fell to his knees before being beheaded by Bemus.

Hari, Vladsun, Bemus, Golnesa, and Scourge banded together and ordered the others to make sure everyone got out of the castle. The five remaining High Guardians turned as a unit towards Mercury, who appeared to be enjoying the violence. Together, they slayed several more Wintersun soldiers as they fought towards the enemy leader.

A volley of arrows were sent on them from across the hall, Scourge leaped into action, his massive frame moving to shield the other High Guardians from them. With an almost superhuman agility, he intercepted the shafts, deflecting them with his shield. But even as he sought to protect his allies, tragedy struck. A single arrow found its mark, piercing through and burying itself deep into his neck.

For a moment, he stood there, his eyes wide with shock as he grasped at the arrow protruding from his flesh. Blood gushed from the wound, staining his armor crimson as he staggered backward, his strength faltering with each passing second.

With a final, desperate effort, Scourge fought to maintain his footing, his face contorted in a grimace of pain and defiance, but it was clear that his wounds were too severe and his strength too depleted to continue the fight. He collapsed to his knees, his life pooling beneath him as he slumped forward.

Golnesa's heart pounded with a mixture of terror and rage as she fought the sight of her fallen allies. With every swing of her blade, she felt a surge of adrenaline coursing through her veins, driving her forward even as fear gnawed at the edges of her mind.

With a defiant roar, she pushed through her fear, her sword cleaving through the air with lethal precision. As a Hawke soldier fell before her, she turned to face the next opponent, but her streak was short-lived. Out of the corner of her eye, she saw the fallen soldier stir, his hand reaching out to grab her from behind. He had pulled her with him, dragging her toward a shattered window. Golnesa's scream echoed through the room as she was pulled through with him, her body disappearing from view as she plummeted to the ground below.

Hari teared up and darted along the edge of a nearby tabletop, his breath ragged with exertion. Then, several Wintersuns emerged from the corners and Hawkes flew in from the windows, their weapons glinting just as his emblem did in the light. Before he could react, spears pierced his flesh, sending shockwaves of agony through his body.

He stumbled, his legs giving way beneath him as he fell to the ground. Blood spurted from his wounds, staining the floor crimson as he coughed, each breath more labored than the last. Despite the pain, a grim chuckle escaped his lips, mingling with the sound of his ragged breathing.

As the others continued fighting, his laughter grew weaker, interspersed with gasps of agony, until his body lay still, his life extinguished by the merciless blades of his assailants.

In a flurry of motion, Vladsun surged forward, his muscles tensed as he shoved aside a Wintersun assailant looming over Amelia. With a swift, lethal strike, he dispatched his adversary, buying her precious moments to flee to safety.

Surrounded by a swarm of enemy soldiers, Vladsun found himself outnumbered. One by one, the soldiers closed in, driving their swords deep into Vladsun's body with merciless precision. Despite his formidable skill, he was soon overwhelmed by the sheer ferocity of their assault. He stumbled, his strength failing him as darkness closed in around him, his sacrifice remembered as a testament to his loyalty.

Bemus remained alone in the dining hall. He spat on the ground and shouted at Mercury, "You want a fight? Come and fight me instead of letting your lackeys have all the fun."

Mercury held up his hand, signaling the soldiers to wait. He stared down Bemus and said, "You know, death by my hand is not quick."

Bemus stood his ground and retorted, "Nor by mine. Let's dance, shiny boy."

Mercury drew a sword from a sheath on his back. Bemus rushed in to fight. They traded blows with skill and speed, but the fight did not last long. Mercury pushed Bemus back into a wall, drew a dagger, and plunged it into his shoulder.

Bemus yelled in pain, kicked Mercury back, and pulled out the dagger. He licked his own blood off the blade before throwing it aside.

Mercury smirked as if he was amused and rushed back in to continue fighting. They traded a few more blows before Mercury kicked Bemus in the knee so hard that his leg folded backwards. Bemus dropped his sword and held his broken leg.

Mercury did not hesitate and began beating Bemus' head in with his fist. After a few blows, he began dragging him to a burning table.

Once they got close to the flame, Mercury squatted down and said, "I warned you it would not be quick."

He snapped his fingers and waved at a large chunk of burning table. Several soldiers used their spears to flip over the burning debris exposing a bed of hot coals.

Mercury put his boot on the back of the neck of Bemus and plunged his head into the red-hot coals. A few of the Wintersun soldiers grimaced as Bemus screamed in pain and the smell of burning flesh filled the room.

In the end, Bemus stopped struggling and went limp as his screams stopped. Mercury turned to his troops. "I want every person in this castle dead. If you find Azrael, Victor, the sword, or the book, you will bring them to me. Now go!"

The soldiers saluted their leader and rushed out into the halls to continue the slaughter. Mercury kicked Bemus' corpse and walked out of the room. He saw the fire had reached other parts of the castle as well and was spreading. A few servants and guests lagged behind in their escape and were dispatched by his men.

Mercury made his way to the castle entrance. One way or another he was resolved to find the other two totems and destroy them to complete his revenge.

Meanwhile, outside, Azrael and Victor had just witnessed the blast from the vase being broken. Victor shouted, "What was that?"

Azrael grabbed Victor by his vest and pulled him close with a look of fear in his eyes. "They must have broken the vase. I warned you that this could happen. Look at the devastation! The whole damn castle is on fire, and that is the effect while it was being suppressed by a battalion of Wintersun. We need to get the book and the sword out of here. Now! Victor? Are you listening?"

Victor seemed stunned and was watching the castle burn. He looked back at Azrael with masked despair and said, "Hell of a first day, huh? You are right, we need to move. Go back to your castle and I will go back to mine. Once we regroup we can deal with this new threat."

Azrael agreed. They parted ways, grabbed horses, and made their escape as the Wintersun army descended the castle steps.

Mercury watched the two ride off before summoning his horse and looking to the Wintersun soldiers. "Stay here, I will ride after the Zeller Grand Emperor with the Hawkes. He has the enchanted book and I will stop at nothing to get it. I wish you to slaughter every last one of them and prepare for my return. Do you understand?"

The Wintersun soldier saluted. "Yes, sir."

Mercury screamed, "Then go! What are you waiting for?"

The soldier scrambled off to tell the others of Mercury's order. After the golden man mounted his horse, he took off in pursuit of the book and Victor's life.

Chapter 10.5

Victor rode hard and fast all the way back to his castle. Both he and his horse were near the point of collapse when he saw the spires of his castle peeking over the next hill.

He called ahead as best he could, "Open the gates! Hurry!"

As he got closer, he could see the massive gates opening. He breathed a sigh of relief.

In that instant, a searing pain caused him to double over and fall off his horse. Victor reached down with a shaking hand and felt a thick metal protruding from where his left kidney was. He looked down and saw he was bleeding and he could not break off the shaft. Two guards rushed to his side. One slapped his horse to spur it inside the gates while the other dragged him back to the safety of the courtyard.

The first guard turned to say something, but another bolt shot out of his mouth, shattering his teeth and spraying the other guard and

Victor with blood. Several more bolts fell around Victor and the guard as they made it inside the gates that were already closing.

      The guard called over a doctor and Victor groaned in pain as the doctor pulled out the bolt. He grabbed the guard by the collar and pulled him closer. "Listen, Mercury and his soldiers are coming. They must have bolt guns. Get the defenses set up. We have no time. We must defend the castle."

      The guard ran off to spread the word. Victor looked at the doctor and asked, "How bad is it?" The man hesitated. Victor shouted this time, "How bad is it?"

      The doctor went pale in the face and stammered out, "It is not good, sir. You need rest and time to heal or it could be the end of you."

      Victor spat on the ground and pushed the doctor away. "I will be fine," he said as he stood up. Loud booms were heard from the front gate. Victor shouted at the doctor, "Go! Get Thaw and bring him to me."

The doctor gulped and pointed up to the castle ramparts, where Thaw was commanding the soldiers along the walls. More loud noises penetrated through the castle walls as Hawke soldiers attacked the gates and smoke began to rise from outside the walls.

Victor chose to not hesitate and rushed into the castle. He turned to close the front doors, and as he did, he saw the door burst apart, sending splinters of wood everywhere. He paused to look through the smoke at a Hawke soldier who appeared to be carrying a black cauldron on his back.

The soldier stuck a flaming torch into the cauldron and began running towards the castle, but took three steps inside the courtyard before a Zeller guard ran up and stabbed him in the heart. The Wintersun soldier cackled and embraced the Zeller guard. As he struggled to free himself, he screamed in fear, "Get back!"

The cauldron on the Wintersun's back emitted billows of black smoke and there was an explosion. In an instant, both men disappeared.

Victor grimaced at the explosion and finished closing the next door. He grabbed a polearm and barricaded himself in, but he knew it would not stop them. Instead of waiting, he began making his way to the library near the back of the castle.

Guards rushed past Victor towards the doors, swords at the ready. He held on to the book and pushed forward. He was still bleeding and could feel himself growing weaker.

He was almost to the library when there was another explosion. The doors burst open with such force that it cracked the walls and rubble rained down on the soldiers.

Victor turned pale as he saw a full battalion of Hawke soldiers marching up the castle steps. He turned away and continued to the library. He could tell from the screams behind him that the battle was not going in their favor.

Victor reached the library and looked over his shoulder to see the Hawke soldiers slaughtering their way through the halls. As the Grand Emperor ducked into the dark room, he cursed at himself. Victor carried himself down the main aisle, stopping after a few rows of books.

He drew his sword and pointed it off to his left. "Come out now," he growled.

To his surprise, it was his younger cousin Vincent. "What are you doing here?" he hissed.

Vincent's teeth rattled as he replied, "When the fighting started, I hid in here hoping it would just go away."

Victor was about to say more when the door to the library swung open. He threw the book to Vincent and pressed himself up against a bookshelf. He held a finger to his lips to signal silence. Vincent nodded and retreated back into the darkness.

Victor waited for the intruder to come closer. Then with all the strength he had left, Victor raised his sword up to his chest, spun out from behind the bookshelf, and brought the blade towards the intruder. He plunged it deep into the torso of Mercury, piercing through the middle of his heart.

The golden man coughed up blood and smiled, which confused Victor. He looked down to see that Mercury had plunged a blade of his own into his stomach. The golden man fell to the ground trying but failing to pull out his blade before fainting. Victor managed to retrieve the weapon that was within him, but then struggled to keep his intestines from coming out. He too fell to the ground, losing even more blood.

He called to Vincent in a weak voice, "Boy, come here. It is safe."

Vincent emerged from the shadows still holding the book against his chest with both hands.

"Listen to me. The last Overseer split into three powerful totems that kept each other in check. One of them was broken before I came here. Azrael of the Diamond Mortem has a sword, which is the second totem, and you hold the third. It must not fall into the wrong hands because it is beyond any power we can comprehend. Do you understand me, child?"

Vincent nodded as Victor grunted and coughed up even more blood.

With his final breath, he wheezed a grave warning, "Listen closely — do NOT read this book of 'Peace' you hold in your hands, anyone foolish enough to open its pages, even *you*, will unleash a destructive power the likes of which this world has never known."

All Glory to God

Special Thanks

Urban City and 3rd Degree Entertainment for all contributions great and small, and not allowing me to settle for less than what I'm worth.

Red Rook Films: Elizabeth Salazar, Caleb Baccus, and Carlos Flores for their friendship and accepting my ideas in their productions.

Individuals: Charlotte Carrendar, Lahdo Esso, Angelis Cordero, Timothy Weber, and Denton Lewis for their inspiration and assistance in creating this fictional world.

And thank you to all readers and those who helped turn this fantasy of mine into a reality. There will be more.

Rest in Peace Victor.

Made in the USA
Columbia, SC
11 July 2024

b53d026a-45b1-4924-98ef-64176e1e49faR03